Bodega Language.

Behavioural psychologists say individuals give themselves away by their unconsidered gestures.

But an unswerving dedication to *one well considered gesture* is what marks out The Macallan Malt Whisky.

Every drop of The Macallan has been—and always will be — matured exclusively in oaken casks that have previously contained Dry Oloroso and other rare sherries. *Some gesture!*

This is the ancient and now *absurdly costly* way of mellowing pure malt spirit. You can buy perfectly good whisky made without employing this traditional method. But ... one sip of The Macallan ... and *your tongue will tell you the difference.*

To join our small (but devoted) band of merry malt sippers, please call 1-800-428-9810.

THE MACALLAN.
THE SINGLE MALT SCOTCH.

The Paris Review is published quarterly by The Paris Review, Inc. Vol. 39, No. 144, Fall 1997.
Business Office: 45–39 171 Place, Flushing, New York 11358 (ISSN #0031-2037). Paris Office:
Harry Mathews, 67 rue de Grenelle, Paris 75007 France. London Office: Shusha Guppy, 8 Shawfield
St., London, SW3. US distributors: Random House, Inc. 1(800)733-3000. Typeset and printed in
USA by Capital City Press, Montpelier, VT. Price for single issue in USA: $10.00. $14.00 in Canada.
Post-paid subscription for four issues $34.00, lifetime subscription $1000. Postal surcharge of $10.00
per four issues outside USA (excluding life subscriptions). Subscription card is bound within magazine. Please give six weeks notice of change of address using subscription card. *While The Paris
Review welcomes the submission of unsolicited manuscripts, it cannot accept responsibility for
their loss or delay, or engage in related correspondence. Manuscripts will not be returned or
responded to unless accompanied by self-addressed, stamped envelope. Fiction manuscripts
should be submitted to George Plimpton, poetry to Richard Howard, The Paris Review, 541 East
72nd Street, New York, N.Y. 10021.* Charter member of the Council of Literary Magazines and
Presses. This publication is made possible, in part, with public funds from the New York State Council
on the Arts and the National Endowment for the Arts. Periodicals postage paid at Flushing, New
York, and at additional mailing offices. **Postmaster:** Please send address changes to 45-39 171st
Place, Flushing, N.Y. 11358.

Petaluma

1ST. AVE. AT 73RD. ST., NEW YORK CITY
772·8800

©1987 John Fischer

Czesław Miłosz

An International Festival

Readings, Discussions, Exhibits

Robert Hass, Seamus Heaney,
Edward Hirsch, Jane Hirshfield,
Denise Levertov, Leonard Nathan,
Adam Michnik, Robert Pinsky,
Tomas Venclova, Helen Vendler,
Adam Zagajewski,

and . . . Czesław Miłosz

Friday, April 24 – Monday, April 27, 1998
Claremont McKenna College
Claremont, California

For more information contact Robert Faggen
(909) 607-3005
or fax 621-8579

BENNINGTON
WRITING
SEMINARS

*MFA in Writing and Literature
Two-Year Low-Residency Program*

A. BLAKE GARDNER

FICTION
NONFICTION
POETRY

Jane Kenyon Poetry Scholarship available

For more information contact:

Writing Seminars, Box PA
Bennington College
Bennington, VT 05201
802-442-5401 ext. 4452
Fax 802-442-6164

YMCA National Writer's Voice
A Network of Literary Arts Centers at YMCAs

☆ **Core Centers**: *Billings, MT • Scottsdale, AZ • Fairfield, CT • Chicago, IL • Lexington, KY • Minneapolis, MN • Chesterfield, MO •
Bay Shore, NY • New York, NY • Silver Bay, NY • Detroit, MI • Tampa, FL*

△ **New Centers**: *Huntington, NY • Atlanta, GA • Charlottesville, VA • Providence, RI • Miami, FL • Quincy, IL •
Wethersfield, CT • Gardena, CA • Manchester, NH • Everett, WA*

◯ **Armed Services Center**: *Springfield, VA •*

✳ **Program Schools**: *Tempe, AZ • Mobile, AL • Pawling, NY • Des Moines, IA • Houston, TX • Denver, CO •
San Francisco, CA • Tampa, FL • Columbus, OH • Springfield, MA • Baltimore, MD • Long Beach, CA • Tacoma, WA •
West Chester, PA • Rockford, IL • Nashville, TN • Billings, MT • Honolulu, HI • Boston, MA •
Black Mountain, NC • Rochester, NY (Program Schools offer year-round training in literary arts program development to YMCA staff.)*

■ **YMCA National Writer's Voice Office • YMCA of the USA National Office**
*International Centers in development: *France, Israel, Italy and South Africa*

YMCA Writer's Voice centers meet the particular needs of their communities
through public readings, workshops, writng camps for youth, magazine publishing,
in-school residencies, and other literary arts activities while offering national
programs such as the National Readings Tour, the National Readings Network, The
Writers Community Writer-in-Residence Program, and the Body-in-Question
Reading & Discussion Program. Centers also participate in national conferences,
funding initiatives, and program sharing.

Contact your local YMCA or the YMCA National Writer's Voice Office
5 West 63rd Street • New York, NY 10023 • 212.875.4261

*A program of the YMCA of the USA, funded by the YMCA, Lila Wallace-Reader's Digest Fund,
National Endowment for the Arts, National Endowment for the Humanities, The William Bingham
Foundation, and the Lannan Foundation, as well as many regional, state, and local organizations.*

DIRT ANGEL
Stories by Jeanne Wilmot

An electrifying debut, *Dirt Angel*
is informed by an original voice from
the urban landscape of cross-over
culture. The negotiations between
lovers, lifestyles, girlfriends, races,
siblings find their place on these
pages in highly charged and authentic
ways. Passionate, sensual, violent,
and tender, *Dirt Angel* is a stunning
collection by a bold new talent.

"A strong, original work with a vivid flow of language
and landscape. Altogether a striking and memorable
performance." —Elizabeth Hardwick

"With her first book, Jeanne Wilmot, like her fast-talking,
fast-walking protagonists, has hip-hopped onto fiction's
center stage, and she nails our attention there from the first
page to the last. A remarkable debut." —Russell Banks

"Wilmot's stories are fierce, exacting, often dazzlingly
smart and penetrating. They regularly mimic life's
elusiveness, and in those moments of evanescence and
clarity they are actually breathtaking." —Richard Ford

Ontario Review Press
Distributed by George Braziller, Inc.
(212) 889-0909 • Fax (212) 689-5405

The Paris Review

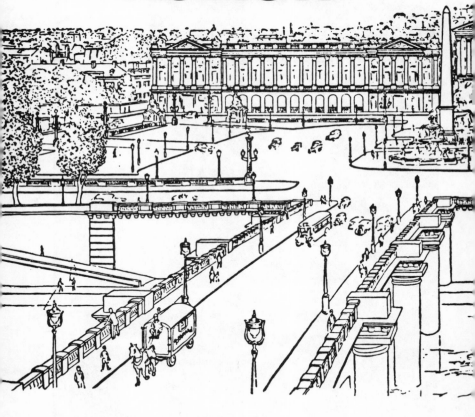

Editorial Office:
541 East 72 Street
New York, New York 10021
HTTP://www.voyagerco.com

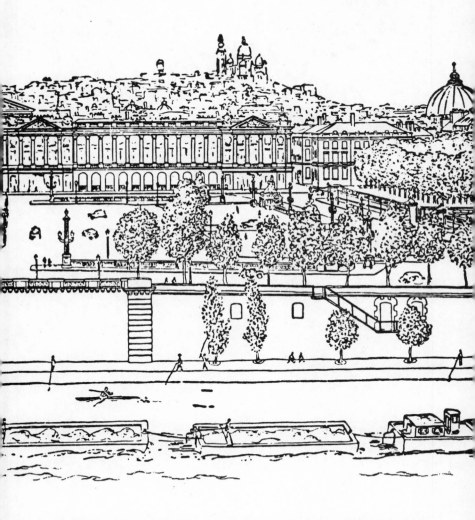

Business & Circulation:
45-39 171 Place
Flushing, New York 11358

Distributed by Random House
201 East 50 Street
New York, N.Y. 10022
(800) 733-3000

Table of contents illustration by Pierre Constanca, Untitled drawing.
Frontispiece by William Pène du Bois.

Number 144

Interviews

Seamus Heaney	*The Art of Poetry LXXV*	88
Robert Pinsky	*The Art of Poetry LXXVI*	180

Fiction

Jane Avrich	*The Great Flood*	282
Peter Matthiessen	*Lost Man's River*	20
Rick Moody	*The Mansion on the Hill*	214
Kate Walbert	*The Blue Hour*	139
David Foster Wallace	*Brief Interviews with Hideous Men*	39

Features

Aldo Buzzi	*A Self-Interview*	152
Elias Canetti	*Selected Notes from Hampstead*	254

Art

Betsy Rosenwald	*Wind*	cover
Frank Yamrus	*Six Bodies*	69

Poetry

Michael Blumenthal	*Falling Asleep at the Erotic Mozi*	168
Anne Babson Carter	*A Morning View of Bluehill Village*	28
Brad Davis	*Two Poems*	77
Ben Downing	*The Calligraphy Shop*	29
Clayton Eshleman	*Giverny*	275
Marilyn Hacker	*Two Poems*	267
Carol Vanderveer Hamilton	*Narcolepsy*	272
Richard Kenney	*Venice and Mars*	82
Karl Kirchwey	*Syracuse*	276
Kenneth Koch	*My Olivetti Speaks*	171
Yusef Komunyakaa	*Memory Cave*	26
Timothy Liu	*Three Poems*	279
Joanie Mackowski	*Waiting*	79
Corey Marks	*American Monochrome*	34
Deborah Pease	*What Is the Word for Window?*	33
Maura Stanton	*The Last Judgment*	169
Terese Svoboda	*Old God*	170
Wisława Szymborska	*Negative*	76
John Updike	*Two Cunts in Paris*	166
Sidney Wade	*Three Poems*	269
David Yezzi	*Two Poems*	37

Notes on Contributors   289

from Lost Man's River

Peter Matthiessen

At Lost Man's Key

We took the sailing skiff. There was no wind. In the light of the moon, I rowed Papa upriver on the incoming tide and on past Possum Key to the eastern bays. In all that long journey, he never twitched, never uttered a sound, but sat there jutted up out of the stern like an old stump, silhouetted on the moonlit water. That black hat shaded his face from the moon, his eyes were hidden.

Some time after midnight, we went ashore on Onion Key and slept a little. I was exhausted when he woke me in the dark, and I asked why we had to leave there before daybreak. A hard low grunt of warning meant I was not to speak again.

It was cold before daybreak, with a cold mist on the water. I rowed hard to get warm. Descending Lost Man's River, there was breeze, and I raised the sail. That old skiff slipped swiftly down the current in the early mists and on across the empty grayness of First Lost Man's Bay, the dark bulk of him, still mute, hunched in the stern.

At first light, we slid the skiff into the mangroves and waded around to the sand point on the south end of the Key. Already afraid, I dared not ask why we were sneaking up on Bet and Wally when our intent was to run those Tuckers off the claim. I guess I knew he had not come there to discuss things. In that first dawn of the new year, my teeth were chattering.

We slipped along through the low wood. Soon we could see between the trees the stretch of shore where their small sloop was moored off the Gulf beach. Their driftwood shack with palm-thatch roof was back up on the shell ridge, in thin shade. Like most Islanders, they rose at the first light, and Wally Tucker was already outside, perched on a driftwood log mending his galluses. He must have been expecting trouble, because his rifle was leaned against the log beside him.

Papa gave me a kind of a funny wince, like he had no choice about what he had to do. Then he moved forward out of the sea grape with his old double-barrel down along his leg, crossing the sand in stiff short steps, like a bristled-up male dog. He made no sound that I could hear, yet Wally, being extra wary, must have picked up some tiny pinching of the sand. His gallus strap and sail needle and twine fell from his hand as he whirled, reaching for his gun, but in that instant he stopped that hand and moved the other one out to the side before slowly raising both.

Tucker swallowed, as if sickened by the twin muzzle holes of that raised shotgun. Seeing no mercy in my father's face, he did not ask for any. He held my eye for a long moment, as if there were something I could do. He spoke to me while he watched Papa, saying, "Please, Rob. Take care of poor Bet." Perhaps he forgave me, perhaps he knew I was there against my will. Then he looked his executioner squarely in the eye, as if resigned to his fate. Papa knew better. Cursing, he swung the shotgun up in a quick snap as the man spun sideways toward his gun, and the scene exploded in red haze as Wally, blown clean over that log, fell twisted to the sand. A voice screamed. "Oh Christ Jesus no!" It was not Bet, as I first thought, but me.

Bet ran outside, holding a pot, and she screamed, too, at

the sight of her beloved, kicking and shuddering on the red
sand. Surely they had expected something, for she kept her
head and did not run toward her young husband. She dropped
her pot and lit out for the woods, very fast for any woman
close to term. I see her still, her white shift, sailing over that
pale sand like a departing spirit.

Your father—our father—murdered Wally in cold blood.
I never knew till he had done it that this was his intention
even before we departed Chatham Bend. And perhaps he
hadn't really known it either, for his face looked unimaginably
sad and weary, as if the last of his life anger had drained out
of him. He seemed bewildered, like someone arrived in a dark
realm of no return. In that moment—for all took place while
the ghostly form of that young girl was still crossing the beach
ridge into the trees—what struck me as most strange was his
quiet demeanor, that unnatural and horrifying calm.

"You see that, boy? He tried to kill me," Papa said dully.

Leaning his shotgun on the driftwood where Wally himself
had perched moments before, he eased himself down, seating
himself, and planted his hands upon his knees, his boots not
two feet from the body, which was still shuddering like a felled
steer. Then he reached into his coat and took out his revolver,
extending it butt first. In my crazed state, I imagined he was
inviting me to execute him, and I took the gun and pointed
it at his blue eyes. I was gagging and choking, knowing there
would be no future, that my life was finished. I think I might
have pulled the trigger if he had not smiled. I stared at him,
and my arm lowered. Then he pointed at the sea wood, saying,
"I forgot to bring a dog. If she gets too deep into the brush,
we just might lose her." And he mentioned the families down
on South Lost Man's Beach who might come to investigate
the shot. We could not lose much time hunting her down.

I stood stupidly, unable to take in what he was saying.
Patiently he explained that Bet was a witness. I must go after
her at once. "We cannot stay here," he repeated gently. And
still I did not move. "You came this far, Rob. You better
finish it."

I gasped, teeth chattering, whole body shuddering. I was

fighting with all my might not to be sick. I yelled, "*You* finish
it!" He gazed where she had gone. "I would take care of it
myself," he said, "but I'd never catch her. It is up to you."
I started yelling. Shooting these poor young people in cold
blood was something terrible and crazy, we would burn in
hell!

He was losing patience now, although still calm. He folded
his arms upon his chest and said, "Well, Rob, that's possible.
But meanwhile, if she gets away, we are going to hang."

I would not listen. I couldn't look at Wally's body without
retching, so how could I run down his poor Bet and point a
gun at her and take her life? I wept. "Don't make me do it,
Papa! I can't do it!"

"Why, sure you can, Son, and you best jump to it, because
you are an accomplice," Papa told me. "It's your life or hers,
look at it that way."

"You told me we were coming here to settle up our claim!"

"That's what we did," he said. He stood up then and turned
his back to me, looking out toward the Gulf horizon. "Too
late to talk about it now," he said.

I was running. I was screaming the whole way. Whether
that scream was heard there on that lonely river or whether
it was only in my heart I do not know.

Being so cumbersome, poor Bet had not run far. In that
thick tangle, there was no place to run to. I found sand scuffs
where she had fallen to her knees and crawled in under a big
sea grape. Panting like a doe, she lay big-bellied on her side,
wide-eyed in shock. I stopped at a little distance. Seeing me,
she whimpered, just a little. "Oh Rob," she murmured. "We
did you no harm."

I called out, "Please, Bet, please don't look! I beg of you!"
I crept up then and knelt beside her, and she breathed my
name again just once, oh so softly, as if trying to imagine
such a person.

I never expected death to be so . . . intimate? That white
skin pulsing at her temple, the sun-filled hair and small pink
ear, clean and transparent as a seashell in the morning light—

so full of life! Her eyes were open and she seemed to pray, her parted lips yearning for salvation like a thirsting creature. She never looked into my eyes nor spoke another word on earth, just stared away toward the bright morning sea.

Raging at myself to be merciful and quick, I grasped my wrist to steady my gun hand. Even so, it shook as I raised the revolver. Already steps were coming up behind, crushing the sand, and hearing them, her eyes flew wider. Before she could shriek, I placed the muzzle to her ear, forcing my breath into my gut to steel myself and crying aloud as I pulled back on the trigger, pulled her life out of her. My head exploded with red noise. Spattered crimson with her life, I fainted.

For a while after I became aware, I lay there in the morning dance of sea grape leaves reflected on the sand. Light and branches, sky and turquoise water — all was calm, as in a dream of heaven.

I forced open my eyes. I yelled in terror. She was gone. Closing my eyes again, I prayed for sleep. I prayed that nothing had taken place, that the dream of trees and sky and water might not end.

The murderer came and leaned and shook my shoulder. Gently, he said, "Come along now, Son, it's time to go." He had already hauled the bodies out into the river. Alive and unharmed in the warm womb of its mother, the unborn kicked in its blind premonitions beneath the sunny riffles of the current.

I struggled to stand up but I could not. The weakness and frustration broke me, and I sobbed. I saw the boot prints and the sand kicked over the dark bloodstain, like a fatal wound and shadow on the earth.

He leaned and took me underneath one arm and lifted me easily onto my feet. He used a brush of leaves and twigs to scrape the brains and bloody skull bits from my breast, for I had fallen down across her body. Never before had this man touched me with such kindness, nor taken care of me in this strong loving way. I actually thought, What took so long? After all these years, he loves me! But his compassion — if that is what it was — had come too late. My life was destroyed beyond the last hope of redemption. What had happened here had bound me like a shroud. I was a dead man from that day forward, forever and ever and amen.

I retched and fought away from him but fell, too weak to run. He bent again and lifted me, half-carried me toward the skiff.

With hard short strokes he rowed upriver, against the ebb tide. His heavy coat lay on the thwart beside me. He himself seemed stunned, half-dead, he had forgotten the revolver. My hand found the gun furtively, over and over, whenever he turned to see the course ahead. I wanted to take it, cover it with my shirt, but I felt too shaken and afraid. In that long noon, ascending Lost Man's River, I realized I should have killed him when he first gave me that gun, to spare Bet and her unborn. Instead I had taken those two lives and lost my own.

Yusef Komunyakaa

Memory Cave

A tallow worked into a knot
of rawhide, with a ball of waxy light
tied to a stick, the boy
scooted through a secret mouth
of the cave, pulled by the flambeau
in his hand. He could see
the gaze of agate eyes
& wished for the forbidden
plains of bison & wolf, years
from the fermented honey
& musty air. In the dried
slag of bear & bat guano,
the initiate stood with sleeping
gods at his feet, lost
in the great cloud of their one
breath. Their muzzles craved
touch. How did they learn
to close eyes, to see into
the future? Before the Before:
mammon was unnamed & mist
hugged ravines & hillocks.
The elders would test him
beyond doubt & blood. Mica
lit the false skies where
stalactite dripped perfection
into granite. He fingered
icons sunlight & anatase
never touched. Ibex carved
on a throwing stick, reindeer
worried into an ivory amulet,
& a bear's head. Outside,

the men waited two days
for him, with condor & bovid,
& not in a thousand years
would he have dreamt a woman
standing here beside a man,
saying, "This is as good
as the stag at Salon Noir
& the polka-dotted horses."
The man scribbles *Leo loves
Angela* below the boy's last bear
drawn with manganese dioxide
& animal fat. This is where
sunrise opened a door in stone
when he was summoned to drink
honey wine & embrace a woman
beneath a five-pointed star.
Lying there beside the gods
hefty & silent as boulders,
he could almost remember
before he was born, could see
the cliff from which he'd fall.

Anne Babson Carter

A Morning View of Bluehill Village

Farnsworth Art Museum

All he could see from this scene over Bluehill, Maine
(no distortions here: the work is from a seagirted light),
is enough of a world for any man, it seems plain

from his painting dated 1824, September. Trailing a rain
Fisher climbed up to get the angle right; to sight
all he could see from this scene over Bluehill, Maine—

distinctly no anthill: it looms more a mountain
at sea—as clarity would unveil the view from this height
is enough of a world for any man. It seems plain

he set to as though knowing a sea captain
would pause 100 years later and hail: "How right!"
all he could see from this scene over Bluehill, Maine.

(Even now, gazing at these houses piping like shanty re-
    frains
down salted inlets, we are instilled with what, overnight
is enough of a world for any man.) It seems plain-

ly so American: three frocked figures in meadow of
    purslane;
a horse, a cemetery, stone wall; that our eye delights
all he could see from this scene over Bluehill, Maine
is enough of a world for any man, it seems plain.

Ben Downing

The Calligraphy Shop

My God, they were all so beautiful,
each parchment trumpeting its cursive praise
of Allah, whose residence in Istanbul

seemed tenuous throughout the vulgar maze
of kitsch and gizmos the Grand Bazaar's become.
Here at last, I thought, He'd find a phrase

or two to please Him—not the vendors' dumb,
kilowatt promotion of their crap,
but silent decibels of script, its un-

or otherworldly characters trapped
in suspended eloquence. As if on ice
a figure-skating rubricant had mapped

his arabesques with slathered blades, the rise
and roller-coaster dip of letters swelled
even past my ignorance; my eyes

alone could estimate, yet not quite melt,
the igneous devotion frozen there.
Did it matter exactly what they spelt?

Arcs, crescents, diamonds punctuating the air
above them: an abstract caravan
of lines carried over crystal-clear

its cargo, the sweet imbroglio of man
and deity snagged (I romanticized)
within those desert skeins. The Koran

fanned out across the walls in bearably sized
divisions of its heat, the surahs all
cooling under glass—some plain, some surprised

alchemically into animals.
There were verses crammed to fit a camel's back,
Kufic exhortations strung along the tail

of tigers like a lash, delicate black
songbirds caged in painstaking minuscule,
and, beside them, brute raptors shellacked

to paper by religion. Such midnight oil
they must have torched, these anonymous
masters of kinetic penmanship, such toil

lavished on the strictly frivolous!
But would their occidental counterparts
have recognized the brotherhood of bliss

between them, the consanguinity of art,
or would the monks behind the Book of Kells
have cried for heathen blood and torn apart

their genius as the stuff of infidels?
As I was pondering this, the store's
proprietor approached, offering his help

in that skewed, courtly English foreigners
can so disarm us with. He laid out
his treasures patiently: which ones were

Turkish, Urdu, what they were about,
the deep antique and the relatively new.
Then, perceiving my attention caught

by a small one high up on the wall, he drew
it closer. Although less extravagant
than others, it fascinated through

sheer obsessiveness, for the inscription went
hypnotically snaking down a gyre.
"Ah yes," said my host. "It's Kurdish, meant

to rid a house of demons, djinn, whatever
pesky spirits skulk around. Place a bowl
beneath it, then wait for ghosts to gather.

They will amass, unable to control
their belletristic curiosity.
Once they start to read they'll read the whole,

the spiral pulling them inexorably
toward its center, from where they drop
into the dish—now disposable, you see."

And so was I. Powerless to stop
gawking at the paranormal bait
before me, suckered by its agitprop,

toppled by an agile nib, I let
my skeptical guard fall peacefully. Outside,
a muezzin was warbling, from his minaret,

torrid plangencies of prayer and pride
upbraided, his spectral keening parallel
or woven with the printed one I tried,

but failed, to resist, susceptible
as I was that blazing August afternoon
to the Byzantine embellishments of quill

searing the mere vellum. I've come to burn,
since then, with a greedy rage to reproduce
its tyrannies, inflicting in turn

(on fellow ghosts) capture, jail, the gentle noose
of amazement; I've come to hunt its cold,
fatally calibrated charm, its ruse

of hanging there in ambush, growing old.

Deborah Pease

What Is the Word for Window?

> *Where is it all gone? Where is it? Oh, my God, my God*
> *I've forgotten . . . It's muddled in my head . . . I don't*
> *remember the word for window in Italian . . . I've for-*
> *gotten everything, every day forgetting, and life slips*
> *away and will never return, never, we'll never go to Mos-*
> *cow . . .*
>
> —Irina in *The Three Sisters*
> by Anton Chekhov

But suppose, Irina, you find yourself asking:
What is the word for window?
And a voice, your own or someone else's, replies
In a not-so-patient tone: Window.
Window is the word for window.
Imagine, Irina, this is clear enough and yet
It still doesn't make sense since window
Is window but that isn't quite what you meant, window
Isn't the word you want for window, it's something
Else, behind the word, far away from any window
You are looking at, or through, now, another
Phenomenon or landscape or a different smell—
Furniture polish instead of wilting daisies—
A different feeling, a source, an essence,
A certain day or time of day in a certain place . . .
But, yes, it's all muddled, just as you say,
One clings to bits of knowledge, facts
(The word for window in Italian), one begins to see
The hopes of a great journey are in vain, then,
Irina, one goes much further, as you will know
When you see a window
With no name in any language.

Corey Marks

American Monochrome

If I tell a story of America it will be with the needle
splitting Demuth's needle-pocked skin—how his blood blooms
in insulin as he hunches his shoulder to shield the syringe

from the crowds around him who stare into the arcs of acrobats
pinwheeling through the splayed open air of the circus tent.
Before the thumbstroke and glide he watches his blood fade

and thinks of the garden he wandered in Paris before he col-
    lapsed
and the weakness and craving became a disease, before it be-
    came
a word. The garden where another man kneeled

in front of a wash of lilacs and coughed once, a dry, shallow
    cough . . .
Or I'll tell it with the watery fade of color from his brushpoint
into the melting flight of the acrobats, how the distant hand
    of one

becomes lost behind the yellow body of another and how,
as it passes into the other man's crotch, the hand dissolves
into the paper, into a forgiveness for desire, and not a denial,

not the precise denial in the incorruptible geometries
of his Lancaster, the razor-incised pencil line and oil, black win-
    dows
red buildings, black smokestacks speaking balloons of white
    smoke.

And if Demuth wanted to paint America, it was in the way
    a razor

is a reduction of slag and smoke calling out the emptiness
behind the black flattened windows, the hands and faces

and bodies vanished as though Demuth scorched his city
into the precision of machine, absolved of its makers,
and not in the way a sailor gently traces a razor along his arm,

inscribing the skin with a heart, with initials — *C* and
  D . . .
but he is simply color faded onto paper, a man grabbing his
  cock
and turning his arm toward the absent brushstroke. Even so,

if I'd bent closer, and if the guard hadn't told me sharply
to step back, I would have seen the lines carved in flesh welling
with blood . . . And the plume of blood washing into the
  clear syringe

has nothing to do with America, and everything
with the pale flowers Demuth painted when he was too weak
to leave his home — hyacinth, iris, zinnia, cineraria.

He would wake and swing to the edge of his bed, disentangling
from the sheets rumpled and stained only by sleeplessness
as his mother leaned just outside the room, watching

through the half-open door. He would reach for his brush
and the rough-surfaced paper and paint whatever brilliant
  measure
his mother had set beside him as he slept, stilling the flowers'

dissolution in water color, and making it clearer . . . But when
  Demuth
wandered the Paris garden he didn't think of the flowers, not
  yet,
but of how he could seduce America into his brushstroke.

And if I say the coughing man, too, thought of America, that
    he was writing
a country he'd never seen into a novel he never quite finished;
that when he returned to Prague his cough deepened, and
    he scrawled

when his larynx was fire: *The lilac — dying it drinks and goes
on swilling;*
or even if I simply say when he left the garden he looked away
from Demuth's glance, and flicked a smear of dirt off his
    knee —

you must forgive me this distortion, this smudging of my
    story.
Let it fade the way Demuth's brushes bleed into his cups of
    water
as he finally turns away from the dissected air of the circus
    tent,

from the acrobats dressed in red and black and not in yellow,
    spinning
into each other's grasps. He packs the brushes and pocked
    tubes
and walks outside to pour the color-tainted water at the base

of a straw-strewn cage. And when he looks into the black bars
he feels himself dissolving, caving in to the absence in his
    blood.
He reaches for the metal and thinks the cage waits for some-
    thing new.

Two Poems by David Yezzi

The Hidden Model

a pentimento

What vague dispassion or crisis of hope
entered the artist's head when, leaving off
his study of a woman, he began,

still on the same stretcher, another work—
this one, too, the portrait of a girl
but with, restorers tell us, different eyes

and gown, an altogether different grin?
His reused canvas (probably prescribed
by a lack of means) was not unusual,

though certainly there'd been a loss of paint:
umbers crowded at their vanishing,
or his crisp siennas fixed as auburn hair.

What care he took to cover them, beginning
so nearly with the features of the old,
obliterating, reshaping a cheek

or caressing the neck another way
till slowly, finally, he would repent
the promise in the former figure there.

Beyond the gossip of historians,
nothing of his first model is known,
nothing, that is, the naked eye can hold

as proof her smaller hands had come before.
Still, some shadings of the face persist,
a capsule of that day that she'd been glad

to sit a second hour by him, posing.
Had he known outright he'd never finish it?
Perhaps just this: that such work's never lost,

that what eluded each false start might serve
to save his latest version, the crisis turned
by a surer hand, rehearsing what was missed.

Morandi's Bottles

His slender Moselles would, in truth, describe
the scumbled shapes of autumn, color leached
as from a cheek, sallow, opaque; or five
green Burgundies might best contrive to teach
suave consolations of the midday sun,
despite what light his studio could hold;
for deeper shades of solitude he'd run
the throat of a Chianti, inked in bold,
netting with his crosshatch all he saw
suggested — ruined cityscapes, stone pines,
the shape a shoulder makes, or nature pausing —
that the mundane might offer with its lines
what sighs beneath the surface, even there,
of the unillumined world where it comes clear.

from Brief Interviews with Hideous Men

David Foster Wallace

#6   *E——— on "How and Why I Have Come to be Totally Devoted to S——— and Have Made Her the Linchpin and Plinth of My Entire Emotional Existence"*

And yet I did not fall in love with her until she had related the story of the unbelievably horrifying incident in which she was brutally accosted and held captive and raped and very nearly killed.

Q.

Let me explain. I'm aware of how it might sound, believe me. I can explain. In bed together, in response to some sort of prompt or association, she related an anecdote about hitch-hiking and once being picked up by what turned out to be a psychotic serial sex offender who drove her to a secluded area and raped her and would almost surely have murdered her had she not been able to think effectively on her feet under enormous fear and stress. Irregardless of whatever I might have thought of the quality and substance of the thinking that enabled her to induce him to let her live.

Q.

Neither would I. Who would, now, in an era when every — when psychotic serial killers have their own trading cards? I'm concerned in today's climate to steer clear of any suggestion of anyone quote asking for it, let's not even go there, but yet rest assured it gives one pause about the capacities of judgment involved, or at the very least in the naïveté —

Q.

Only that it was perhaps marginally less unbelievable in the context of her type, in that this was what one might call a quote Granola Cruncher, or post-Hippie, New Ager, what have you, in college where one is often first exposed to social taxonomies we called them Granola Crunchers or simply Crunchers, terms comprising the prototypical sandals, unrefined fibers, daffy arcana, emotional incontinence, flamboyantly long hair, extreme liberality on social issues, financial support from parents they revile, bare feet, obscure import religions, indifferent hygiene, a gooey and somewhat canned vocabulary, the whole predictable peace-and-love post-Hippie diction that im—

Q.

A large outdoor concert-slash-performance-art community festival thing in a park downtown where — it was a pickup, plain and simple. I will not try to represent it as anything nicer than that, or more fated. And I'm going to admit at the risk of appearing mercenary that her prototypical Cruncher morphology was evident at first sight, from clear on the other side of the bandstand, and dictated the terms of the approach and the tactics of the pickup itself and made the whole thing almost criminally easy. Half the women there — it is a less uncommon typology among young educated girls out here than one might think. You don't want to know what kind of festival or why the three of us were there, trust me. I'll just bite the political bullet and confess that I classified her as a strictly one-night objective, and that my interest in her was almost entirely due to the fact that she was extraordinarily pretty. Sexually attractive, sexy. She had a phenomenal body, even under the poncho. It was her body that attracted me. Her face was a bit strange. Not homely but eccentric. Tad's assessment was that she looked like a really sexy duck. Nevertheless *nolo* to the charge that I spotted her on her blanket at the concert and sauntered carnivorously over with an overtly one-night objective. And, having had some prior dealings with the Cruncher genus prior to this, that the one-night proviso was due mostly to the grim unimaginability of having to *talk* with a New Age brigadier for more than one night. Whether or not you approve I think we can assume you understand.

Q.

That essential at-center-life-is-just-a-cute-pet-bunny *fluffiness* about them that makes it exceedingly hard to take them seriously or to end up not feeling as if you're exploiting them in some way.

Q.

Fluffiness or daffiness or intellectual flaccidity or a somehow smug-seeming naïveté. Choose whichever offends you least. And yes and don't worry I'm aware of how all this sounds and can well imagine the judgments you're forming from the way I'm characterizing what drew me to her but if I'm to really explain this to you as requested then I have no choice but to be brutally candid rather than observing the pseudosensitive niceties of euphemism about the way a reasonably experienced, educated man is going to view an extraordinarily good-looking girl whose life philosophy is fluffy and unconsidered and when one comes right down to it kind of contemptible. I'm going to pay you the compliment of not pretending to worry whether you understand what I'm referring to about the difficulty of not feeling impatience and even contempt —

the blithe hypocrisy, the blatant self-contradiction — the way
you know from the outset that there will be the requisite
enthusiasms for the rain forest and spotted owl, creative meditation, feel-good psychology, macrobiosis, rabid distrust of
what they consider authority without evidently once stopping
to consider the rigid authoritarianism implicit in the rigid
uniformity of their own quote unquote nonconformist uniform, vocabulary, attitudes. As someone who worked himself
through both college and two years now of postgraduate school
I have to confess to an almost blanket — these rich kids in torn
jeans whose way of protesting apartheid is to boycott South
African pot. Silverglade called them the Inward Bound. The
smug naïveté, the condescension in the quote compassion they
feel for those quote unquote trapped or imprisoned in orthodox American lifestyle choices. So on and so forth. The fact
that the Inward Bound never consider that it's the probity
and thrift of the re— to occur to them that they themselves
have themselves become the distillate of everything about the
culture they deride and define themselves as opposing, the
narcissism, the materialism and complacency and unexamined
conformity — or the irony that the blithe teleology of this quote
impending New Age is exactly the same cultural permission
slip that Manifest Destiny was, or the Reich or the dialectic
of the proletariat or the Cultural Revolution — all the same.
And it never *even occurs* to them their certainty that they are
different is what makes them the same.

Q.

You would be surprised.

Q.

All right and the near-contempt here specifically in the way
you can glide casually over and bend down next to her blanket
to initiate conversation and idly play with the blanket's fringe
and create the sense of affinity and connection that will allow
you to pick her up and somehow almost resent that it's so
goddamn easy to make the conversation flow toward a sense
of connection, how exploitative you feel when it is so easy to

get this type to regard you as a kindred soul — you almost know what's going to be said next without her having even to open her pretty mouth. Tad said that she was like some kind of smooth blank perfect piece of pseudo-art you want to buy so you can take it home and sm—

Q.

No, not at all, because I am trying to explain that the typology here dictated a tactic of what appeared to be a blend of embarrassed confession and brutal candor. The moment enough of a mood of conversational intimacy had been established to make a quote confession seem even remotely plausible I deployed a sensitive-slash-pained expression and quote confessed that I'd in fact not just been passing her blanket and even though we didn't know each other had felt a mysterious but overwhelming urge just to lean down and say hi but no something about her that made it unimaginable to deploy anything less than total honesty forced me to confess that I had in fact deliberately approached her blanket and initiated conversation because I had seen her from across the bandstand and had felt some mysterious but overwhelmingly sensual energy seeming to emanate from her very being and had been helplessly drawn to it and had leaned down and introduced myself and started a conversation with her because I wanted to connect and make mutually nurturing and exquisite love with her, and had been ashamed of admitting this natural desire and so had fibbed at first in explaining my approach, though now some mysterious gentleness and generosity of soul I could intuit about her was allowing me to feel safe enough to confess that I had, formerly, fibbed. Note the rhetorically specific blend of childish diction like *Hi* and *fib* with flaccid abstractions like *nurture* and *energy*. This is the lingua franca of the Inward Bound. I actually truly did like her, I found, as an individual — she had an amused expression during the whole conversation that made it hard not to smile in return, and an involuntary need to smile is one of the best feelings available, no? A refill? It's refill time, yes? No?

Q. . . .

And that prior experience has taught that the female Granola Cruncher tends to define herself in opposition to what
she sees as the essentially unconsidered and hypocrisy-bound
attitudes of quote mainstream women and is thus essentially
unoffendable, rejects the whole concept of propriety and
offense, and views so-called honesty of even the most brutal
or repellent sort as evidence of sincerity and respect, getting
quote real, *id est* the impression that you respect her per-
sonhood too much to ply her with implausible fictions and
leave very basic energies and desires uncommunicated. Not
to mention, to make your indignation and distaste complete,
I'm sure, the fact that extremely, off-the-charts pretty women
of almost every type have, from my experience, tend all to
have a uniform obsession with the idea of *respect*, and will
do almost anything anywhere for any fellow who affords her
a sufficient sense of being deeply and profoundly respected.
I doubt I need to point out that this is nothing but a particular
female variant of the psychological need to believe that others
take you as seriously as you take yourself. There is nothing
particularly wrong with it, as psychological needs go, but yet
of course we should always remember that a deep need for
anything from other people makes us easy pickings. I can tell
by your expression what *you* think of brutal candor. The fact
is that she had a body that my body found sexually attractive
and wanted to have intercourse with and it was not really any
more noble or complicated than that. And she did indeed turn
out to be straight out of Central Granola-Cruncher Casting, I
should stress. She had some kind of monomaniacal hatred for
the American timber industry, and professed membership in
one of these apostrophe-heavy near-Eastern religions that I
would defy anyone to pronounce correctly, and believed
strongly in the superior value of vitamins and minerals in
colloidal suspension rather than tablet form, et cetera, and
then, when one thing had been led stolidly by me to another
and there she was in my apartment and we had done what I
had wanted to do with her and had exchanged the standard

horizontal compliments and assurances, she was going on about her imported denomination's views vis-à-vis energy fields and souls and connections between souls via what she kept calling quote focus, and using the, well, the quote L-word itself several times without irony or even any evident awareness that the word has through tactical overdeployment become compromised and requires invisible quotes around it now at the very least, and I suppose I should tell you that I was planning right from the outset to give her the special false number when we exchanged numbers in the morning, which all but a very small and cynical minority always want to. I.e. exchange numbers. A fellow in Tad's torts study group's great-uncle or grandparents or something have a vacation home just outside town and are never there, with a phone but no machine or service, so when someone you've given the special number calls the special number it simply rings and rings, so for a few days it's usually not evident to the girl that what you've given her isn't your true number but for a few days allows her to imagine that you've just been extremely busy and scarce and that this is also perhaps why you haven't called her either. Which obviates the chance of hurt feelings and is therefore, I submit, good, though I can well im —

Q.

The sort of glorious girl whose kiss tastes of liquor when she's had no liquor to drink. Cassis, berries, gumdrops, all steamy and soft. Quote unquote.

Q. . . .

Yes and in the anecdote there she is, blithely hitchhiking along the interstate, and on this particular day the fellow in the car that stops almost the moment she puts her thumb out happens to — she said she knew she'd made a mistake the moment she got in. Just from what she called the energy field inside the car, she said, and that fear gripped her soul the moment she got in. And sure enough, the fellow in the car soon exits the highway and exits off into some kind of secluded area, which seems to be what psychotic sex criminals always

do, you're always reading *secluded area* in all the accounts of
quote *brutal sex slayings* and *grisly discoveries* of *unidentified
remains* by a scout troop or amateur botanist, et cetera, common knowledge which you can be sure she was reviewing,
horror-stricken, as the fellow began acting more and more
creepy and psychotic even on the interstate and then soon
exited into the first available secluded area.

Q.

Her explanation was that she did not in fact feel the psychotic energy field until she had shut the car's door and they
were moving, at which time it was too late. She was not melodramatic about it but described herself as literally paralyzed
with terror. Though you might be wondering as I did when
one hears about cases like this as to why the victim doesn't
simply bail out of the car the minute the fellow begins acting
erratic or begins casually discussing how much he loathes his
mother and dreams of raping her with her LPGA-endorsed
sand wedge and then stabbing her 106 times, et cetera. But
here she did point out that the prospect of bailing out of a
rapidly moving car and hitting the macadam at sixty miles
an — at the very least you break a leg or something, and then
as you're trying to drag yourself into the underbrush of course
what's to keep the fellow from turning around to come back
for you, which in addition let's keep in mind that he's now
going to be additionally aggrieved about the rejection implicit
in your preferring to hit the macadam at sixty m.p.h. rather
than remaining in his company, given that psychotic sex
offenders have a notoriously low tolerance for rejection, and
so on.

Q.

Something about his aspect, eyes, the quote energy field
in the car — she said she knew instantly in the depths of her
soul that the fellow's intention was to brutally rape, torture,
and kill her, she said. And I believed her here, that one can
intuitively pick up on the epiphenomena of danger, sense
malevolence in someone's aspect — you needn't buy into en-

ergy fields or ESP to accept mortal intuition. Nor would I even
begin to try to describe what she looks like as she's telling the
story, reliving it, she's nude, hair spilling all down her back,
sitting meditatively cross-legged amid the wrecked bedding
and smoking ultralight Merits from which she keeps removing
the filters because she claims they're full of additives and un-
safe — as she's sitting there *chain-smoking*, which was so pat-
ently contradictory that I couldn't even bring — and some kind
of blister on her Achilles tendons, from the sandals, leaning
with her body to follow the oscillation of the fan, so she's
moving in and out of a wash of moon from the window whose
angle of incidence itself alters as the moon moves across the
window — all I can tell you is that she was lovely. The bottoms
of her feet dirty, almost black. The moon so full it looks
swollen. And long hair spilling all over, more than — beautiful
lustrous hair that makes you understand why women use con-
ditioner. Tad's boon companion Silverglade telling me she
looks like her hair grew her head instead of the other way
around and asking how long estrus lasts in her species and
droll ho ho. My memory is more verbal than visual, I'm afraid.
It's on the sixth floor and my bedroom gets stuffy, she treated
the fan like cold water and closed her eyes when it hit her.
And by the time the psychotic fellow in question exits into
the secluded area and finally comes straight out and indicates
what his intentions are — apparently detailing certain events
and procedures and implements — she's not the least bit surprised, she said she'd known the kind of hideously twisted
soul-energy she'd gotten in the car into, the kind of pitiless and
unappeasable psychotic he was and what they were heading for
in this secluded area, and concluding that she was going to
become just another grisly discovery for some amateur botanist
a few days hence unless she could focus her way into the sort
of soul-connection that would make it difficult for the fellow
to murder her. These were her words, this was the sort of
pseudo-abstract terminology she — and yet at the same time
I was engrossed enough in the anecdote now to simply accept
it as a kind of foreign language without trying to judge it or
press for clarification, I just decided to assume that *focus* was

her apostrophic denomination's euphemism for prayer, and that in a desperate situation like this who was in a position to judge what would be a sound response to the sort of shock and terror she must be feeling, who could say with any certainty whether prayer wouldn't be appropriate. Foxholes and atheists and so forth. What I remember best is that by this time it was, for the first time, taking much less effort to listen to her—she had an unexpected ability to recount it in such a way as to deflect attention from herself and displace maximum attention onto the anecdote itself. I have to confess that it was the first time I did not find her a bit dull. Care for another?

Q.

That she was not melodramatic about it, the anecdote, telling me, nor affecting an unnatural calm the way some people affect an unnatural nonchalance about narrating a horrific incident that is meant to heighten their story's drama and/or make them appear nonchalant and sophisticated, one or the other of which affects is often the most annoying part of listening to certain types of attractive women structure a story or anecdote—that they are used to high levels of attention, and need to feel that they control it, always trying to control the precise type and degree of your attention instead of simply trusting that you are paying the appropriate type and degree of attention. I'm sure you've noticed this in attractive women, that paying attention to them makes them immediately begin to pose, even if their pose is the affected nonchalance they affect to portray themselves as unposed. But she was, or seemed, oddly unposed for someone this attractive with this dramatic a story to tell. It struck me, listening. She seemed truly affectless in relating it, open to attention but not solicitous—or contemptuous, or affecting disdain or contempt, which I hate. Some beautiful women, something wrong with their voice, some squeakiness or lack of inflection or a laugh like a machine gun and you flee in horror. Her speaking voice is a neutral alto without squeak or that drawled long *O* or vague air of nasal complaint that—also mercifully light on the *likes* and *you knows* which make you chew your knuckle.

Nor did she giggle. Her laugh was fully adult, full, good to hear. And that this was my first hint of sadness or melancholy, as I listened with increasing attention to the anecdote, that the qualities that I found myself admiring in her narration of the anecdote were some of the same qualities about her that I'd been contemptuous of when I'd first picked her up in the park.

Q.

Chief among them that — and I mean this without irony — she seemed quote *sincere* in a way that may in fact have been smug naïveté but was powerful and very attractive in the context of listening to her encounter with the psychopath, in that I found it helped me focus almost entirely on the anecdote itself and thus helped me imagine in an almost terrifyingly vividly realistic way what it must have *felt* like for her, for anyone, finding yourself by nothing but coincidence heading into a secluded woody area in the company of a dark man in a dungaree vest who says he is your own death incarnate and who is alternately smiling with psychotic cheer and ranting and apparently gets his first wave of jollies by singing creepily about the various sharp implements he has in the Cutlass's trunk and detailing what he's used them to do to others and plans in exquisite detail to do to you. It was tribute to the — her odd affectless sincerity that I found myself hearing expressions like *fear gripping her soul*, unquote, less as televisual clichés or melodrama but as sincere if not particularly artful attempts to describe what it must have felt like, the feelings of shock and unreality alternating with waves of pure terror, the sheer emotional *violence* of this magnitude of fear, the temptation to retreat into catatonia or shock or the delusion — yield to the seduction of the idea, riding deeper into the secluded area, that there simply must be some sort of mistake, that something as simple and random as getting into a 1987 maroon Cutlass with a bad muffler that just happened to be the first car to pull over to the side of a random interstate could not possibly result in the death not of some other person but your own personal death at the hands of someone whose reasons have nothing to do with you or the qualities of your character, as if everything you'd ever been told about the relation between character and intention and outcome has been a fiction from start to—

Q.

—to finish, that you'd feel the alternating pulls of hysteria and dissociation and bargaining for your life in the way of foxholes or simply to blank catatonically out and retreat into the roar in your mind of the ramifying realization that your whole seemingly random and somewhat flaccid and self-indulgent but nevertheless fundamentally blameless life had somehow been connected all along in a terminal chain that has justified or somehow connected, causally, to lead you ineluctably to this terminal unreal point, your life's quote unquote point, its as it were sharp point or tip, and that canned clichés such as *fear seized me* or *this is something that happens to other people* or even *moment of truth* now take on a horrendous neural resonance and vitality wh—

Q.

Not of—just of being left narratively alone in the self-sufficiency of her narrative aspect to contemplate how little-kid-level *scared* you'd be, how much you'd despise and resent this sick twisted shit beside you ranting whom you'd kill without hesitation if you could while but at the same time feeling involuntarily the very highest respect, almost a deference— the sheer agential *power* of one who can make you feel this frightened, that he could bring you to this point simply by wishing it and now can, if he wished, take you past it, past yourself, turn you into a *grisly discovery, brutal sex slaying,* and the feeling that you'd do absolutely anything or say or trade anything to persuade him to simply settle for rape and let you go, or even torture, even willing to bring to the bargaining table a bit of nonlethal torture if only he'd settle for hurting you and choose to drive off and leave you hurt and breathing in the weeds and sobbing at the sky and traumatized beyond all recovery instead of as nothing, yes it's a cliché but this is to be *all*? this was to be the *end*? and at the hands of someone who probably didn't even finish Manual Arts High School and had no recognizable soul or capacity for empathy with anyone else, a blind ugly force like gravity or a rabid dog, and yet it was *he* who wished it to happen and who had the power and certainly the implements to make it happen, implements he names in a maddening singsong about knives and wives and scythes and awls, adzes and mattocks and other implements whose names she did not recognize but still even so *sounded* like wh—

Q.

Yes and a good deal of the anecdote's medial part's rising action detailed this interior struggle between giving in to hysterical fear and the level-headedness to focus concentration on the situation and to figure out something ingenious and persuasive to say to this sexual psychotic as he's driving deeper into the secluded area and looking ominously around for a propitious site and becoming more and more openly raveled and psychotic and alternately smiling and ranting and invoking God and the memory of his brutally slain mother and gripping the steering wheel so tightly that his knuckles are gray.

Q.

That's right, the psychopath is also a mulatto, although with aquiline and almost femininely delicate features, a fact that she has omitted or held back for a good portion of the anecdote. She said it hadn't occurred to her as important. In today's climate one wouldn't want to critique too harshly the idea of someone with a body like that getting into a strange automobile with a mulatto. In a way you have to applaud the broad-mindedness. I didn't at the time of the anecdote even really notice that she'd omitted the ethnic detail for so long, but there's something to applaud there as well, you'd have to concede, though if—

Q.

The point being that she thinks rapidly on her feet and determines that her only chance of surviving this encounter is to establish a connection with the quote soul of the sexual psychopath as he's driving them deeper into the woody secluded area looking for just the right spot to pull over and brutally have at her. That her object is to focus very intently on the psychotic mulatto as an ensouled and beautiful albeit tormented person in his own right instead of merely a threat to her or a force of evil or the incarnation of death. Try to bracket any New Age goo in the terminology and focus on the tactical strategy itself if you can because I'm well aware that what she is about to describe is nothing but a variant of the hoary old *love-will-conquer-all* bromide but bracket your contempt for a moment and see the concrete ramifications of — in this situation in terms of what she has the courage and apparent conviction to actually attempt here, because she says that sufficient love and focus can penetrate psychosis and evil and establish a quote soul-connection, unquote, and that if the mulatto can be brought to feel even a minim of this alleged soul-connection there is some chance that he'll be unable to follow through with actually killing her. Which is of course on a psychological level not implausible at all, since sexual psychopaths are well known to depersonalize their victims and liken them to objects or dolls, *Its* and not *Thous* so to speak, which is often their explanation of how they are able to inflict unimaginable brutality on a human being, namely that they do not see them as human beings at all but merely as objects of the psychopath's own needs and intentions. But yet love and empathy of this kind of connective magnitude demand quote unquote *total focus,* she said, and her terror and totally understandable concern for herself were at this point distracting to the extreme, so she realized that she was in for the most difficult and important battle of her life, she said, a battle that was to be engaged completely within herself and her own soul's capacities, which idea by this time I found extremely interesting and captivating, particularly because she is so unaffected and seemingly sincere when *battle of one's*

life is usually such a neon indication of melodrama or manipu-
lation of the listener, trying to bring him to the edge of his
seat and so forth.

Q.

I note with interest that now you are interrupting me to
ask the same questions I was interrupting her to ask, which
is precisely the sort of convergence of—

Q.

She said the best way to describe focus to a person who
hadn't undertaken what were apparently her denomination's
involved and time-consuming series of lessons and exercises
was to envision focus as intense concentration further sharpened and intensified to a single sharp point, to envision a
kind of needle of concentrated attention whose extreme thin-
ness and fragility were also, of course, its capacity to penetrate,
and that but the demands of excluding all extraneous concerns
and keeping the needle thinly focused and sharply directed
were extreme even under the best of circumstances, which
these profoundly terrifying circumstances were of course not.

Q.

Thus in the car, under let's now keep in mind enormous
duress and tension, she marshals her concentration. She stares
directly into the sexual psychopath's right eye—the eye that
is accessible to her in his aquiline profile, as he drives—and
wills herself to keep her gaze on him at all times. She wills
herself not to weep or plead but merely to use her penetrating
focus to attempt to feel and empathize with the sex offender's
psychosis and rage and terror and psychic torment, and says
she visualizes the focus piercing through the mulatto's veil of
psychosis and penetrating various strata of rage and terror and
delusion to touch the beauty and nobility of the generic human
soul beneath all the psychosis, forging a nascent compassion-
based connection between their souls, and she focuses on the
mulatto very intently and tells him what she saw in his soul,
which she insisted was the truth. It was the climactic struggle
of her spiritual life, she said, what with all the under the

circumstances perfectly understandable terror and loathing of the sex criminal that kept threatening to dilute her focus and break the connection. But yet at the same time the effects of her focus on the psychotic's face were obvious—when she was able to hold the focus and penetrate him and hold the connection the mulatto at the wheel would become quiet, as if preoccupied. His right profile would tense and tighten hypertonically and his dead eyes filling with anxiety and conflict at feeling the delicate beginnings of the sort of connection with another soul he had always both desired and always also feared in the very depths of his psyche, of course.

Q.

Just that it's commonly acknowledged that a primary reason your prototypical sex killer rapes and kills is that he regards rape and murder as his only viable means of establishing some kind of meaningful connection with his victim. That this is a basic human need. I mean some sort of connection of course. But also frightening and susceptible to delusion and psychosis. It is his twisted way of having a, quote, relationship. Most conventional relationships terrify him. But with a victim, raping and killing, the sexual psychotic is able to forge a quote unquote connection via his ability to make her feel intense fear and agony, while his exultant sensation of total Godlike control over her—what she feels, whether she feels, breathes, lives—this allows him some margin of safety in the relationship.

Q.

Simply that this is what first seemed somehow ingenious in her tactics, however daffy the terms—that it addressed the psychotic's weakness, his grotesque shyness as it were, the terror that any conventional, soul-exposing connection with another human being will threaten him with engulfment and-slash-or obliteration, i.e. that *he* will become the victim. That in his cosmology it is either feed or be food—God how lonely, do you feel it?—but that the brute control he and his sharp implement hold over her very life and death allow the mulatto to feel that here he is in one hundred percent total control of the relationship and thus that the connection he so desperately needs will not expose or engulf or obliterate him. Nor is this of course all that substantively different from a man sizing up an attractive girl and approaching her and artfully deploying just the right diction and pushing just the right buttons to induce her first to go out with him and then to come home with him, never once saying anything or touching her in any way that isn't completely gentle and pleasurable and seemingly respectful, leading her gently and respectfully to his satin-sheeted bed and in the light of the moon making exquisitely attentive love to her and making her come over and over until she's quote begging for mercy and is totally under his emotional control and feels that she and he must be deeply and unseverably connected for the evening to have been so perfect and mutually respectful and fulfilling and then lighting her cigarettes and engaging in an hour or two of pseudo-intimate postcoital whispering in his wrecked bed and seeming very close and content when what he really wants is to be in some absolutely antipodal spot from wherever she is from now on and is thinking about how to give her a special disconnected telephone number and never contacting her again. And that an all too obvious part of the reason for his cold and maybe somewhat victimizing behavior is that the potential profundity of the connection he has worked so hard to make her feel frightens him. I know I'm not telling you anything you haven't already decided you know. With your slim chilly smile. You're not the only one who can read people, you know. He's a fool because he thinks he's made a fool of her, you are thinking. Like he got away with something. The satyrosaurian sybaritic heterosapien male, the type you short-haired catamenial bra-burners can see coming a mile away. And pathetic. He's a predator, you believe, and he too thinks he's a predator, but he's the really frightened one, he's the one running.

Q.

I am just inviting you to consider that it isn't the *motivation* that's the psychotic part. The variation is simply the psychotic

one of substituting rape, murder, and mind-shattering terror
for making exquisite love and giving a false number whose
falseness isn't so immediately evident that it will hurt someone's feelings and cause you unease.

Q.

And please know that I'm quite familiar with the morphology behind these bland little expressions of yours and the
affectless questions. I know what an excursus is and I know
what a dry wit is. Do not think you are getting out of me things
or admissions I'm unaware of. Just consider the possibility
that I understand more than you think. Though if you'd like
another I'll buy you another no problem.

Q.

All right. Once more, slowly. That literally killing instead
of merely running is the killer's psychotically literal way of
resolving the conflict between his need for connection and his
terror of being in any way connected. Especially, yes, to a
woman, connecting with a woman, whom the vast majority
of psychotics on record do hate and fear, often due to twisted
relations with the mother as a child. The psychotic sex killer
is thus often symbolically killing the mother, whom he hates
and fears but of course cannot literally kill because he is still
enmeshed in the infantile belief that without her love he will
die. The psychotic's relation to her is one of both terrified
hatred and terror and desperate pining need. He finds this
conflict unendurable and must thus symbolically resolve it
through psychotic sex crimes.

Q.

Hers had little or no—she seemed simply to relate what
literally happened without commenting one way or the other,
or reacting. But nor was she disassociated or monotonous.
There was a disingen—an equanimity about her, a sense of
residence in herself or a type of artlessness that did, does, that
resembled a type of intent concentration. This I had noticed
at the park when I first saw her and crouched by the blanket,

since a high degree of unself-conscious concentration is not standard issue for a beautiful Cruncher on a wool blanket sitting contra—

Q.

Well still, though, it's not exactly what one would call esoteric is it since it's in the air, and common knowledge about childhood's connection to adult sex crimes in the popular culture constantly, presently. Turn on the news for Christ's sake. It doesn't exactly take a von Braun to connect problems with connecting with women to problems in the childhood relation to the mother. It's in the air.

Q.

That it was a titanic struggle, she said, in the Cutlass, heading deeper into the secluded area, because whenever for a moment her terror bested her or she for any reason lost her intense focus on the mulatto, even for a moment, the effect on the connection was obvious—his profile smiled and his right eye again went empty and dead as he recrudesced and began once again to singsong psychotically about the implements in his trunk and what he had in store for her once he found the ideal secluded spot, and she could tell that in the wavering of the soul-connection he was automatically reverting to resolving his connectionary conflict in the only way he knew. And I clearly remember her saying that by this time, whenever she succumbed and lost her focus for a moment and his eye and face reverted to creepy psychotic unconflicted relaxation, she was surprised to find herself feeling no longer paralyzing terror for herself but a nearly heartbreaking sadness for him, for the psychotic mulatto. And I'll say that it was at roughly this point of listening to the story, still nude in bed, that I began to admit to myself that not only was it a remarkable postcoital anecdote but that this was, in certain ways, rather a remarkable woman, and that I felt a bit sad or wistful that I had not noticed this level of remarkability when I had first been attracted to her in the park. This was while the mulatto has meanwhile spotted a site that meets his criteria and has

pulled crunchingly over in the gravel by the side of the secluded woody area's road and asks her, somewhat apologeti-
cally or ambivalently it seems, to get out of the Cutlass and
to lie prone on the ground and to lace her hands behind
her head in the position of both police arrests and gangland
executions, a well-known position obviously and no doubt
chosen for its associations and intended to emphasize both
the ideas of punitive custody and death. She does not hesitate
or beg. She had long since decided that she must not give in
to the temptation to beg or plead or cajole or in any way
appear to resist him. She was rolling all her dice on these
daffy-sounding beliefs in connection and nobility and compassion as more fundamental and primary components of soul
than psychosis or evil. I note that these beliefs seem far less
canned or flaccid when someone appears willing to stake their
life on them. This was as he orders her to lie prone in the
roadside gravel while he goes back to the trunk to browse
through his collection of torture implements. She says by this
time she could feel very clearly that her acerose focus's connective powers were being aided by spiritual resources far greater
than her own, because even though she was in a prone position
and her face and eyes were in the clover or phlox in the gravel
by the car and her eyes tightly shut she could feel the soul-
connection holding and even strengthening between her and
the mulatto, she could hear the conflict and disorientation in
the psychotic sex offender's footsteps as he went to the Cutlass's
trunk. She was experiencing a whole new depth of focus. I
was listening to her very intently. It wasn't suspense. Lying
there helpless and connected, she says her senses had taken
on the nearly unbearable acuity we associate with drugs or
extreme meditative states. She could distinguish lilac and shat-
tercane's scents from phlox and lambsquarter, the watery mint
of first-growth clover. Wearing a corbeau leotard beneath a
kind of loose-waisted cotton dirndl and on one wrist a great
many bracelets of pinchbeck copper. She could decoct from
the smell of the gravel in her face the dank verdure of the
spring soil beneath the gravel and distinguish the press and
shape of each piece of gravel against her face and large breasts

through the leotard's top, the angle of the sun on the top of
her spine and the swirl in the intermittent breeze that blew
from left to right across the light film of sweat on the top of
her back and shoulder blades. In other words what one might
call an almost hallucinatory accentuation of detail, the way
in some nightmares you remember the precise shape of every
blade of grass in your father's lawn on the day your mother
left him and took you to live at her sister's. Many of the cheap
bracelets were gifts, apparently. She could hear the largo tick of
the cooling auto and bees and bluebottle flies and stridulating
crickets at the distant treeline, the same volute breeze in those
trees she could feel at her back, and birds — imagine the temptation to despair in the sound of carefree birds and insects
only yards from where you lay trussed for the gambrel — of
tentative steps and breathing amid the clank of implements
whose very shapes could be summoned by the sounds they
made against one another when stirred by a conflicted hand.
The cotton of her dirndl skirt the light sheer unrefined cotton
that's almost gauze.

Q.

It's a frame for butchers. Hang by the hind feet to bleed.
It's from the Hindu for *leg*. It never occurred to her to get
up and run for it. A certain percentage of psychotics slice
their victims' Achilles tendons to hobble them and preclude
running for it, perhaps he knew that was unnecessary with
her, could feel her not resisting, not even considering resisting,
using all her energy and focus to sustain her feeling of connection with his conflicted despair. She says she felt terror but
not her own. She could hear the sound of the mulatto finally
extracting some kind of machete or bolo from the trunk, from
her description, then a brief half-stagger as he tried to come
back up along the length of the Cutlass to where she lay prone,
and heard then the groan and sideways skid as he went to his
knees in the gravel beside the car and was sick. Puked. Can
you imagine. That *he* is now the one puking from terror.
She says by this time something was aiding her and she was
completely focused. That by this time she was focus itself, she

had merged with connection itself. Her voice in the dark is uninflected without being flat — it's matter-of-fact the way a bell is matter-of-fact. It feels as if she's back there by the road. A kind of scotopia. How in her oneiric state of heightened attention to everything around she said the clover smells like weak mint and the phlox like mown hay and she feels the way that she and the clover and phlox and the dank verdure beneath the phlox and the mulatto retching into the gravel and even the contents of his stomach were all made of precisely the same thing and were connected by something far deeper and more elemental than what we limitedly call quote unquote love, what from her perspective she calls connection, and that she could feel the psychotic fellow feeling the truth of this at the same time she did and she could feel the plummeting terror and infantile conflict this feeling of connection aroused in his soul and stated again without drama or self-satisfaction that she felt this terror, not her own but his. That when he came to her with the bolo or machete and a hunting knife in his belt and some kind of ritualistic design like a samekh or palsied omicron drawn on his tenebrous brow in the blood or lipstick of a previous victim and turned her over into a rape-ready supine position in the gravel he was crying and chewing his lower lip like a frightened child, making small lost noises. And that she kept her eyes on his as he raised her poncho and gauzy skirt and cut away her leotard and underthings and raped her, which given the kind of surreal clarity of sensuous discernment she was experiencing in her state of total focus imagine what this must have felt like for her, being raped in the gravel by a weeping psychotic whose knife's butt jabs you on every thrust, and the sound of bees and meadow-birds and the distant whisper of the interstate and his machete clanking dully in the stone on every thrust, she claiming it took no effort of will to hold him as he wept and gibbered as he raped her and stroking the back of his head and whispering small little consolatory syllables in a soothing maternal singsong. By this time I found that even though I was focused very intently on her story and the rape in the road my own mind and emotions were also whirling and making connections and associations, for instance it struck me that this behavior of hers during the rape was an unintentional but tactically ingenious way to in a way prevent it, or transfigure it, the rape, to transcend its being a vicious attack or violation, since if a woman as a rapist comes at her and mounts her can somehow choose to *give* herself, sincerely and compassionately, she cannot be violated or raped, no? That through some sleight of hand of the psyche she was now giving herself instead of being quote taken by force, and that in this ingenious way, without resisting in any way, she had denied the rapist the ability to dominate and take. And, from gauging your expression, no I am not suggesting that this was the same as her asking for it or deciding she wanted it unquote, and no this does not keep the rape itself from being a crime. And in no way had she intended acquiescence or compassion as a tactic to empty the rape of its violating force, nor the focus and soul-connection themselves as tactics to cause in him conflict and pain and gibbering terror, so that at whatever point during the transfigured and sensuously acute rape she realized all this, saw the effects her focus and impossible feats of compassion and connection were having on his psychosis and soul and the pain they were in fact causing him, it became complex—her motive had been only to make it difficult for him to kill her and break the soul-connection, not to cause him agony, so that the moment her compassionate focus countenanced not just his soul but the effect of the compassionate focus itself on that soul it all became complex, an element of self-consciousness had been introduced and now was itself the object of focus, like some sort of diffraction or regress of self-consciousness and consciousness of self-consciousness. She didn't talk about this division or regress in any but emotional terms. But it was going on—the division. I was experiencing the same thing, listening. On one level my attention was intently focused on her voice and story. On another level I—it was as if my mind were having a garage sale. I kept flashing back to a lame joke during a freshman religion survey we all had to take as an undergrad—the mystic approaches the hot-dog stand and tells the vendor "Make me one with every-

thing." It wasn't the sort of division where I was both listening
and not. I was listening both intellectually and emotionally.
This religion survey was popular because the professor was so
colorful and such a stereotypical example of the sixties mental-
ity, several times during the semester he returned to the point
that distinctions between psychotic delusions and certain kinds
of religious epiphanies were very slight and esoteric and had
used the edge of a sharpened blade to describe the line between
them, and at the same time I was also remembering in near-
hallucinatory detail that evening's outdoor concert and festival
and the configurations of people on the grass and blankets
and the parade of lesbian folk singers on the poorly amplified
stage, the very configuration of the clouds overhead and the
foam in Tad's cup and the smell of various conventional and
nonaerosol insect repellents and Silverglade's cologne and bar-
becued food and sunburned children and how when I first
saw her seated foreshortened behind and between the legs of
a vegetarian-kabob vendor she was eating a supermarket apple
with a small supermarket price sticker still affixed to it and that
I'd watched her with a detached amusement to see whether she
would eat the sticker without taking it off. It took him a long
time to achieve release and she held him and gazed at him
lovingly the entire time. If I had asked a you-type question
such as did she really *feel* loving as the mulatto was raping
her or was she merely *conducting herself in a loving manner*
she would have gazed blankly at me and had no idea what I
was talking about. I remembered weeping at movies about
animals, as a child, even though some of these animals were
predators and hardly what you would consider sympathetic
characters. On a different level this seemed connected to the
way I had first noticed her indifference to basic hygiene at the
community festival and had formed judgments and conclu-
sions on that basis. Just as I can watch you forming judgments
based on the openings of things I'm describing that then prevent you from hearing the rest of what I try to describe. It's
due to her that this makes me sad for you instead of pissed
off. And all this was going on simultaneously. I felt more
and more sad. I smoked my first cigarette in two years. The

moonlight had moved from her to me but I could still see
her profile. A saucer-sized circle of fluid on the sheet had
dried and vanished. You are the sort of auditor for whom
rhetoricians designed the Exordium. From below in the gravel
she subjects the psychotic mulatto to the well-known Female
Gaze. And she describes his facial expression during the rape
as the most heartbreaking thing of all. That it had been less
an expression than an anti-expression, empty of everything
as she unpremeditatedly robbed him of the only way he'd ever
found to have power. His eyes were holes in the world. She
felt heartbroken, she said, as she realized then that her focus
and connection were inflicting far more pain on the psychotic
than he could ever have inflicted upon her. This was how she
described the division. A hole in the world. I began in the
dark of our room to feel terrible sadness and fear. I felt as
though there were far more genuine emotion and connection
in that anti-rape she suffered than in any of the so-called
lovemaking I spent my time pursuing. Now I'm sure you know
what I'm talking about now. Now we're on your terra firma.
The whole prototypical male syndrome. Eric drag Sarah to
teepee by hair. The well-known Privileging of the Subject.
Don't think I don't speak your language. She finished in the
dark and it was only in memory that I saw her clearly. The
well-known Male Gaze. Her pose a protofeminine seated con-
traposto with one hip on a Nicaraguan blanket with a strong
smell of unrefined wool to it with her trust me on this *breathtaking* legs sort of curled out to the side so her weight was
on one arm stiff-armed out behind her and the other hand
held the apple — am I describing this right? can you — the toile
skirt, hair that reached the blanket, the blanket dark green
with yellow filigree and a kind of nauseous purple fringe, a
linen singlet and vest of false buckskin, sandals in her rattan
bag, bare feet with phenomenally dirty soles, beyond belief,
their nails like the nails of a laborer's hands. Imagine being
able to console someone as he weeps over what he's doing to
you as you console him. Is that wonderful, or sick? Have you
ever heard of *couvade*? No perfume, the slightest scent of
some unsoftened soap like those cakes of deep-yellow laundry

soap one's aunt tried to—I realized I had never loved anyone.
Isn't that trite? Like a canned line? Do you see how open I'm
being with you here? Who would go to the trouble of kabobing
only vegetables? I had to respect her blanket's boundary, on
the approach. You do not stroll up out of the blue and ask
to share someone's wool blanket. Boundaries are an important
issue with this type. I assumed a sort of respectful squat off
its fringe with my weight on my knuckles so that my tie hung
straight between us like a counterweight. As we casually
rapped and chatted and I deployed the blunt-confession-of-
true-motive tactic I watched her face and felt as though she
knew just what I was doing and why and was both amused
and responsive, I could tell she felt some affinity between us,
an aura of connection, and it's sad to recall the way I viewed
her acquiescence, the fact of her response, a little disappointed
that she was so easy, her easiness was both disappointing and
refreshing, that she was not one of these breathtaking girls
who believe themselves to be too beautiful to approach and
view any man as a supplicant or libidinous goon, the chilly
ones, and require tactics of attrition rather than feigned affinity, an affinity that is heartbreakingly easy to feign, I have to
say, if you know your female typologies. I can repeat that if
you like, if you want to get it exact. Her description of the
rape, certain logistics I'm omitting, was lengthy and detailed
and rhetorically innocent. I felt more and more sad, hearing
it, trying to imagine what she had been able to do, I felt more
and more sad that on our way out of the park I'd felt that
tiny stab of disappointment, even maybe anger, wishing she'd
been more of a challenge. That her will and wishes had opposed my own just a little. This is called Werther's Axiom,
whereby quote The intensity of a desire D is inversely propor-
tional to the availability of D's gratification. Known also as
Romance. And sadder and sadder that it had not once, it
seemed—you'll like this—occurred to me before what an
empty way this was to come at women, then. Not wicked or
predatory or culpable—empty. To gaze and not see, to eat
and not be full. Not just to feel but *be* empty. While meanwhile, within the narrative itself, she, deep inside the psychotic

"The Paris Review remains the single most important little magazine this country has produced."

—T. Coraghessan Boyle

THE
PARIS
REVIEW

Enclosed is my check for:

☐ $34 for 1 year (4 issues)
(All payment must be in U.S. funds. Postal surcharge of $10 per 4 issues outside USA)

☐ Send me information on becoming a *Paris Review* Associate.
Bill this to my Visa/MasterCard:
Sender's full name and address needed for processing credit cards.

_____
Card number   Exp. date

☐ New subscription   ☐ Renewal subscription
☐ New address

Name _____

Address _____

City _____ State _____ Zip code _____

Please send gift subscription to:

Name _____

Address _____

City _____ State _____ Zip code _____

Gift announcement signature _____

call (718)539-7085

Please send me the following:

☐ The Paris Review T-Shirt ($15.00)
Color _____ Size _____ Quantity _____
☐ The following back issues: Nos. _____

See listing at back of book for availability.

Name _____

Address _____

City _____ State _____ Zip code _____

☐ Enclosed is my check for $ _____
☐ Bill this to my Visa/MasterCard:

_____
Card number   Exp. date

BUSINESS REPLY MAIL

FIRST CLASS   PERMIT NO. 3119   FLUSHING, N.Y.

POSTAGE WILL BE PAID BY ADDRESSEE

THE PARIS REVIEW
45-39 171 Place
FLUSHING NY   11358-9892

No postage
stamp necessary
if mailed in the
United States

BUSINESS REPLY MAIL

FIRST CLASS   PERMIT NO. 3119   FLUSHING, N.Y.

POSTAGE WILL BE PAID BY ADDRESSEE

THE PARIS REVIEW
45-39 171 Place
FLUSHING NY   11358-9892

whose penis is inside her, seeing the palm's web as he tenta-
tively attempted to stroke her head in return, and seeing the
fresh cut and realizing it was his own blood the fellow had
used for his forehead's mark. Which is not a rune or glyph
at all, I knew, but a simple circle, the Ur-void, the zero,
that axiom of Romance we call also mathematics, pure logic,
whereby one does not equal two and cannot. And that the
quote rapist's mocha color and aquiline features could well
be brahminic instead of negroid. These and other details she
withheld—she had no reason to trust me. And nor can I—
and I can't for the life of me recall whether she ate the sticker,
nor what became of the apple at all. Terms like *romance* and
love and *soul* that I believed could be used only with quotation
marks, exhausted clichés. Believe that I felt the mulatto's fath-
omless sadness, then. I—

   Q.

   It's not a good word, I know. It's not just quote *sadness* the
way one feels sad at a film or a funeral. A falling, plummeting
quality, a timelessness. The way in winter the light gets just
before dusk. Or that—all right—how, say, at the height of
lovemaking, the very height, when she's starting to come,
when she's truly responding to you and you can see it in her
face that she's starting to come, her eyes widening in that way
that is both surprise and recognition, which not a woman alive
can fake or feign if you really look hard at her eyes, you know
what I'm talking about, that apical moment of maximum
human sexual connection when you feel closest to her, *with*
her, so much closer and finer than your own coming, which
always feels more like losing your grip on the person who's
grabbed you to keep you from falling, a neural sneeze that's
not even in the same ballpark's area code as *her* coming, and—
and I know what you will make of this but I'll tell you anyhow—but how even this moment of maximum connection
and joint triumph and joy at making them start to come has
this void of piercing sadness to it of their eyes as they widen
to their very widest point and then as they come begin to
close, the eyes do, and you feel that familiar blade of sadness

inside your exultation as they arch and pulse and their eyes
close and you can feel that they've closed their eyes to shut
you out, you've become an intruder, their union is now with
the feeling itself, that behind those lids the eyes are rolled
around and staring inward, into some void where you who
brought them there can't follow. That's shit. I'm not putting
it well. I can't make you feel what I felt. You'll turn this into
Narcissistic Man Wants Woman's Gaze On Him At Climax,
I know. Well I don't mind telling you I'd begun to cry, at
the anecdote's climax. Not loudly, but I did. Neither of us
were smoking by now. We were both up against the head-
board, facing the same way, though addorsed is how I remember us for the story's last part, when I wept. Memory is strange.
I do remember listening for some acknowledgment from her
that I was crying. I felt embarrassed—not for crying, but for
wanting so badly to know how she took it, whether it made
me seem sympathetic or selfish. She stayed where he left her
all day, supine in the gravel, weeping, she said, and giving
thanks to her particular religious principles and forces. When
of course as I'm sure you could have predicted I was weeping
for myself. He left the knife and drove off in the Cutlass,
leaving her there. He may have told her not to move or do
anything for some specified interval. If he did, I know she
obeyed. She said she could still feel him inside her soul, the
mulatto—it was hard to break the focus. I felt certain that
the psychotic had driven off somewhere to kill himself. It
seemed clear from the anecdote's outset that someone was
going to have to die. The story's emotional impact on me was
profound and unprecedented and I will not even try to explain
it to you. She said she wept because she realized that as she
stood hitchhiking her religion's spiritual forces had guided
the psychotic to her, that he had served as an instrument of
growth in her faith and capacity to focus and alter energy fields
by the action of her compassion. She wept out of gratitude, she
says. He left the knife up to the handle in the ground next to her
where he had thrust it, apparently stabbing the ground dozens of
times with desperate savagery. She said not one word about
my own weeping or what it signified to her. I displayed far

more affect than she did. She learned more about love that day with the sex offender than at any other stage in her spiritual journey, she said. Let's both have one last one and then that will be it. That her whole life had indeed led inexorably to that moment when the car stopped and she got in, that it was indeed a kind of a death, but not at all in the way she had feared as they entered the secluded area. That was the only commentary she indulged in, just at the anecdote's end. I did not care whether it was quote true. It would depend what you mean by true. I simply didn't care. I was moved, changed — believe what you will. My mind seemed to be moving at the quote speed of light. I was so sad. And that whether or not what she believed happened happened — it seemed true even if it wasn't. That even if the whole focused-soul-connection theology, that even if it was just catachretic New-Age goo, her belief in it had saved her life, so whether or not it's goo becomes irrelevant, no? Can you see why this, realizing this, would make you feel conflicted in — of realizing that your entire sexuality and sexual history had less genuine connection or feeling than I felt simply lying there listening to her talk about lying there realizing how lucky she'd been that some angel had visited her in psychotic guise and shown her what she'd spent her whole life praying was true? You believe I'm contradicting myself. But can you imagine how any of it felt? Seeing her sandals across the room on the floor and remembering what I'd thought of them only hours before? I kept saying her name and she would ask *What?* and I'd say her name again. I'm not afraid of how this sounds to you. I'm not embarrassed now. But if you could understand, have I — can you see why there's no way I could let her just go away after this? Why I felt this apical sadness and fear of the thought of her getting her bag and sandals and New-Age blanket and leaving and laughing when I clutched her hem and begged her not to leave and said I loved her and closing the door gently and going off barefoot down the hall and my never seeing her again? Why it didn't matter whether she was fluffy or not terribly bright? Nothing else mattered. She had all my attention. I'd fallen in love with her. I believed she could save me.

I know how this sounds, trust me. I know your type and I know what you're bound to ask. Ask it now. I felt she could save me I said. Ask me now. Say it. I stand here naked before you. Judge me, you chilly cunt. You dyke, you bitch, cooze, slut, gash, cunt. Happy now? All judgments confirmed? Be happy. I do not care. I knew she could. I knew I loved her. End of story.

Six Bodies

Frank Yamrus

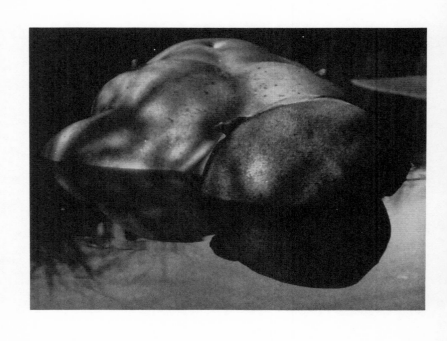

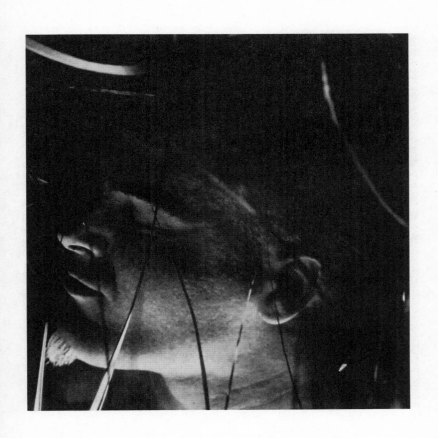

Wisława Szymborska

Negative

In the dun-colored sky
A cloud even more dun-colored
With the black outline of the sun.

To the left, that is, to the right
A white cherry branch with black flowers.

On your dark face, light shadows.
You have sat down at a small table
And laid your grayed hands on it.

You give the impression of a ghost
Who attempts to summon the living.

(Because I'm still counted among them,
I should appear and knock:
Good night, that is, good morning,
Farewell, that is, hello.
Not being stingy with questions to any answer
If they concern life,
That is, the storm before the calm.)

> —*translated from the Polish*
> *by Joanna Trzeciak*

Two Poems by Brad Davis

Simple Enough

In my home we take turns with the remote
and whoever's turn it is calls the show.

Rule two: a change of turn must occur
on the half hour at the commercial break.

If there's a question of whose turn is next
the clicker always travels clockwise.

What more is there to know? We speak
in tongues. We live nowhere near the water.

Where am I going with this?
I'm holding the remote and it's my call.

If someone would write it I'd read cover
to cover *The Sociology of Druthers*.

But I'm stalling. Silence and glossolalia
come easier to me than this posturing,

this fidgeting with the clicker. Last night
I dreamt of falling into snow.

In Your Absence

I sit. She cooks.
It's not what it looks like.
But then, what *does* it look like?
Is she pretty?
How old am I?

She cooks. I think
creole, barbecue, stir-fry, anything
at all other than what you won't be eating
with me tonight at this counter
in this small town.

What does it look like
now? A man, a woman, a roadside diner.
It's all so damn small from the moon!
Remember? We woke up
that morning—men were on the moon,

and that photograph, "earthrise,"
right there, front page—remember?
They were your words: *so damn small.*
So damn perfect—that photograph—
tore my world to confetti.

Across the counter she waits. I think
I'll say it: *The usual.* New England boiled dinner
with milk and a side of onion rings.
For one. As always,
she cooks. I remember.

Joanie Mackowski

Waiting

The café walls are covered with pictures of flying parrots;
I take a table, rest my arms; the table gently tips.
A dozen strangers sit and sit and talk, all they do is lovely,
and tea leaves circle in their cups like hawks above the valley.

A woman reads a magazine, flecks ashes on the table;
a man pushes his plate away while fifty angels pull.
Outside a light snow's coming down; it heaps the cars with
    pillows.
The waitress hums a tune off-key and stacks a plate with apples.

I'm waiting on this cloudy evening, in fumes of cake and
    diesel,
so I find a book. It's not mine; it must be somebody's. "O-
klahoma is part of the great plains, rich with swaying grasses;
every winter is cold as death, and every summer blazes."

I find that book predictable, so I go to find another,
but the shelf is nearly empty now—only one book there:
a pictorial history of bullfighting, written by Señor Pendu;
it's always nice to be reminded that knowledge is abundant.

The spine is stained with coffee, the pages in shreds and tatters;
but it's chock full of glossy photos of famous matadors.
On another page, five fearsome bulls wait beneath a tree;
I read, "The arena's full of blood, sand, grace and poetry."

I thumb through pages absently while waiting for a fellow.
A man approaches my table; he pauses, then says, "hello."

I not quite sure if he's the fellow I agreed to meet—
does our memory make us strong, or does it make us timid?

The sky outside is charcoal gray, the clouds in shapes like
   carrots;
the air in here is charcoal gray because of the cigarettes.
All the glowing cigarette butts are wee lighthouses in a row!—
cars outside flick their headlights on to know the world they
   narrow.

While waiting for God's fingertips at last to touch Adam's,
I count the ridges on the forehead of each sad Madame.
There're fourteen thousand seven hundred and a dozen ridges;
where the land is flat as milk the sky bends down and drinks.

The teacups knock about like bones, the chairs like summer
   thunder.
A woman puts her fork down; she smells of lavender.
Out in the street a car doesn't stop, so it bends another's
   fender.
The woman runs out through the door screaming "our brains
   are starving!"

While waiting, I've forgotten why, in Café Paradiso,
I try an arcane meditation, and I feel my body dissolve.
The sugar is not so enlightened, and floats in my tea like
   diamonds—
it must *demand* its nothingness, *demand* to lose its dazzle.

A gentleman on a bicycle pedals before the windows;
let's all turn into seagulls now and go wherever the wind goes.
Let's all be free as milkweed, free as the eye's wonders,
and inside every sugar bowl's an Oklahoma winter.

Let's all be as free as atoms, as free as Armageddon,
as free as all of god's angels who can't count up to ten.
Let's all crawl into burlap bags and play with roadside kittens;
let's live by the airport and stuff our ears with cotton.

While waiting for my rendezvous, I order a turkey sandwich
and finally hear the thread-like voice coming from my wrist-
   watch.
"Tut tut," it says, "your eight ball's sunk. Life's moving on
   without you."
Oh well, I say, so long, farewell, auf Wiedersehen, adieu—

but still waiting for their destinies in a stupid café
twenty tea drinkers get on their knees, clasp their hands and
   pray.
It's good to pray while the tea steeps or whenever there's time
   to kill;
the waitress prances like a horse, laughs, "life is such a tickle."

While waiting agitatedly in the paradise I made, o-
lé, olé! the vases say and throw their roses down.
So I draw my little sword, I kill the stumbling bull,
and blood, sand, grace and matadors fall onto my pillow.

Richard Kenney

Venice and Mars

—for Harry Ford

The Venetian Republic regarded the art of mirror-making as a state secret, to be conserved by any sanction necessary, including the most extreme.

●

Scuola Veneziana, copia di un affresco perduto, secolo XV (?)—

●

       Brass plaque; canvas protected behind a lexan
veil in the Lost Museum's millennial simulacra
(locked) collection: *copy . . . original . . . Venetian
   school . . .*
see here, through the glaze of old cobalt, locust-
wing of crazed and flaking lacquer, ocher,
mercury, this queer, clichéd seascape: coasting
vessel (Venice in the middle distance) steeped
in storm-light, lateen spars pressed over, tipped
like gauge needles buried in the red—

●

                    And here, *Venice*
(as though this were the painting!) as, here, mirror
at its mouth, a medieval, closed, stone Europe,
dead or sleeping, trailing a ruffed wrist in the tepid
Mediterranean here, this one city open like a vein . . .

●

And the world about to change forever. Retouch the
   narrative:

not *History*, the *Birth of the Renaissance*, per se,
but rather this paint rendering of the awful vernal
instant itself: a tale of intrigue, of murder, maybe, or narrow
escape. Observe two figures: one, on a writ
of the Council of Ten, secretly impersonates
the City; he's taken passage on a fast ship. His intercept
lies in the future of this painting, there at the vanishing
point —

•

Towards which a second, masked figure's set
his own course, some days before, by the slow
land route. Watch his carriage. His eyes are mirrors. Illegal
knowledge spurs him.

•

In the past of this painting, lantern glow
late, at the lost articles division of the Guild
of Venetian Glassmakers, where a fresh-cut goose quill
scritches, *tic tic*. Tycho sleeps, and Kepler; Galileo's
moon, too, is smooth as these dark canals.
Still, something's up: a spirit level
tips —

•

As, hove to in an equinoctial gale
off the half-spilled Adriatic slope, a galeass
lies over in the dark, her glass still falling.
Folded parchment weeps against wet skin
below, where, a punched sail bag, serge and voile,
on Guild retainer, our milky-cheeked assassin
swallows, redoubles in the dark, swallows,
pressing his veined eyes, watermarked, the will
of Venice an inky cobweb in his stocking.

•

                                                    Still,
on balance, this chop may be negotiable:
brine in the dark canal, where hammer and anvil,
gimballing, hang cocked to smash one polished
optical effect, a purloined notion cushioned,
curved in the ark of another brain's blue heaven, lurching
north now, under a plumed hat, by fast night coach . . .

•

So ends an age. *O, Renaissance!* This vanity
reflects: no crosshairs raised here since the Milvian
Bridge: so, each millennium, the clergy
changes costume, muttering the old remarriage
services: earth and sky, love and
war—repairing constellated ceilings, hemming
veils, repapering the text—whose black event-
horizon, closed, leaks X rays nonetheless: slight mirage,
a bone or two, and thus antiquity's
declassified.

•

          Secrets! Since then, what leak, what hemorrhage
of hot self-knowledge, what dead sky-scrawled, half-
    mistaken quid-
ity at what price? Venusian swamps drained. Martian
towpaths drifted over with red sand, now—and ridge
and rille and moon and star, the whole numeric, mirror-
handed, death-haunted dream! The New Myth! Mercury
in place at last!

•

          But, too, it's had its awkward
side: apocalypse: that clipped ulp of heavy hydrogen

gone up, as gas will, O, and *Kyrie,*
what won't stay hid! The whole reliquary, quark
and string come loose, and what left now but candle-lit
vigil, divination of the vapor trails that thread the black
   reaches
of our children's dreams, where even light can't
leap a straight line through. What whistling in the dark watch
now, our poor priests' teeth clicking *tic tic*, wit-
less clock like a geiger counter in the background, Trojan
women shrieking like our radars through the night —

                    •

                                    Dish

and goblet shatter on that shrill note. How can one age
change into another? Turn the glass: antiquity
advances like the desert now, like déjà
vu, where all originals are lost in the white
future of this painting.

                    •

                          But how shall this catastrophe occur,
you'll ask? A great museum fire, Lascaux
and metro saved, maybe, the rest to hell? Not arson,
then? The last curator whispers *mirrors,*
see? This small reflecting telescope some careless
hand's turned skywise on the windowsill . . . a sunny
afternoon . . . oil paint . . . a thread of smoke . . .

                    •

                                    Alas!

As fire draws water, so in the skull's low basin
sun once drew dewdrops of the eye's clear humors:
what clear look led Tycho to Kepler
to the ellipse of Mars? By what lost taxidermy
DNA's stitched up from nothing, what poor Sinbad's

sojourn up among the rat-faced hominids whom
God left too long in the dark, striking copies
of themselves —

•

        Now this, the mirror's backtalk: demi-
gods, a conscious artifact! supreme Daedal-
ian moment, O, where the flat ancestral ocean cap-
illaries inland: here the spice route intersects
the silk road, one and minus one, where the optic
nerve ends, where the little man at the masthead's drill
eye catches sun-glint from the camel's burnished cheekplate,
   and syntax
of the sandstorm comes at last to glass.

•

                How Aladdin's
smoke slips back! — the earth tips west again; new djinn
appear, and find their way to this condition,
paint in a square vitrine. This lunatic tale, too, cirque
and mare, what consequence it limns! A little unlit
tinder, flint at the species' origin,
H_2 to something else, smeared on a polished dish
in an alternative universe . . . and look, now this: one
   small silicíc
chip gone stolen: lo! Europe and Heaven transformed! Latin
on the moon! The sun's old compact pocked and cracked.
   The Doge
can't sleep! Serene Republic sunk, unless — what? — one sick
cutthroat tossing in his berth revives, a lateen
sail shakes out and fills, slack canthus
at the corner of this blue-white, weeping sky —

•

Sic
semper, etc., you'll say, *that's empire*. And thus,
this painting: Venice, in a dust of ocher, *secco*
as it always seems, in retrospect. The spirit
level tips with a ship's inclinometer at land's
end, *so*, and one bone bubble full of mathematics seeks
another, rising up the map behind Piero
della Francesca's antique cornstalk lances
clacking and crossing like searchlights in the dark, *x*,
x, here, here, the mirror-maker's secret
broken once for all for another thousand
years' bad luck—

•

O, red sky in the—

•

Thus endeth
this tail of the dispensation of Venice, where sand annealed
to glass once, ground to a fineness first here, as an ill-
wind storming at the Martian surface, or the polished sand-
glass where we dreamt the Renaissance, and dream our
    own death
too, certainly, in this city of lost originals,
this city of dreams and vexed dreams, *anno*
mirabilis x x x x x, come now, reflecting these canals.

its pecked-at ripeness that looks ~~through~~ scars of ~~it~~
and moves on

its blood-prick testing ~~you want~~ ~~clearance from,~~ clearance from,

THE HAW LANTERN

Fires were taboo all over Ireland
when the high king in Tara saw the blaze
of the Easter fire Patrick lit at Slane.
Next came their confrontation of the hill,
the king's conversion and our heritage
dwindling down to poor hindsights like this:
the illumination we'd be fitter for
burns out of season in a wintry haw,
crab of the thorn, a small light for small people,
asking no more from them but that they keep
the wick of self-respect from dying out,
not dazzling them with rewards or terrors,
~~not long to blind them to consoling them.~~

And another story, where the old Greek roams
with his lantern, seeking for one just man -
I would end up in my own version of that one
being scrutinized from behind the haw
he holds up at eye level on its twig,
flinching before its bonded flesh and stone,
its pecked-at ripeness a~~nd tested staying power~~
I love possessively ~~and am~~ dismissed by.
                    yet
            and wait to be dismissed by

The ~~one~~ illumination we ~~are up to~~ might still be fit for,
burning out of season : ~~a~~ the wintry haw,
crab of the thorn , small light for small people

Then there's the story where an old Greek man

                              /

          ~~and pricked blood~~ and probed
            its blood-prick testing ~~that~~ I want
I want to pass   to pass

A manuscript page for the title poem of The Haw Lantern.

Seamus Heaney

The Art of Poetry LXXV

*Born in County Derry, Northern Ireland, in 1939, Seamus
Heaney was the eldest of nine children in a Catholic family.
After receiving a degree in English from Queen's University
in 1961, Heaney worked as a school teacher, then for several*

years as a freelancer. In 1975, he was appointed to a position in the English department at a college of education in Dublin, where he trained student teachers until 1981. Harvard University invited him for one term in 1979 and soon after, a part-time arrangement was proposed, allowing Heaney to teach the spring semester then return to Ireland and his family. In 1984 he was elected the Boylston Professor of Rhetoric and Oratory at Harvard. As well, from 1989 to 1994 he was Professor of Poetry at Oxford University. After being awarded the Nobel Prize for Literature in 1995, Heaney resigned from the Boylston Chair, but will still be affiliated with Harvard as a visiting poet-in-residence. He now lives in Dublin with his wife, Marie, with whom he has three children.

Heaney is the author of twelve collections of poetry, includ-ing Death of a Naturalist *(1966),* Door into the Dark *(1969),* Wintering Out *(1972),* North *(1975),* Field Work *(1979),* Sweeney Astray *(1984),* Station Island *(1985),* The Haw Lan-tern *(1987),* Seeing Things *(1991) and* The Spirit Level *(1996). His prose has been collected in three books:* Preoccupations *(1980),* The Government of the Tongue *(1989) and* The Re-dress of Poetry *(1995). His works also include a version of Sophocles'* Philoctetes, The Cure at Troy *(1990) and a transla-tion, with Stanislaw Baranczak, of Jan Kochanowski's* Laments *(1995).*

This interview took place over three mornings in mid-May of 1994 in Heaney's rooms at Harvard's Adams House. (It was briefly updated after Heaney received the Nobel.) A crab-apple tree was in full blossom outside his living-room window. At the end of the month, Heaney would return to Ireland. Throughout our conversation, student voices and laughter drifted from the corridor. The phone rang steadily, until it was unplugged. Tea was served with Pepperidge Farm cookies. A coffee table and two large oak desks were covered with neat piles of correspondence, manuscripts, committee paperwork, literary magazines, books, et cetera. Heaney sat on the sofa in the glow of a lamp. A comfortable mix of tidiness and clutter made it easy for us to begin. A bouquet of lilacs drooped in a vase nearby. On the mantel there were family snapshots:

his sons at the Wicklow cottage, all three children in Dublin
with their mother, his good friend Bernard McCabe leaping
joyfully into the air in Italy. Also, there was a Spode plate
with an image of Tintern Abbey reproduced on it and a framed
print called "The Tub of Diogenes," both cherished birthday
presents—Heaney had recently turned fifty-five. And there
was a postcard of Henri Rousseau's painting The Muse and
the Poet. *At each session, Heaney wore a suit, pressed white*
shirt and tie. His Doc Martens were polished. His white hair,
though neatly shorn, was tousled. He had traveled extensively
in recent weeks, and though his brown eyes were heavy-lidded,
his mind was alert and mischievous. After each session, we
had a glass of Jack Daniels.

INTERVIEWER

As you end your twelfth year at Harvard, what are your
impressions of American students?

SEAMUS HEANEY

When I came here first I was very aware of their eagerness
to be in contact with the professor. At home in Ireland, there's
a habit of avoidance, an ironical attitude towards the authority
figure. Here, there's a readiness to approach and a desire to
take advantage of everything the professor has to offer. That
unnerved me a bit at the start, but now I respect it. Also, the
self-esteem of American students tends to be higher. They
come to college with positive beliefs in their abilities, whatever
they are.

INTERVIEWER

Do you feel that teaching all these years has affected your
writing?

HEANEY

Well, it's bound to have affected my energy levels! I remember Robert Fitzgerald warning me, or at least worrying for me,

on that score. But for better or worse—I now feel for worse, earlier on I felt for better—I believed that poetry would come as a grace and would force itself through whenever it needed to come. My sense of the world, of what was laid out for me in my life, always included having a job. This simply has to do with my generation, my formation, my background—the scholarship boy coming from the farm. The fact of the matter is that the most unexpected and miraculous thing in my life was the arrival in it of poetry itself—as a vocation and an elevation almost. I began as a school teacher in Belfast in 1962. I taught for one year in St. Thomas's Secondary Intermediate School. I had a good degree in English at Queen's University and felt that I had some literary possibility, but I had no real confidence. Then in November of 1962 I began to write in earnest, and sort of hopefully. As an undergraduate I had contributed poems to the English Society magazine. I had been part of a class that included, among other people, Seamus Deane, who was very much the star of the group, and George McWhirter, now a poet at the University of British Columbia at Vancouver. And there were others with writerly ambitions around Queen's at the time—Stewart Parker, for example, who eventually became a dramatist—so I was one of that crowd. But I didn't have any sense of election or purpose or ambition. My pseudonym at Queen's, in the magazines where I published, was Incertus—Latin for *uncertain*—I was just kicking the ball around the penalty area, not trying to shoot at the goal. Then in 1962 the current began to flow. I remember taking down Ted Hughes's *Lupercal* from the shelves of the Belfast public library and opening it at "View of a Pig," and immediately going off and writing a couple of poems that were Hughes pastiches almost. The first one was called "Tractors"; I remember a line that said "they gargled sadly"—which pleased me a lot at the time. So I sent it out to the *Belfast Telegraph*— not the greatest literary journal in the world, but even so, it published that poem. And that was of immense importance because I knew no one at the paper, which meant that the thing had been accepted on its own merits, such as they were.

INTERVIEWER

You grew up in a family where the men were nonverbal. And you've acknowledged that the idea of rhyme first came to you as a pleasure via your mother. Can you speak a little bit about your home life as a child?

HEANEY

My father was a creature of the archaic world, really. He would have been entirely at home in a Gaelic hill-fort. His side of the family, and the houses I associate with his side of the family, belonged to a traditional rural Ireland. Also, nowadays, I am more and more conscious of him as somebody who was orphaned early on in life. His own father had died suddenly when he was quite young. His mother died of breast cancer. So he and his siblings were then fostered out and reared by aunts and uncles. My father grew up with three bachelor uncles, men who were in the cattle trade in a fairly substantial way, traveling back and forward to markets in the north of England, and it was from them that he learned the cattle trade. So the house where he spent his formative years was a place where there were no women, a place where the style was undemonstrative and stoical. All that affected him and, of course, it came through to us in his presence and his personality.

INTERVIEWER

What about your mother?

HEANEY

Well, my mother was more a creature of modernity. Her people lived in the village of Castledawson, which was in some respects a mill village. Many of the people there worked in Clarke's linen factory. One of her uncles was a stoker in the factory, one of her brothers worked there too, another drove a bread van — held the franchise, as it were, for a Belfast bakery in that Castledawson area. One of her sisters trained as a nurse, another went off to England and was there during the war, married eventually to a miner from Northumberland. I suppose you could say my father's world was Thomas Hardy and my mother's D.H. Lawrence. Castledawson was that kind of terrace-house village, spic-and-span working class. And there was a nice social punctilio about the McCanns—that was my mother's family name; it came out in their concern with dress codes and table manners and things like that. They liked you to have your shoes polished and your hair combed. They had a little allotment garden out at the back and a washhouse with a set of wringers. And I suppose I would call the McCanns democrats. They had a strong sense of justice and civil rights and they were great argufiers. They genuinely and self-consciously relished their own gifts for contention and censoriousness.

INTERVIEWER

What about the Heaneys? Were they democrats?

HEANEY

The Heaneys were aristocrats, in the sense that they took for granted a code of behavior that was given and unspoken. Argumentation, persuasion, speech itself, for God's sake, just seemed otiose and superfluous to them. Either you were an initiate in the code or you weren't. It had to do with their rural background, with the unspoken Gaelic thing that was still vestigially there.

INTERVIEWER

Did they speak Gaelic?

HEANEY

No, not at all. The Irish language hadn't been spoken in that part of Ulster for a century or two. But it sometimes seems to me that the gene pool in the Bann Valley hasn't been disturbed for a couple of thousand years.

INTERVIEWER

Were there books in the house?

HEANEY

Not many. The book environment was in my Aunt Sarah's house. She had trained as a schoolteacher in the 1920s and had got herself a library of sorts. She had a complete set of Hardy's novels, for example, and an early three-volume edition of Yeats's works — plays, stories and poems.

INTERVIEWER

What about your Aunt Mary?

HEANEY

Mary was my father's sister and she lived at home with us. And since I was the first child, I was her favorite. She was a woman with a huge well of affection and a very experienced, dry-eyed sense of the world. All the Heaney women had this inveterate realism that was only equaled by their kindness. They were very unblaming and very — not passive — vigilant. It was a live and let live thing with them, although they were also capable of a withering contempt, an ultimate, dismissive contempt. But then, in between, just tolerance and hauteur. Mary dispensed affection to all of us, but as I say, I was favored because I was the eldest.

INTERVIEWER

You must have very quickly become the fourth adult in the house.

HEANEY

Yes, I did. In my early teens I acquired a kind of representative status, went on behalf of the family to wakes and funerals and so on. And I would be counted on as an adult contributor when it came to farm work — the hay in the summertime, for example. But I remember that kind of responsibility being laid upon me almost formally the morning my brother Christopher was buried. He was our four year old who was killed in a road accident. I must have been thirteen or fourteen at the time. Anyway, I came home from college for the funeral and all the rest of the youngsters were there. And when I began to cry in the bedroom, my father said to me, "Come on now, if you cry, they'll all be crying."

That's memorialized in your poem "Mid-Term Break."

That's right.

What's it been like all these years having a transatlantic existence? Was it a strain on you as a husband and father?

The fact that Marie and the children were here with me in 1979—four months in Cambridge and then another month on Long Island—the fact that we had all been together for that time in Cambridge with friends we'd known even earlier in Ireland, Helen Vendler, for example, and Alfie and Sally Alcorn, that was very important when I was wondering about whether to accept the offer. Daddy wasn't going off into the unknown. There were many people here who knew not just me but Marie and the children also. The question was whether the four-month separation was worth it for the sake of the other eight months at home.

I had a dream, actually, the night before the decision had to be made. I dreamed that I was in the desert and it was night. I needed some place to lie down, some shelter, and came upon this lean-to made of posts angled up against some sort of wall or cliff face. And over the posts there were skins or some sort of covering. I crept in underneath this to sleep for the night and then in the next frame of the dream it's broad morning, sunlight, the cliff face has disappeared, the lean-to is gone, I'm out in the open. What I had taken to be a solid wall had actually been the side of a liner docked in the Suez Canal and during the night the liner had moved on.

So I took this to mean nothing is permanent, that I should go with it — although I'm sure there are other ways of interpreting it.

INTERVIEWER

One could look at the liner as Harvard, too?

HEANEY

Oh, you could indeed! Then, about the same time, we met the Swedish poet Tomas Tranströmer and his wife, Monika, and they said to us, "Look, things will work fine as long as you see each other every six weeks . . . Just don't let more than six weeks go past." So that became the contract. Marie had a sister living in Dublin at that stage, who was a sort of favorite aunt to the children, and she promised she'd stay with them for a week or two every springtime so that Marie could come over and visit me in Cambridge.

INTERVIEWER

Here in your rooms, even though it's clear that you've tried to make a nest for yourself, one can still sense that your life is very much elsewhere.

HEANEY

Yes, that's right. I think, you see, that if I'd got an apartment on Beacon Hill, say, and furnished it for myself, got in my bookcases and *objets* and pictures and made it a comfortable elsewhere, then that would have radically affected my relationship with home. So it was a wonderful thing to be offered this apartment in Adams House by Robert Kiely, who was and still is master. The point is that the apartment here is not an alternative life. It is like nesting on a ledge, being migrant, being in someone else's house, in fact. I am Bob and Jana Kiely's houseguest, more or less. The place I have here is not in any way an alternative to the life I have in Dublin. It's a transient arrangement. And for both me and the family, that has been psychologically very important. Then too I suppose it's fair to say that I came to an arrangement with myself that this period of the year would be an executive rather than a creative time. I would do my teaching, do poetry readings, be busy, be on the job and not worry too much about getting writing done. The other two-thirds of the year at home would be the writing time, the daydream time. And it has turned out, in fact, that the summer is the best time for me to write. When I go home, the actual vegetation and the summertime weather can sometimes work wonders. There's that sheer buildup of need that comes from having been away. And a kind of slaking comes just from being back. That has been the rhythm of it so far.

INTERVIEWER

It really isn't so long ago since you left Northern Ireland and supported yourself as a freelancer. You've just celebrated your fifty-fifth birthday and are now writing from the point of having a good part of your oeuvre behind you, having worked as the Boylston Professor at Harvard and until just recently as Professor of Poetry at Oxford. I wonder how you feel about these two contrasting experiences and if it's any different for you nowadays when you sit down to make a poem?

HEANEY

That experience of twenty years ago, when I left Northern Ireland and went to write full-time in Wicklow, obviously that cannot be repeated. It was crucial and intense. It had to do with that first vital step into risk. I gave up my job at Queen's University in 1972 as a fairly deliberate test of myself and my capacities. I was lucky to have had two books published and a third coming at that stage. I was lucky to have the support of artist friends and poet friends. Two people who were very important at the time were Ted Hughes and the painter Barrie Cooke, who also happens to be a friend of Ted's, one of the pike- and salmon-fishing confraternity. Anyway, they were all in favor of the move. And so, it must be said, was Marie, even though it was a case of going into the wilderness with the family, and putting things on a fairly frugal basis. Would we survive economically? Would I be able to write in a way that would justify leaving the job? So those were intense years, for sure. There was another different crisis later when I decided to leave the freelance life and go back to teaching in Dublin. I had been four years in the cottage in County Wicklow, from 1972 to 1976. For the first three of those years I was freelancing. During the fourth I had begun to teach at the teachers training college at Carysfort. I regretted doing so, of course, at the time. I knew in my writerly being that I was moving off-center but I also had a strong, contrary wish to do the right thing as a parent. I didn't resent going back into teaching, but I did know very clearly that I was abandoning something. Yet because I did know what I was doing, it was mitigated just a little. At any rate, my next book, which came out three years later, is one of my favorites. In its own way it was a book of change also; it moved me from the intensity of *North* to something more measured, in both formal and emotional terms.

INTERVIEWER

Are you speaking of *Field Work*?

HEANEY

Yes. *Field Work* told me that the move into jobsville was workable. It may not have produced crunch writing of the kind that was in *North,* but *North* came out of an unrepeatable period when I had my head down like a terrier at the burrow, going at it hot and heavy, kicking up the mold. That wasn't going to happen twice. *North* was the book *nel mezzo del cammin.* But even if *Field Work* was less obsessive, more formally rangy, full of public elegies and personal love poems and those Glanmore sonnets, it was still a proof that I could write poetry in my new situation. Then three years later I got into the Harvard arrangement and that was even better: eight months at work on my own, four months teaching. All the same, when I was teaching full-time in Carysfort, I did manage to get established in labor with *Station Island*. But maybe I'm making far too much of all this in retrospect, how different one year was from the next. I have begun to think of life as a series of ripples widening out from an original center. In a way, no matter how wide the circumference gets, no matter how far you have rippled out from the first point, that original pulse of your being is still traveling in you and through you, so although you can talk about this period of your life and that period of it, your first self and your last self are by no means distinct.

Still, you speak as if there have been definite periods and divisions. Do you feel guilt about having left the North? In a poem like "Exposure" where you admit, "I am neither internee nor informer; / An inner émigré, grown long-haired / and thoughtful . . ." one senses that you do. Yet could you have written the poems collected in *North* had you not left?

I don't think I could have, no. I got gathered in myself through leaving. I had a great sense of being battened down for action. Separation perhaps, rather than detachment. A certain resolve. The thing is, the Wicklow move was not some sudden transition. We came back from California in 1971 with a half-plan to leave Belfast and live freelance out in the country in Northern Ireland. But even so, leaving the north didn't break my heart. The solitude was salubrious. Anxiety, after all, can coexist with determination. The anxiety in a poem like "Exposure" is about whether the work that comes out of this move is going to be in any way adequate. The poem is asking itself, Is there enough here to hold the line against the atrocious thing that is happening up there? And the poet is saying, What am I doing but striking a few little sparks when what the occasion demands is a comet?

What caused the dramatic change in *North*?

HEANEY

I suppose the corollary of being battened down is being a bit tensed up. At the time when I was writing the poems, I was putting the pressure on myself and feeling, well, exposed as in "Exposure." I associate the poems of *North* with a particular place, the upstairs room of that cottage, me chain-smoking and working against a deadline, looking out into the sunlight, hunched over the table, anxious. And the anxiety is there, I think, in the very constriction of the quatrains of the poems.

INTERVIEWER

Did reading Robert Lowell and W.C. Williams and Robert Creeley influence you? Or was it as a result of translating *Sweeney Astray* that you began to write a much trimmer poem?

HEANEY

Those wafty little quatrains got started when I was in Berkeley, and they make their appearance in *Wintering Out*. Poems like "Westering" and "Anahorish" and so on. But the same kind of hovering four-line stanza is there earlier, in "Bogland" and the last poems in *Door into the Dark*. I had a genuine curiosity about Williams and read him fairly systematically when I was in California. Read him with affection but with puzzlement too. I suppose without knowing it I always wanted the line to have back echo, to sing on a little beyond where it ended, but what Williams seemed to be offering was a music that stopped exactly where the line stopped. No resonance, no back echo, no canorous note. I kept looking and saying, Is this all? and I came to realize that the answer was, Yes, this is all. But then I think that there is a dialogue or tension inherent in all verse between what you might call the strength of stunt in the line and the attractions of stretch. Certainly, after *North,* I very deliberately started on some poems that were more metrically and syntactically articulated. Sonnets. Rhymed pentameters. Things with a bit of lift to them. An element of song. And there's a poem in *Field Work* called "The Singer's House," which is really about the poet's and the poem's right to a tune in spite of the tunelessness of the world around them. The singer is David Hammond who is a good friend and had been a kind of lord of misrule in our early days around Belfast. One of the things that the Troubles did, of course, was to put a damper on all that carousing and freewheeling. People weren't going out at night. And then too, because the old political sediment was being stirred up inside everybody, little standoffs and sidelinings and divisions began to develop among people too. So the mood darkened. And then suddenly, ten years later, I was out at the Hammonds' summerhouse on the Atlantic coast in Donegal and we had this wonderful exalted evening. Singing, drinking, the whole "jocund company" mood. And it was a terrific reminder that what we call in the abstract *song* is a really vital category and one to be pursued without apology. So "The Singer's House" came out of that. In fact, the formal impulse in a lot of those poems in *Field Work* is an example of this Cavalier principle exerting itself against the Roundhead who is inside me too. I mean, who wouldn't like to write Mozartian poetry?

INTERVIEWER

What would Mozartian poetry be?

HEANEY

It would have all of the usual life in it. But it would have great formal acceleration. I recently read Christopher Marlowe's "Hero and Leander" and got this terrific lift from it because of the way it was rejoicing in its own resources as an invention. It gave you a music that was trampolining off itself, glamorous and delicious and self-conscious. There was genuine sweetness and swank in the writing, but underneath all that banner-flying beauty and merriment, there was terrific veteran knowledge. Real awareness of hurt and vindictiveness and violence. And there was wiliness. I thought it was astonishingly mature poetry to have been written by a young man. The poem has a Prospero awareness of all the penalties but it still retains an Ariel ability to keep itself sweet and lively.

INTERVIEWER
You don't think of anything you've written as Mozartian?

HEANEY
I don't, no.

INTERVIEWER
Doesn't a new risk introduce itself with time, that is the risk of being too much like oneself, or repeating oneself?

HEANEY
I suppose you inevitably fall into habits of expression. But the fact of the matter is that when you're engaged in the actual excitement of writing a poem, there isn't that much difference between being thirty-five or fifty-five. Getting warmed up and getting into the obsession and focus of writing is its own reward at any moment.

INTERVIEWER
And it's just as difficult now to make it go?

HEANEY
Absolutely. Perhaps more so. In the beginning, I think everybody writes for the high of finishing. There is a sprint towards the completed thing; you urgently want a reward, immediate gratification. But what I enjoy most nowadays is the actual process. When I get an idea, I just want to keep it going for as long as possible. In the beginning, if I thought of an image I sort of pounced on it and rushed through its implications inside — typically — six or eight quatrains. But to-day one of those originating images might suggest another, and the poem might go about its business obliquely and grow in a more zigzaggy, accretionary way. I'm more devoted at the moment to opener, sectioned kinds of things.

INTERVIEWER
Do you think of yourself more as an autobiographical poet, or a social poet or a pastoral poet or a political poet?

HEANEY

If I'm in that panic-stricken situation where someone who has absolutely no familiarity with poetry and no interest in it says to me, "What kind of poetry do you write?" I do tend to say, "Well, it's more or less autobiographical, based on memory." But I would also want to maintain that the autobiographical content per se is not the point of the writing. What matters is the shape-making impulse, the emergence and convergence of an excitement into a wholeness. I don't think I'm a political poet with political themes and a specifically political understanding of the world, in the way that Bertolt Brecht is a political poet or Adrienne Rich or, in a different way, Allen Ginsberg.

INTERVIEWER

Is Yeats a political poet?

HEANEY

Yeats is a public poet. Or a political poet in the way that Sophocles is a political dramatist. Both of them are interested in the polis. Yeats isn't a factional political poet, even if he does represent a definite sector of Irish society and culture and has been castigated by Marxists for having that reactionary, aristocratic prejudice to his imagining. But the whole effort of the imagining is towards inclusiveness. Prefiguring a future. So yes, of course, he is a poet of immense political significance, but I think of him as visionary rather than political. I would say Pablo Neruda is political.

INTERVIEWER

What about W.H. Auden?

HEANEY

Is it too sophisticated to say Auden is a civic poet rather than a political poet?

I remember your saying in an essay that Auden introduced to English writing of his era a regard of contemporary events, which had been neglected.

HEANEY
There are poets who jolt the thing alive by seeming to lift the reader's hand and put it on the bare wire of the present. It's a matter of cadence and diction quite often. But Auden did set himself up for a while very deliberately as a political poet. Certainly up until the early 1940s. And then he becomes, if you like, a meditative poet. A bit like Wordsworth. At first a political poet with a disposition that is revolutionary. And then come the second thoughts. But as Joseph Brodsky said to me once upon a time, intensity isn't everything. I believe Joseph was thinking then of Auden, the later Auden. The early Auden *is* intense, there's a hectic staccato artesian kind of thing going on, there's immense excitement between the words and in the rhythms. There's the pressure of something forcing through. And then that disappears. In the 1950s and 1960s you have the feeling that things are being inspected from above. I suppose the transition comes when he writes those sonnet sequences at the end of the 1930s, marvelous, head-clearing sequences like "In Time of War" and "The Quest," all vitality and perspective and intellectual shimmer. There is that sense of experience being invigilated and abstracted from a great height, but what is still there in that middle period is the under-energy of the language. Then finally that just disappears. And a kind of lexical burble begins to take over.

INTERVIEWER
How would you describe your own voice?

HEANEY
I tried very deliberately in *Field Work* to turn from a broody, phonetically self-relishing kind of writing to something closer

to my own speaking voice. And I think that from *Field Work* onwards I have been following that direction. It's a very different kind of linguistic ambition now from what I was after in *Death of a Naturalist* or *Wintering Out* or *North*. Those books wanted to be texture, to be all consonants, vowels and voicings, they wanted the sheer materiality of words. When I began, I was trying for concreteness and I was encouraged in this by Philip Hobsbaum, who liked my work when it was read at the workshop he ran in Belfast in the mid-sixties. The Group, as it was called.

INTERVIEWER

I've heard it said that your new poems—and I would include in this statement, all of "Squarings"—are part of a movement in poetry to go back to, not a Wordsworthian innocence, but a place pre-language, pre-nationalism, pre-Catholicism. Before all that is codified. Is this true?

HEANEY

Well, in "Squarings," there is a definite impatience and a definite desire to write a kind of poem that cannot immediately be ensnared in what they call the "cultural debate." This has become one of the binds as well as one of the bonuses for poets in Ireland. Every poem is either enlisted or unmasked for its clandestine political affiliations.

INTERVIEWER

Is that why "Squarings" is stripped of local reference, for instance?

HEANEY

But I think of them as intensely, intimately local.

INTERVIEWER

Yet there are no place names.

HEANEY

True enough.

INTERVIEWER

In the section about shooting marbles, for example, one could be in County Derry or Milwaukee; it's as if the action or experience of the poem were intended to be universal, rather than parochial.

HEANEY

I'm glad you think that. What I loved about those poems was the old sense of a sprint. The twelve-line form was just chanced upon at the start, but then it became a willfulness. I had a year off from teaching and dedicated myself to following the impulse of the sprint. Those poems were, in a way, written against the clock. In a couple of hours, an hour, even less; I'd have a go and revise it later. There was an air of devil-may-careness, abandon, a certain hurtle. And I was very grateful for that because the title sequence of *Station Island* had been an entirely different kind of writing. Something that had been slowly accrued.

INTERVIEWER

It is another example of a long poem.

HEANEY

But a slow poem too. There were sections put in and sections taken out. It was written, as it were, responsibly. The speaker in the poem was consonant with the writer behind it. There was a sense of public confessing.

INTERVIEWER

But there are characters and voices.

HEANEY

Yes, that's true. It has a certain heaviness of being about it. Different, as I say, from the devil-may-careness of "Squarings." The needle is always swinging between two extremes with me. One is the gravitas of subject matter, a kind of surly nose-to-the-groundness, almost a nonpoetry, and the other

is the lift and frolic of the words in themselves. I like poetry
that doesn't fancy itself up to be poetry.

Do you mean by the nature of its subject?

Yes, but I also like a touch of rough and readiness in the
language. Something in words that makes you realize all over
again what Louis MacNeice means when he says "world is
suddener than we fancy."

In writing "Squarings," where so much is stripped away,
did you feel you'd used up allegory and myth, which are fre-
quent in earlier books?

I didn't set out to avoid allegory and myth. Those modes
are forever available, and I'd hate to cut myself off from them.
It's more that the "Squarings" were a given note. An out-of-
the-blueness. The first one came through unexpectedly, but
feeling as if it had been preformed. This was after I'd finished
an assignment I'd been worrying about, a selection of Yeats's
poems with a long introduction for *The Field Day Anthology
of Irish Writing*. I'd been working for weeks in the National
Library in Dublin and on the day I finished, in the library,
the first words of the first poem in "Lightenings" came to
me, as if they had been embossed on my tongue: "Shifting
brilliances. Then winter light / In a doorway, and on the
stone doorstep / A beggar shivering in silhouette. / / So the
particular judgment might be set . . ." I felt exhilarated. The
lines were unlike what I'd been writing. So I just went with
it. The excitement for me was in a pitch of voice, a feeling
of being able to make swoops and connections, being able to
get into little coffers of pastness, things I had remembered
but never thought of writing about. For example, there's one

about crossing the Bay Bridge in San Francisco. It used to be
that when I was coming over from the San Francisco Airport—
I was teaching at Berkeley then, during 1970, 1971—there
would be one or two young soldiers in the back of the bus,
traveling across to Treasure Island Military Base, headed for
Vietnam. I remember feeling at that time that it was like
being in a death carriage. But somehow I did not feel that it
was a part of my subject, it was too implicated in the American
crisis. And yet it stayed in my mind, and I just took this flash
photograph of it when I was doing the twelve-liners. At that
time I was able to range all over the place, whatever kind of
melt or skim or glancing was going on. And I gave myself
permission, as they say, to go with it. The arbitrariness of the
twelve-line form, the impulse and swiftness of it made me
feel different from myself for a while. But I didn't have any
project of going beyond myth or allegory.

INTERVIEWER

Do you think losing both your parents affected your work?
In a way, in "Squarings," there is an obliteration of the past,
which is what comes with the death of one's parents.

HEANEY

I was at each deathbed, in the room with my siblings. Moments of completion. Both of them died peacefully—"got
away easy," as they might have said themselves. There wasn't
much turmoil or physical distress. My father died of cancer;
of course, there was a period of deterioration, but at the end
the actual hour-by-hour decline was relatively predictable and
relatively untroubled. My mother died from a stroke much
more quickly, inside three days. Again, we all had time to
assemble. There was a sense of an almost formal completion.
But also a recognition that nothing can be learned, that to be
in the presence of a death is to be in the presence of something
utterly simple and utterly mysterious. In my case, the experience restored the right to use words like *soul* and *spirit,* words
I had become unduly shy of, a literary shyness, I suppose,

deriving from a misplaced obedience to proscriptions of the abstract, but also a shyness derived from a complicated relationship with my own Catholic past. In many ways I love it and have never quite left it, and in other ways I suspect it for having given me such ready access to a compensatory supernatural vocabulary. But experiencing my parents' deaths restored some of the verity to that vocabulary. These words, I realized, aren't obfuscation. They have to do with the spirit of life that is within us.

INTERVIEWER

In your poem "Terminus" you describe a state of in-betweenness that characterizes your way of seeing the world. One might argue that a state of in-betweenness is necessary to be a writer, a poet. Do you feel your in-betweenness in the public arena of politics has won you the enmity of some of your countrymen?

HEANEY

I suppose the enmity comes from people who think I'm not sufficiently in-between. Some people in Northern Unionist quarters, for example, might see me as a typical Irish nationalist with an insufficient sympathy for the Unionist majority's position in the North. The in-betweenness comes into play more problematically in relation to the nationalist and republican traditions in Ireland. I am certainly a person with an Ireland-centered view of politics. I would like our understanding and our culture and our language and our confidence to be Ireland-centered rather than England-centered or American-centered. And there are two strains of Irish politics deriving from this. One is constitutional nationalism; that is to say, nationalist politics as they have been practiced by elected Irish representatives in the nineteenth century at Westminster, and then since 1921 at Stormont in the North and in the Dail in the Republic, and practiced most conspicuously over the last thirty years by John Hume. On the other hand, there is the strain of republican separatism, a more uncompromising ap-

proach to national independence represented most notably
by Gerry Adams and Sinn Fein and most atrociously by the
IRA. Now people with a strong republican commitment would
probably consider me to have been insufficiently devoted to
their program and policies and insufficiently vocal against what
they see as imperial British activities in Northern Ireland. In
1979, for example, on a train, I actually met a Sinn Fein official
who upbraided and challenged me on this score. Why was I
not writing something on behalf of the republican prisoners
who were then on what was called "the dirty protest" in the
Maze Prison? These were people striking for the right to be
treated as political prisoners. Thatcher was insisting on treating
them as what she called ODCs—Ordinary Decent Criminals.
The Tories were attempting to define the IRA as murderers
without any political status whatsoever, attempting to rob
their acts of any aura of political motivation or liberation.
There was a big, big agitation going on in the prison. The
prisoners were living in deplorable conditions. Enduring in
order to maintain a principle and a dignity. I could understand
the whole thing and recognized the force of the argument.
And *force* is indeed the word because what I was being asked
to do was to lend my name to something that was also an
IRA propaganda campaign. I said to the fellow that if I wrote
anything I'd have to write it for myself. He eventually threw
this up against me somewhere, saying that I had refused to
write or speak out against torture. Everything changed for
writers in Northern Ireland once the Provisional IRA began
to inflict their own violence on people. I had been quite propa-
gandistically involved early on in 1968–1970, but it was my
own propaganda, so to speak, expressing a minority viewpoint
in places like the *New Statesman* and *The Listener*.

INTERVIEWER
When you say the minority, do you mean in the North?

HEANEY
Yes. The Catholics. To begin with, the Catholics had this
sense of the moral high ground, which is so enabling. The

system had been rigged against us and when the civil-rights marches began, the official resistance was to the minority *qua* minority. The state machine just worked like that and the point of the new movement was to change it. You felt that being a spokesperson for the shift was honorable and, indeed, imperative. But all that certitude got complicated once the IRA began to speak on your behalf with an exploding bomb. But it should be said that I never thought of my audience as being made up only of Northern Catholics. The reader to whom everything is directed, the one Mandelstam called "the reader in posterity," is as much for me a Northern Protestant as anything else. But listen to what I'm saying! Protestant, Catholic—the point is to fly under or out and beyond those radar systems. Ideally our work is directed towards some just, disinterested point of reception. A locus of justice, a kind of listening post and final appeal court. I regard many of the things I know and have to tell about as deriving from my Catholic minority background in Northern Ireland, but I don't regard that as a circumstance that determines my audience or my posture.

INTERVIEWER
Do you feel the poet has an obligation at a politically diffi-cult time?

HEANEY
I think the poet who didn't feel the pressure at a politically difficult time would be either stupid or insensitive. I take great comfort in this regard from a formulation of Robert Pinsky's in his essay on the responsibility of the poet. He relates the word *responsibility* to its origin in *response* and then to its Anglo-Saxon equivalent in the word *answer*. Pinsky says that as long as you feel the need to answer you are being responsible, because it's in the ground of one's answering being that the responsibility of the poet is lodged. How you actually deliver the answer, of course, is something else. There's a tempera-ment involved. And there's the crucial matter of artistic ability,

whether you are artistically fit to take on what is often recalcitrant subject matter.

INTERVIEWER

But do you think politics can be affected?

HEANEY

Yes, I do think they can be affected. I think there's far too much mealymouthedness about that. Auden's remark that poetry makes nothing happen is used too often to foreclose the question. I do believe, for example, that Robert Lowell had a political effect. I'm not saying that because of the thematic content of his work, but because he had established a profile and an authority as a poet.

INTERVIEWER

Do you mean visibility?

HEANEY

Visibility, yes, but visibility in itself isn't enough. There are other poets with visibility. Lowell manifested a kind of *gravitas*. His enemies might say he represented portentousness, but that's neither here nor there. There was a sense that he stood for something. When he intervened in public matters, when he decided to decline an invitation from the White House, say, that had a political effect. And when he took part in the march on the Pentagon, it had meaning because of the regard in which he was held, as poet and patrician. Come to think of it, Philip Larkin had a definite political influence also. He fortified a certain kind of recalcitrant Englishness. His masquerade encouraged a strain of xenophobia and a strain of philistinism in English life. I'm not saying there's anything philistine about his melodies. But there was nothing admirable in his pronouncements about art and life, all those statements to the effect of, "Oh, I don't know. I just love Margaret Thatcher. I don't read poetry in translation and I would never dream of going abroad." That kind of lowest-common-denominator stuff, which he famously paraded in his *Paris Review* interview, that kind of thing actually works itself into the culture. Larkin's antiheroics and his absconding from anything visionary or bold did have its effect. And I would say that Hugh MacDiarmid had an effect too — very different — in Scotland. Norman MacCaig once said that the Scottish nation should observe two minutes of pandemonium every year on the anniversary of MacDiarmid's death. In Ireland, of course, we observe two weeks of summer school every year in memory of Yeats. And rightly so.

INTERVIEWER

Don't you argue in an essay — using the example of Jesus writing in the sand — that poetry has the power to suspend violence? You suggest that it wasn't important what Jesus wrote in the sand, but it was the unexpected gesture of his turning away from the stoning of a prostitute and writing in the sand that stops the stoning or suspends it.

HEANEY

Yes. Debate doesn't really change things. It gets you bogged in deeper. If you can address or reopen the subject with something new, something from a different angle, then there is some hope. In Northern Ireland, for example, a new metaphor for the way we are positioned, a new language would create new possibility. I'm convinced of that. So when I invoke Jesus writing in the sand, it's as an example of this kind of diverting newness. He does something that takes the eyes away from the obsession of the moment. It's a bit like a magical dance.

INTERVIEWER

It's a marvelous trope for writing.

HEANEY

People are suddenly gazing at something else and pausing for a moment. And for the duration of that gaze and pause, they are like reflectors of the totality of their own knowledge and/or ignorance. That's something poetry can do for you, it can entrance you for a moment above the pool of your own consciousness and your own possibilities.

INTERVIEWER

Do you see your "Bog Poems," as they are called, as an example of this kind of diversion and entrancement?

HEANEY

I see the Bog Poems in Pinsky's terms as an answer. They were a kind of holding action. They were indeed a bit like the line drawn in the sand. Not quite an equivalent for what was happening, more an attempt to rhyme the contemporary with the archaic. "The Tollund Man," for example, is the first of the Bog Poems I wrote. Essentially, it is a prayer that the bodies of people killed in various actions and atrocities in modern Ireland, in the teens and twenties of the century as well as in the more recent past, a prayer that something would come of them, some kind of new peace or resolution. In the understanding of his Iron Age contemporaries, the sacrificed body of Tollund Man germinated into spring, so the poem wants a similar flowering to come from the violence in the present. Of course it recognizes that this probably won't happen, but the middle section of the poem is still a prayer that it should. The Bog Poems were defenses against the encroachment of the times, I suppose. But there was always a real personal involvement — in a poem like "Punishment," for example.

INTERVIEWER

In what respect?

HEANEY

It's a poem about standing by as the IRA tar and feather these young women in Ulster. But it's also about standing by as the British torture people in barracks and interrogation centers in Belfast. About standing between those two forms of affront. So there's that element of self-accusation, which makes the poem personal in a fairly acute way. Its concerns are immediate and contemporary, but for some reason I couldn't bring army barracks or police barracks or Bogside street life into the language and topography of the poem. I found it more convincing to write about the bodies in the bog and the vision of Iron Age punishment. Pressure seemed to drain away from the writing if I shifted my focus from those images.

INTERVIEWER

So often your poems are about the disenfranchised (as in a poem like "Servant Boy") or the victimized (as in "Punishment)—do you feel yourself to be among them as an Irish Catholic coming from a country with tanks, posted soldiers and other degradations?

HEANEY

I don't think consciously in that way. I would hate to think of the poems as a parade of victim entitlement. Something that irks me about a lot of contemporary writing is the swank of deprivation. One of the poets who meant most to me and whom I now believe I have always underrated as an influence is Wilfred Owen. The influence wasn't quite at the level of style, more in the understanding of what a poet ought to be doing. I think Owen's assault upon the righteousness that causes breed in people, and his general tilting of poetry's sympathies towards the underground man, I think all that had an effect upon my notion of what poetry's place in the world should be. At any rate, in the early 1970s I did surely identify with the Catholic minority. A poem like "The Ministry of Fear" is a very deliberate treatment of the subject of minority-dom. An attempt to encompass that element of civic reality. It's written in blank verse; there's not much sport between the words of it.

INTERVIEWER

Do you think that the search for an Irish identity is a common thread among Irish poets? Is there a true bearer of Irishness? Is it the peasantry, the middle class, the gentry?

HEANEY

I don't think that there is one true bearer of Irishness. There are different versions, different narratives, as we say, and you start out in possession of one of these. Maybe righteously in possession, as one of Yeats's Anglo-Irish, say, — "no petty people" — or as one of my own "big-voiced scullions." But surely you have to grow into an awareness of the others and attempt to find a way of imagining a whole thing. That really is the challenge, to open the definition and to make the domain of Irishness in Ireland — I hate to use the word *pluralist,* it's so prim and righteous — to make it open and available, and by now I think it really is a bit like that. The problem is that some people loathe being included within the category of Irishness in the first place. Northern Protestant loyalists, people from a Unionist background — they are simply repelled by the notion of being nominated Irish, never mind the prospect of being co-opted, forcibly or constitutionally, into an integrated Irish state. So you want to respect their refusal since it is based on definite historical and ethnic grounds. But at the same time, for fifty years the other side of that refusal has been their bullying attitude to the nationalist minority, saying in effect, "Because *we*'re not going to be Irish, you can't be Irish either. We refuse you that identity. In our six-county state, you're British, willy-nilly, so you can take it or leave it." So while I believe that the Protestants must be granted every cultural and personal and human right to define themselves, they must not be given a veto on the political future (which has been the case for decades, through Westminster's ideological solidarity with the Unionists); they must not be granted the right to base the ethos of a new Northern Ireland upon their loyalism and loyalties alone.

INTERVIEWER

In your poem "The Mud Vision" you describe an apparition like a rose window of mud. What was the vision there and did you believe it?

It superimposes two things. First there was this moment in the 1950s when the Virgin was supposed to have appeared to a woman in County Tyrone. It wakened up the whole country. I remember feeling this huge sense of animation and focus and expectation and skepticism all at once. It was a current that flowed in and flowed out of this one little place, which was as a matter of fact the place my wife comes from, Ardboe, on the shores of Lough Neagh. And even though I did not believe that the mother of God had stood there on a hawthorn bush at the end of a local garden, I was tuned in to the animation. So that memory of a community centered and expectant and alive to vision is behind the poem. But the actual mud-vision idea came from seeing a work by the English artist Richard Long, a big flower-face on a wall, made up entirely of muddy handprints. It began as a set of six or eight petals of mud and then moved out and out concentrically until it became this huge sullied rose window. So the poem you are asking about was written by a man who had known the excitement of Ardboe in his early life gazing up in later life at this thing on the wall of the Guinness Hopstore in Dublin. I was wanting to write about contemporary Ireland, the Republic of Ireland, as a country with a religious subconscious but a secular destiny — at the point of transition from the communality of religious devotion to the loneliness of modernity and subjectivity. The community in the poem has lost the sense of its own destiny and of any metaphysical call. And it is exposed to the challenge of making a go of it in a more secular world. There's a sense of disappointment in the poem. A sense of having missed an opportunity.

INTERVIEWER

Returning for a moment to your Catholic roots, I wonder, do you believe in Satan?

HEANEY

That's a good question. I haven't thought of him for years. But his name is very thrilling. It really does bring me to my senses.

INTERVIEWER
But that's not to say you believe in him?

HEANEY
I don't know. He's still sort of alive and well when I remember that old prayer they used to intone at the end of Mass about Satan roaming through the world seeking the ruination of souls.

INTERVIEWER
Speaking of roaming round the world, do you collect anything?

HEANEY
Nothing systematic, but I am a bit of a fetishist, so stuff does gather up around me. Stones, bits of stick, birch bark, postcards, boxes, paintings, many paintings over the years and books, of course. I have two bits of birch from New England, for example. One is a beautiful objet trouvé, a bit like a tilted-back human torso, a hollow section of birch trunk, a birch-bark Apollo. I picked it up off the ground years ago when we were visiting Don Hall and Jane Kenyon up at Eagle Pond. And I have this other thing I got recently when I traveled up with Bill and Beverley Corbett to Dunbarton in New Hampshire to see Robert Lowell's grave. I found a birch stick beside the burial ground and then found myself holding on to it. That's what happens. I've got stones from Beeny Cliff and bits of granite from Joyce's Tower and sea-green slate from Yeats's. A stone from Delphi. A view of Tintern Abbey. Orpheus on a vase. And on a plate. And on a medal.

INTERVIEWER
Since you grew up on a farm, I wonder if you have any pets or animals at home?

HEANEY
Well, our attitude towards cats and dogs in the first life, in County Derry, was one of benign neglect. Affection, but

no signs of affection. The dogs and cats were part of the life, definitely valued, but they weren't exactly petted. They were kept out of the house, on the whole. But now at home in Dublin we have a dog named Carlow, and Carlow is in the house all the time. There's no farm for him to roam in. He's a sheepdog, all the same, and a sheepish dog too. And there's some debate among us as to whether he's a culchie or a yuppie.

INTERVIEWER

What's a culchie?

HEANEY

Oh, a rough-diamond country type at large in the city. I mean some of the family think of him as Carlo without the final *w*, a yuppified class of a character with aspirations to be an opera singer, perhaps; but to me he retains the *w*, like the Irish county, a Carlow who plays Gaelic football and maybe even the occasional game of hurling.

INTERVIEWER

If you could be an animal what would it be?

HEANEY

I might enjoy being an albatross, being able to glide for days and daydream for hundreds of miles along the thermals. And then being able to hang like an affliction round some people's necks.

INTERVIEWER

What about architecture? If you could be a building, what would you be?

HEANEY

The Pantheon. Why not? Paul Muldoon once made me a "monumental / Emmenthal" when he assigned the poets their identities as cheeses. When I went to Rome, of course, I went to St. Peter's Square and found it an overwhelming experience, partly because of the magnificent architectural sweep of it, but partly too because I had seen so many pictures of it and because I knew that if my father and mother had been alive, they'd have got terrific pleasure from the thought of my going there. It would have had a real religious dimension for them . . . I suppose I am just trying to explain to myself why the tears came to my eyes when I went into it. A sudden irrigation. But I'm afraid I ended up returning over and over again to the Pantheon.

INTERVIEWER

Do you have a special affection for Italy?

HEANEY

I do, yes. It's a place I feel I could live in — Tuscany, especially. Again, it may have to do with an early conditioning among all those Christian images. In Northern Europe and in North America, they have all peeled away by now from the actual environment: churches, statues, crucifixes, images of the Madonna, the Holy Family and so on — even in Ireland those things have evaporated out of topographical significance. And what has disappeared with them is the big unifying dream. But in Italy, the images and the humanist/Christian culture that put them in place seem to be saying that the dream is still a possibility. The Italians aren't any more religious but the images are still on show there and still promise; they don't feel environmentally or architecturally superceded and so they still promote the possibility of meaning — to this child of the rural Catholic 1940s, at any rate. Maybe it's just that you are more animated by the aesthetic in Italy.

INTERVIEWER

Do you ever feel confined by the personal mythologies that take over a life? For instance, the public's perception of the semiwildman from County Derry farmland who goes south, makes good and ends up Boylston Professor at Harvard?

HEANEY

Well, I'd go back to the image of the concentric ripples. They are always on the move and invisible to themselves. It's the person looking at the pool from the bank who sees the process as a pattern. The public's perception is just that, and you can never share it, even if you wanted to. And your own perception of yourself is always going to be very different. Imagine if you were an oyster. The public would see you as an infrangible nut, a kind of sea-raid shelter, but you would feel yourself all mother-of-pearly inwardness and vulnerability.

But to answer your question about the Boylston Professorship and "making good" and all that. I've worked for my living in institutions for most of my life. I see nothing wrong with it. Of course, there is something perilous about it if you are a poet. You are cushioned from a certain exhilarating exposure to risk when you have a salary and a "situation in life." But it's better to recognize that and get on with the job than to live on the cushion and still go around pretending that you are somehow a free bohemian spirit. Some writers within the academy have this *nous autres, les écrivains* attitude, taking their big stipend and all their freebies and travel grants and Guggenheims but manifesting a kind of *mauvaise foi* by not admitting that their attachment to the academy is their own decision, as it were, and instead just going around mocking this dreary milieu they have opted for. It's an understandable defense mechanism, but it gets on my nerves. It's a sign that they have fallen for the myth of their own creativity. And that they're too anxious about that public perception you ask about—since the myth prescribes the garret rather than the Guggenheim.

INTERVIEWER

As you know, there is a Ted Hughes poem that says everything is inheriting everything. One might argue that there are three literary bloodlines leading to the poetry of Seamus Heaney: the Gerard Manley Hopkins, D.H. Lawrence, Dylan Thomas, Hughes connection, a kind of outburst poetry; and then there's the poetry of the intellectualizing line of wit, coming from Auden, Larkin and Lowell; and finally there are the others who present a kind of documentation of farmland and farm life, including Thomas Hardy and Patrick Kavanagh. I know it is a bit of a game to ask you this, and that it detracts from each writer in the fullest sense, but if I repeated each name, could you say in a sentence or two what draws you to each, beginning with Hopkins?

HEANEY

With Hopkins the sense of the powerline of English language trembling under the actual verse line. The sense of big voltage.

INTERVIEWER

Dylan Thomas?

HEANEY

The rhapsodic thing for sure. I can't remember whether I heard Thomas's voice before I read him in a book. "Poem in October" meant a lot to me. And "Fern Hill," "Over Sir John's Hill," "In the White Giant's Thigh," "I see the boys of summer."

INTERVIEWER

And Lawrence?

HEANEY

Lawrence meant a lot to me too for a while. But for different reasons from Thomas and Hopkins. I liked the plainspokenness. I'm thinking of *Pansies*. He fortified the refuser in me. "The feelings I don't have, I won't say I have. The feelings you say you have, you don't have. If you want to have any feelings, we better give up the idea of having feelings altogether," that sort of stuff, you know? Lawrence came through strongest as a prose writer through *Sons and Lovers*. That really rocked you on your keel. But in my early twenties I did respond to the head-on antiromantic note in him, those poems where he's saying, "Let's clean up this emotional morass. Let's sweep all this mush off the floor."

Ted Hughes?

He was a poet who had plugged into the powerpoint of Hopkins and was giving out the live energy.

Auden?

It took me about twenty years, reading Auden on and off, to come to the high regard for him I have now. He didn't mean much to me as a young writer. But as I got older and lived with all that was happening in Ireland during my thirties and forties, Auden's punishment of the artistic with the ethical became very interesting to me. And all his dualisms. His formulation of the split in every poet between the Ariel and the Prospero. Between the pleasure-giving singer, the music-maker and the wisdom-speaker. The whole question of why he suppressed his poem "Spain" and whether that was right. His suppression of "September 1, 1939." Maybe you have to be a bit older to appreciate the drama of those decisions and the seriousness of his concern. In fact, by the earnestness of his attention to his own texts, Auden shows that he doesn't really believe that "poetry makes nothing happen." He was deeply, deeply worried about truth-telling in poetry, about the effect of a word or a work once it was released into the world. He would have agreed with Czeslaw Milosz that as a poet you should try to be sure that it is good spirits, not evil ones, who possess you when you are carried away in your writing.

What about Larkin?

A great enrichment to me as a reader. I'm not sure that as
a writer I got anything much. When we were young poets
together in Belfast, Michael Longley and his wife Edna were
always forwarding the Larkin-Wilbur line. And I would line
up on the Lowell-Hughes side of things. It was partly because
the sound I made in my lines was closer to the Anglo-Saxon
roughage of Hughes and the head-on, less melodious note of
Lowell. Michael, on the other hand, and Derek Mahon, were
sponsors of immaculate melody. But still, that makes my attitude sound more prejudiced than it ever was. Larkin is one
of the few who can make a catch in the breath.

And Lowell?

Lowell was a classic even when I was an undergraduate. I
read "The Quaker Graveyard" in *The Penguin Book of Contemporary American Poetry* and was kind of goggle-eyed and
goggle-eared, so to speak. Then I read the book about him
by Hugh Staples, where "The Quaker Graveyard" is compared
to Milton's "Lycidas." So you can imagine my awe when I met
him. And my joy when we got on together. This was the early
seventies. At that time, *Notebook* and then *History* and *For
Lizzie and Harriet* and *The Dolphin* were coming out. The
odd thing is, it was the blunt instruments in those books,
those blank sonnets, that were Lowell's strongest influence on
my writing. The literary critic in me says *Life Studies* is the
real goods, and then "For the Union Dead" and "Near the
Ocean," great public poems of our era: what I call the eques-
trian Lowell, the Lowell profiled nobly against his times. These
poems do succeed magnificently, but in *Notebook* and its
progeny he practiced a revenge against his own eloquence,

and I found something heroic about the wrongheadedness
and dare of that.

INTERVIEWER
In your elegy for Lowell, by the way, why does he say at
the end, "I'll pray for you"?

HEANEY
I suppose the fact that it is true is no reason why it should
be there . . . He did actually say it to me, at the end of a
week I'd spent in his company at an arts festival in Kilkenny
in 1975. We'd come up to Wicklow to this small house where
we were living, really very confined; a couple of bedrooms
and a living room and a kitchen. When Cal came in the kids
were running around and I remember him saying to me, "You
see a lot of your children," because, of course, he lived in this
mansion in Kent—Milgate—where there was a nanny in the
west wing with Sheridan, and Cal and Caroline had separate
work rooms, and came together to dine in the evening.

INTERVIEWER
So he said "I'll pray for you" because of your children?

HEANEY
It was when he was taking his farewells. He didn't mention
the children, but there was a tenderness in it. And I think it
was partly his way of saying, "I was once a Catholic too." Also
a way of saying that he knew that I was out there in the cottage
putting myself to the test as a writer. And he could probably
see that there was something isolated and frail about the venture. But then too, there may have been the faintest backlight
of irony in what he said, a hamming up of the old Catholic
bit, I don't know. But there was kindness, I know, and he
probably foreknew that what he said in farewell would be
remembered. Anyhow, I took it as a positive, ironically hedged
goodness.

INTERVIEWER
What about Hardy?

HEANEY

From the moment I read "The Oxen," the moment I read
the opening chapters of *Return of the Native*, I was at home
with him—something about the vestigial ballad atmosphere,
the intimacy, the oldness behind and inside the words, the
peering and puzzlement and solitude. He was there like a
familiar spirit from school days. I remember hearing the poem
"Weathers" read on the BBC radio when I was eleven or twelve
and never forgetting it. "The Oxen" I learned by heart around
that time also. I loved the oddity and previousness of the
English in it. "The lonely barton by yonder coomb"—that
can still make me feel sad and taken care of all at once, *le
cor au fond du bois* with a local accent.

INTERVIEWER
Kavanagh?

HEANEY

I was sort of pupped out of Kavanagh. I read him in 1962,
after I'd graduated from Queen's and was teaching at St.
Thomas's, where my headmaster was the short-story writer
Michael McLaverty. He lent me Kavanagh's *Soul for Sale*,
which includes "The Great Hunger," and at that moment the
veil of the study was rent: it gave me this terrific breakthrough
from English literature into home ground.

INTERVIEWER

Are you aware of a great deal of cross-fertilization between
Irish and American poetry? Do you think there is still an
Anglo-American matrix?

HEANEY

Definitely. But this is not a new thing. Irish poets of the
1950s were very deliberately involved in absorbing and coming

to terms with American poetry. John Montague had been a graduate student in Berkeley; Snyder and Creeley and Carlos Williams were among the people he had met and been influenced by. There was genuine cross-fertilization there because Montague perceived that these writers could help to develop a new ecology in Irish poetry, more erotic, more Olsonian, a "global regionalism," as he called it. Before Paul Muldoon lit out for the territory, there was a move on to go west. Thomas Kinsella, for example, began under the sway of Auden, but in a very deliberate way moved towards Pound. This was fundamentally an aesthetic move, a case of opting for a more cantified way of getting at personal and mythological matter, but there was also something Hiberno-countercultural about it, a shrug at the English models.

INTERVIEWER

It is notable that if you look at a handful of American universities, you find Paul Muldoon, Derek Mahon, Eamon Grennan, Eavan Boland and Seamus Heaney.

HEANEY

And John Montague is over there in Albany. Well, maybe the forms of Irish poetry and of Irish society are still in some uneasy, self-questioning relation to the determining power and example of England and English and the whole Anglo tradition. There's something fleet and volatile in Ireland, and in the young people especially — they would recognize their vibe, if you'll pardon the expression, in a line like "O my America, my new found land." Paul Muldoon is a clear example of that. His phantasmagoria had always involved two Americas: the native American experience and that other LA-Hollywoody-Raymond Chandlery scene. And then there was the power surge that came from America to the women's movement. Sylvia Plath and Adrienne Rich were animating and ratifying for Eavan Boland. Eamon Grennan is a genuine dual citizen, on the campus at Vassar, but as Irish as the strand at Ventry. And Derek Mahon had already been to Lowell country back in the seventies, when he was knocking around Cambridge and then writing his own Marvellian octosyllabics in the wake of Lowell's *Near the Ocean* volume.

INTERVIEWER

What about your critics? Is there one you find especially perceptive?

HEANEY

Well, reading Helen Vendler is always a corroboration. She is like a receiving station picking up on each poem, unscrambling things out of word-waves, making sense of it and making sure of it. She can second-guess the sixth sense of the poem. She has this amazing ability to be completely alive to the bleeper going off at the heart of it, sensitive to the intimacies and implications of the words and your way with them, and at the same time she has the ability to create the acoustic conditions where you can hear the poem best, the ability to set it within a historical context and to find its literary coordinates. And then there is just the sheer undimmed enthusiasm. Helen has been a friend to me as well as a critic, and the friendship has been tonic because all that critical élan comes out in her social self as sheer exhilarating intelligence. The great thing about Helen is not just her literary capacity, it's her sense of honesty, justice and truthfulness. I value these things deeply in her as a person and, naturally, they are part of her verity as a critic.

INTERVIEWER

In your poem "The Sounds of Rain," an elegy for your friend Richard Ellmann, you speak of yourself as being "steeped in luck" with good health and love and work. Do you cease to feel "steeped, steeped, steeped in luck"?

HEANEY

No. I still think I have been inordinately lucky. I regard first of all the discovery of a path into the writing of poems as luck. And the salute that my early poems received and the consequent steadying of direction and identity in my life all coinciding with, as you say, love—I do regard it as a real benediction. And, of course, there's the whole matter of friendships and family solidarity and the trust of cherished ones.

INTERVIEWER

How did you meet your wife?

HEANEY

I met her at a dinner in Belfast at the university. It was a valedictory event for one of the chaplains and she came as the guest of someone else. I talked to her across the table and arranged to pair off with her at the end of the meal. I walked her back to her apartment and on the way called into my own flat to get a book that I lent her and then told her that I would need it back on the following Thursday. So on the Thursday I met her again and we went to a party being run by this marvelous character called Sean Armstrong (Sean was shot in the early days of the Troubles and there's a poem about him in *Field Work,* and about that night at his place, the one called "A Postcard from North Antrim"). Anyhow, we stayed late at the party, and I dallied around her apartment later still and by the wee hours we had more or less proposed to each other.

INTERVIEWER

You've been married how many years?

HEANEY

Twenty-nine years.

INTERVIEWER

You've written many poems about your wife, but by comparison very few about your children. Do you find the experience of fatherhood unsuitable for the lyric?

HEANEY

There's something traditionally sanctioned about the woman as the beloved, as the locus of the lyric. You're playing the old tunes again, to some extent unthinkingly. With the children I suppose I felt I would be intruding on them. I read an interview recently, for example, with Michael Yeats—who's now a man in his seventies—and he said a poet shouldn't write about his children until they've left school. A parent has a sort of emotional upper hand. It's not that the children aren't very dear to me.

INTERVIEWER

Do any of your children write?

HEANEY

Michael is a freelance journalist in Dublin and covers the general area of popular culture. Reviews and interviews of bands. Columns on concerts and movies. Does it all with some brio. But none of them so far does creative writing.

INTERVIEWER

Does your son that's in a rock band write songs?

HEANEY

No, but he's part of the whole band-buzz that's come to life in Dublin recently. He's a drummer and a good one. And Catherine is still in college. Who knows what Catherine will do?

INTERVIEWER

How do your poems begin? When you write, do you finish everything you begin?

HEANEY

I finish nearly everything. But I don't always get to the finish with that sense of rightness and supply that you're always longing for. And like everybody else, I don't understand where the sense of rightness comes from in the first place. You live for that given joy, that feeling that the words are coming out like *fiats,* that now you are Sir Oracle and can issue the edict. I'm what Tom Paulin once called a binge writer. My typical surge would last three or four months. Not every day necessarily but in a coherent self-sustaining action, when you have that happy sense of being confirmed. When you're high as a kite, really, on a high that only poetry can give.

INTERVIEWER

How much is form and prosody on your mind when you're writing, as you begin a poem?

HEANEY

It's hard to be exact about that. Form and prosody aren't usually on anybody's mind until after the first line or two. There's a summons in those first words; they're like a tuning fork and if things go right the tune of the whole poem will get established and sustained in the opening move or movement. Usually, to tell you the truth, I just follow my ear. If I'm working with pentameters, I do often beat out the line with my fingers—Marie used to tell me to watch the road when she'd see me starting to tap the steering wheel. But early on I tended to go more with the camber and timbre of my voice and didn't think too much about keeping the accent or being metrically correct. In fact, I intended the thing to be a bit bumpy and more or less avoided correctness of that kind. If anything has happened over the years, it's that I've become more conscious of the rules. I take more care with the *tum-ti-tum* factor. And I'm not sure whether that is a good thing or a bad thing. Hopkins was my first love, after all.

INTERVIEWER

Is irony something you prize in poetry?

HEANEY

I have no prejudice in favor of it. The word can suggest at worst a knowingness of tone that just irks me. I like irony that is

tragic-historical rather than emotionally protective. Zbigniew
Herbert, for example. Or something mordant to the point of
savagery, like Joyce or Flann O'Brien or Milosz in a poem like
"Child of Europe."

INTERVIEWER

Do you think you can make generalizations about the poetry
of Ireland? That it is musical or rhythmic, self-consciously so?
Or that it is not experimental? That there are no Ashberys or
Ginsbergs? That emotional expression is constrained? Or that
it is searching for an Irish conscience? That it is rural rather
than urban?

HEANEY

I don't think any one of those things could be maintained
with confidence any more. For example, the poetry of Medbh
McGuckian represents something experimental. She seems to
me to have access to a language you might call Kristevan,
something that could be set beside Ashbery. Not influenced
by Ashbery, however. Medbh is sui generis. And there's Paul
Durcan, for example, in the Republic of Ireland, and Paul
has brought this liberationist disruptive surreal satirical element into play. It's not Irish in an expected way. It's certainly
not rural. It's deadpan and passionate all at once, it's saying
something like "The spoof will make you free." In its way,
it's out to forge the uncreated conscience of the race but it's
very aware that forgery has always been a problem dogging
this matter of conscience. And of course you could say that
too about the work done by the other Paul—Paul Mulboon,
as I once called him. Muldoon is a mixture of attachments
and detachments that are as much part of his genius as they
were of Joyce's. He's an heir to the mordant thing in Stephen
Dedalus but he's also swimming in the meltdown of English
after *Finnegans Wake*. And he swims in the wake of the Irish
language too, and picks up on that unsentimental, unpathetic
pride in wordcraft, in being a penman. He's bardic in that
strictly professional sense. He'd find the god Lugh in the word

ludic, and that would only be the start of it. Yet it's all grounded in his need to answer. But if he heard me saying so, he'd probably remember that *anser* is the Latin for goose and start to cackle. He has a merry way with weighty matters. And others have learned from him — Ciaran Carson, for example, who is very writerly but very roguish and clued in to the local scene in Belfast. I suppose I'm talking about younger writers because they have complicated the picture of Irish poetry. As have the writers of poetry in the Irish language itself. Translation has opened things up. Nuala Ni Dhomhnaill has now a wide audience in English and the paradox is that this has made Irish a kind of world language. And come to think of it, there's nothing emotionally constrained about Nuala's work.

INTERVIEWER

I know you've been criticized by feminist Irish writers recently. What is your response to them?

HEANEY

This is a criticism grounded in a corrective impulse. It insists on rereading the tropes — the trope of Ireland as passive suffering female, the trope of Ireland as ruined maid and so on. . . . All that traditional iconography of Irish poetry is under scrutiny. And sensibilities affected by that kind of thing are being challenged. It flows out of the liberationist, subversive energy that's coursing in the country. And it was inevitable that some poems I've written would come in for ideological stick. And then there's the visibility you referred to earlier on. I think I'm perceived as not only being visible but being in the light, so that opening a few holes in me can be regarded as a contribution to a new illumination scheme.

But in a more general way, the target of Eavan Boland's criticism, for example, has been the idea of poetic authority as it derives from a male invention of tradition. She wants to expose it as a kind of false consciousness, a formation proceeding from Romantic and from some specifically Irish precedents, something that has hampered and disoriented women poets and skewed their chances of self-recognition and transformation. Boland has mobilized a lot of oppositional thinking on this front and has become emblematic of the resurgence of women in and through poetry, and I think male poets have taken cognizance of this as a big element in the intellectual life of the country. It is a part of the new weather in the Irish consciousness. For example, it was behind the feminists' attack on *The Field Day Anthology of Irish Writing* a few years ago. Their anger and complaints were certainly to be expected when you consider that all the directors of the Field Day Theatre Company—of which I am one—were men, and so were all the editors. Astonishing, really. And there was no section in the anthology devoted to that whole new body of Irish feminist discourse which has been emerging over the past three decades. So there was a scandal for feminists in that.

The odd thing is that the anthology was very much a post-colonial reading of the Irish situation and therefore should have been sensitive to the silencings that women and women's writing had undergone, but I think that for everybody involved the pressure at the horizon was from Northern Ireland politics rather than gender politics. The warp in the Field Day glass was very much a matter of the northern background of the directors. But the other truth is that this was and is a magnificent three-volume conspectus and a critical rereading of fifteen hundred years of Irish writing in Latin and Norman French and Irish and English, from the time of St. Patrick to the 1990s. It remains a monument to the genius of Seamus Deane, who was the general editor. It's just a pity that the absent section doomed everything else that was present in those four thousand pages. I suppose one good result has been the fact that a fourth volume edited entirely by women is now in preparation. But it was instructive at the time to watch the proscription in action. Some women writers who were included talked as if they had been left out. And some as if they would have preferred to have been left out. It became a whipping boy, or a boy-whipping. A real hosting of the *she*.

INTERVIEWER

What are your plans for your forthcoming sabbatical?

HEANEY

I plan to stay as still as possible and to get into the habit of going to the cottage in Wicklow — which we were eventually able to buy in 1988. I want to do a lot of reading and take things as they come. The last time I had a year off I was determined not to set up a lot of writing goals. I more or less convinced myself that there was no need to do anything. And that worked. I really got going on those twelve-line poems in *Seeing Things*. So I'm taking the same line now: reading, stillness, maybe a journal, trust in poetry.

During the preparation of this interview for publication, Seamus Heaney received the Nobel Prize in literature. The following brief update seemed necessary.

INTERVIEWER

In your new volume, *The Spirit Level,* do you feel your work has taken you in any new direction . . . as in a poem like "Cassandra"?

HEANEY

"Cassandra" was written very quickly. It came out like a molten rill from a spot I hit when I drilled down into the *Oresteia* bedrock that's under "Mycenae Outlook." When I went home from Harvard in 1994, shortly after our interview that May, the really big shift — big at all levels, personal and public — was the IRA ceasefire the following August. That was a genuine visitation, the lark sang and the light ascended. Everything got a little better and yet instead of being able just to bask in the turn of events, I found myself getting angrier and angrier at the waste of lives and friendships and possibilities in the years that had preceded it. It was 1994 and we had got no further, politically, than we had been in 1974.

Had slipped back, indeed. And I kept thinking that a version
of the *Oresteia* would be one way of getting all of that out
of the system, and at the same time, a way of initiating a late-
twentieth-century equivalent of the "Te Deum." The three
Aeschylus plays could be a kind of rite envisaging the possibility of a shift from a culture of revenge to a belief in a future
based upon something more disinterested. At any rate, I began
to read the Aeschylus, and as I did, I also began to lose heart
in the whole project. It began to seem too trite — art wanting
to shake hands with life. Ideally, what I needed was the kind
of poem Andrew Marvell wrote on Cromwell's return from
Ireland and what I was setting up for was a kind of Jonsonian
masque. At least that's what I began to feel. And then the
figure of the Watchman in that first scene of the *Agamemnon*
began to keep coming back to me with his in-between situation
and his responsibilities and inner conflicts, his silence and his
knowledge, and all this kept building until I very deliberately
began a monologue for him using a rhymed couplet like a
pneumatic drill, just trying to bite and shudder in toward
whatever was there. And after that first movement, sure
enough, the other bits came definitely and freely, from different angles and reaches. In a way, that material had as much
force and underlife for me as the bog bodies.

INTERVIEWER

How did you choose what to say in your Nobel lecture?

HEANEY

Two specific things helped me to get started on that address.
First of all, I read the lecture Kenzaburo Ôe delivered to the
Swedish Academy in 1994 and the direct, personal nature of
what he said inclined me to take a similar approach. And then
one night in Dublin, in the course of conversation with Derek
Mahon, we played with the question of whether or not Yeats
ought to be mentioned in the lecture. Not to do so would
be a bit overweening, but to bring him in could be a bit
overpowering. But even so, we decided he had to be brought

in. And that's how I got started. It should also be said, however, that the lecture was done at a frantic pace. The six weeks between the announcement of the news and the deadline when you have to deliver your manuscript for translation are probably the most hectic and distracting weeks of your life. You're going through the world like a skimming stone. There was nothing for it but to hit the podium at full tilt.

INTERVIEWER

What was your response to receiving the Nobel Prize?

HEANEY

It was a bit like being caught in a mostly benign avalanche. You are totally daunted, of course, when you think of previous writers who received the prize. And daunted when you think of the ones who didn't receive it. Just confining yourself to Ireland you have Yeats, Shaw and Beckett in the first group and James Joyce in the second. So you soon realize you'd better not think too much about it at all. Nothing can prepare you for it. Zeus thunders and the world blinks twice and you get to your feet again and try to keep going.

—Henri Cole

The Blue Hour

Kate Walbert

Today I've been watching it snow and thinking of Dorothy. This was in Rochester, before your sister was born, when you were four or five and your father worked most weekends. (I have always thought it ironic that your father made our living as an efficiency expert, a job that required so many hours of overtime.) We lived in a pink brick Georgian at the end of a cul-de-sac called Country Club Road. Your father had flown out from Detroit to find it and had bought it over one weekend. You were too young to travel at the time so we stayed behind. I remember he called from the Holiday Inn to let me know he had found a house and how, when I asked him to describe it, he said it had an "expansive den."

We moved the following weekend and I suddenly found myself in a pink Georgian in the middle of a Rochester winter. I tried to keep my spirits up. I went around to some of the homes where snowmen had been built, ostensibly looking for playmates for you. Dorothy lived in one of those grand cold Tudors with leaded windows and azaleas and box hedges trimmed into spades. Her Christmas decorations were still out — garlands of evergreen wrapped with white lights and a red-ribboned wreath on the front door. I rang the doorbell and Dorothy opened the door as if expecting me. I remember thinking how much she looked like Audrey Hepburn.

"You're here."

"Marion Clark," I said, holding out my hand.

"Oh," she said, shaking it. "I'm sorry."

"You thought I was someone else?" I said.

She nodded. "Forgive me, it's cold. Come in."

She was a woman who could say *forgive me* without batting an eye.

The inside of her house felt nothing like the outside; it held a sweet thick smell I recognized as incense. There were large pillows scattered around the floor in the living room and plants whose tendrils grew up and over the windows. I accepted her drink offer, though it was two o'clock in the afternoon and, for those years at least, your father and I had a rule about no cocktails before six.

I asked for an old-fashioned. It sounded right. She nodded when I said it as if I had passed a secret test; then she led me into the living room. "You *are* who I was waiting for," she said, ducking out. I sat on the couch. It was draped with a batik fabric that had hundreds of tiny mirrors stitched into it, and I remember how I thought that if light ever got through those heavy webbed-green windows the mirrors would reflect it like so many diamonds, as if the couch were afire.

Dorothy returned with an ornate tray and sat down across from me on one of the floor pillows. "So," she said, handing me my drink. "Let me guess. You're new. You're bored. You're looking for playmates for your child but you're really looking for company."

"I suppose you could say that."

"Well, cheers then," she said, lifting her glass. "To play-mates."

"Salud," I said, I'm sure wanting to sound continental. I felt paltry in comparison to this creature in black silk. I had worn my usual wool slacks and snow boots. How could I have known?

I sipped my drink. She had made it quite strong, and from the first taste I felt transported.

"So," she said. "Let me tell you what there is to know. First off, I'm Dorothy. I don't think I ever said that. Not Dot or Dottie, please, but Dorothy. My mother was very particular about this. Anyone who would call me anything but got a talking to, including teachers and boyfriends. She named me Dorothy after Dorothy Lamour, who I have later come to find out goes by Dot. But Mother's lost so there you have it. Second, I live in this monstrous house with a husband, Rick, and twin sons, Richard and Ross. It was not my idea to go with *R*. In fact, I was completely against it, but Rick insisted so what could I do. I had just been through forty-one hours of labor and you might say my mind was a little foggy and besides, he's from Canada of all places." Dorothy paused and took a sip of her drink. Behind her, through the thick glass, I saw that it had begun to snow, again, and wondered if she wasn't cold in nothing more than silk.

"We moved here about seventeen months ago and the boys think it's great and Rick plays golf and I am bored out of my mind. Rochester, for God's sake. Who would have thought I would end up here? I am the daughter of missionaries. I grew up everywhere, including Calcutta and Beijing, and I am the first to tell you that life is elsewhere. My mother ran away to find it." She took a deeper sip. "Do you know what I mean?"

"I suppose so," I said. I felt hot in my coat, but she hadn't offered to take it. I felt as if I had entered some sort of circus fun house and Dorothy sat before me as the reflection of what I could become, if I squinted my eyes, if I poured a drink at two o'clock and burned incense in Rochester.

"Oh, I'm not saying there's nothing to do here. There's the club and a good bridge group and dances every Saturday and around Christmas they have the Bachelors' Ball, which is really for all the married folk who go and get blasted to the hilt and switch husbands and that sort. We'll talk about that into the next year and the spring and it will give us something to think about come fall, again, when we are feeling kind of blowzy and old and when we unpack the ornaments and find two shattered, again. Too bad you weren't moved in before that, you could have met the gang and added your own rumor to the mill."

I must say it got to a point where I simply watched her mouth move. I could not get past a woman using the word *blowzy* in a sentence and getting away with it. She sounded so grand. She reminded me of a lone exotic fish, the type you might see in one of those overpriced pet stores swimming around and around and around an aquarium, the glass sides of which are nearly opaque from algae let to grow, as if the poor thing has been forgotten.

"Come on," she said at last, draining her drink. "The boys won't be home for an hour and I need to shop. You come. I want help."

I stood. I'm not sure how much time had passed, but I remember thinking that you would be fine, set with a new babysitter. Dorothy walked to the hall closet and put on a very full raccoon coat. Then she opened the front door and stepped out. I followed her around to the garage.

"Don't you need the air?" she said, lighting a cigarette. She stood by the garage door and smoked. "Rick doesn't let me do this in the house and who can blame him, the plants and all. Terrible habit, really. My teeth are yellow. But it gives me something to do, don't you think that? If nothing else, this is something to do." We shared the cigarette, then stamped into the garage and got into her car, the make of which I cannot remember. She was not a woman who would take much stock in automobiles, though she did love clothes and had the most elegant wardrobe of anyone I had ever known, before or since. I remember when I got the news that she was dead my second or third thought was of those clothes, of what they would have chosen to put her in for her burial.

We drove into downtown Rochester fast, through yellow lights just changed to red. She had turned on the radio, and I remember how good it felt to have had one drink and to be riding in the front seat of a warm car in the middle of an afternoon with a new friend. She pulled over once we got to the department store—one of those once-grand chains you find in depressed cities. I felt a bit blue, stepping out of the car into the cold to enter such a faded place. We should have pulled up to Bonwit's and left the keys in the car for the valet. But soon the mood shifted; there were aisles of brightly lit things and a makeup counter where a few well-preserved women stood in lab coats and beckoned us closer. I was game but Dorothy took my hand.

"Come on," she said and led me to the escalator, one of the old kind with wooden railings. We rode up to the sportswear section on the second floor.

"What are we looking for?" I asked her.

"You'll see," she said and smiled.

She led me past sportswear toward the back of the second floor, through a maze of girdled mannequins and mounds of flesh-colored bras and panties on sale. The nightgowns hung along the rear wall, a rack of silky expensive things I would have normally passed right by. Dorothy stood in front of them. "Aren't they divine?" she said.

They were part of some kind of early Easter display—pink and blue and green and yellow silks. "I can't wear yellow, but you," Dorothy said, choosing a yellow one from the rack. "You could do it."

She held the yellow nightgown up to me and admired it. I looked back at her, again thinking of her as some kind of mirror in which I stood reflected. "It's lovely," I said.

Dorothy smiled again. "But you do like it?" she said. I took the hanger from her and carried the nightgown over to the real mirror. It was difficult to tell whether I liked it or not. I felt foolish. There I stood in the middle of a Rochester winter holding a yellow silk nightgown over my wool coat and wool slacks, sure that if I actually tried it on I would look absurd in my thick socks and pale arms.

"It's lovely, really," I said, carrying it back to Dorothy and putting it on the rack. "Perhaps I'll come back for the sales."

Dorothy shrugged. "I think it is a wonderful color for you. Not many can wear yellow," she said.

She stood and stared at me for a moment. I attributed the strangeness I felt to the old-fashioned.

•

She invited me in as we pulled into her garage and I accepted. I had so rarely had company in the afternoons in Detroit. Once inside, she offered another drink. There was something of a party about that day — a new friend, a spontaneous shopping trip, two old-fashioneds before six. I felt as if the world could indeed open up for me and I could step in.

She brought out the fresh drinks on a new tray. I pulled off my snow boots and this time she offered to take my coat and I said yes. I felt so comfortable, as if I could curl up on the mirrored couch and sleep for years. I tried to explain the day to your father that night but I could not find the right words.

With Dorothy, the right words were easy. I told her about our moves, and about you and your birth. I told her how your father and I hoped to have another child soon.

She told me again how the *R* names had been her husband's idea. She told me again that her parents were missionaries and that the white porcelain elephant in the corner had come directly from Burma, before they had shut the gates, and that her mother was a great beauty with blond hair and that everywhere they had gone the people in the villages had been far more interested in looking at her hair than they had been in hearing her preach about God and Jesus.

Then she asked me did I believe in God and Jesus, and at the time I did, so I said yes.

She said there were plenty of churches she could show me, but that she could not go inside. That she had sworn off it like she had sworn off any more children and any more sex with her husband.

It was at that point I said I should go, not because I disliked her using such an unfamiliar word, but rather because I knew that with Dorothy I could say much that I might come to regret, that I could speak words that had been, before this, light as balloons drifting through my mind. To speak them would be to give them heft and weight.

"Good-bye, love," she said at the door, kissing me on both cheeks. "See you tomorrow?"

"Of course," I said.

She held my coat up for me and I put my arms through the sleeves and felt so entirely warm, from her, from this, from the promise of another day, that I walked home slowly through the bitter cold, balancing on the ridged rain gutters that ran on either side of Country Club Road, slipping some on the ice. It was the part of the day I would later come to know as the blue hour. Dorothy said she had picked it up somewhere, she thought perhaps Paris. *L'heure bleu*. She said it seemed to her always the best way to describe that time of early evening when the world seemed trapped in melancholy and all its regrets for all its mislaid plans for the day were spelled in the fading clouds.

This is, quite truthfully, how she would phrase things.

Once home, I picked you up and kissed you, and the two of us drove the babysitter back to wherever she had come from. On our return, we stopped for something at the store. Running in, I reached into my coat pocket for my wallet and felt the silk wadded down so deep, I thought for an instant I had never noticed the fine lining of the wool. Then I pulled it out. The yellow nightgown, of course.

•

You came to despise Rochester winters, could never play outside, or for only a few hours, since I was a nervous mother and didn't want you too long in the cold. You would stand, your nose pressed to the plate-glass door, amphibian-like fingers out and spread wide. You would wish for anyplace else.

But the next afternoon you were still excited by the newness of it, of your room, of places to go. The babysitter arrived particularly buoyant, a fresh-faced high-school girl you might have grown into if we had stayed. You led her up the stairs to the place in the hallway where you had set up your Barbie palace, and I called to both of you that I would be gone a few hours, that I was visiting a friend. That day shone with an unfamiliar light; it had stopped snowing the night before, and a sun that seemed as foreign to that city as a locust storm or a tornado had appeared in the morning through pale clouds. The sky looked like a Renaissance painting of a sky, with pinks and blues and mother-of-pearl grays. It hurt to look at it but that we did, Dorothy and I. She had met me at the door and led me outside, where she told me to stand, my back to her back, and stare straight up. Her hair smelled of something herbal, and I could feel her shoulder blades against my own. She wanted us to have our coats off, to lean against one another and to look straight up and to close our eyes and imagine spring.

"Think of yourself standing in the middle of a whiteout and then suddenly the white is blown away by a giant fan and everything's clear and you can see for miles and miles," she said, and so I tried, but truth be told I have always had a tough time shutting my eyes and seeing myself. All I could do was smell Dorothy's hair and feel her shoulders through her sweater; all I could picture was the one tiny button, looped with silk thread, at the nape of her neck.

•

I visited Dorothy every afternoon and every afternoon she met me at the door, glamorous, as if she had slept in her evening clothes. Winter eventually gave way to a wet spring; the trees shook out their new buds and appeared to blossom, collectively, on one particular day in May. It was a few weeks after that that Dorothy met me at the door and put her hand over my eyes. I felt a flutter — her heart, though it might have been my own eyelashes against her skin. Her perfume smelled of cinnamon and tea.

"As you know," she said, leading me in. "I grew up elsewhere. We were missionaries. Or my parents were. Then my mother split. My mother dressed as a boy, a young Arab boy, and toured northern Africa on horseback. I just found out she died, in a flood." I had heard this story before, or most of it. What I did not know was the part about Dorothy's mother in costume. My understanding was that she had died years before. My initial reaction was then of surprise not at the news of Dorothy's mother's death but at the news that during this long winter spent in Dorothy's living room, Dorothy's mother had roamed the world.

"This arrived yesterday," Dorothy said, taking her hand away. "Ta da!"

Before me, raised awkwardly on the Persian rug I had admired many times on the floor of Dorothy's living room, was a tent unlike any I had ever seen. It had many peaks, for starters, and from each a small flag hung, limply; the fabric was the color of sand and across its surface were painted hundreds, perhaps a thousand pairs of eyes, each startled, each oddly female.

I think I gasped or made some kind of sound that indicated I was truly amazed, because Dorothy put her hand on my shoulder as if to steady me.

"It came in the mail. I think she painted it, I don't know. Anyway, it arrived in a box, with her." Dorothy lit a cigarette. "She wants me to take her somewhere. To spend the night in this and then to throw her out."

"Her?" I said.

Dorothy gestured to a small urn on the coffee table. "Will you come?" she asked.

"Of course," I said without consideration. As I have told you, Dorothy was my friend.

•

We left on a hot June day, the trees now thick with green. Dorothy knew of a lake not far from the city where we could pay a small fee and spend the night. We pitched the tent there, near the car and a stucco structure with showers and bathroom stalls. The lake stretched out endlessly beneath the shadow of a mountain known as Mt. Rattlesnake. It was from the top of it, Dorothy informed me, that we would toss her mother at sunrise.

That night we built a small fire and fried eggs. Dorothy sat on a tree stump and talked. She told me again of her mother, and her brother, who was missing in action in Korea. She told me about her father, whose belief in Jesus, she said, left no room for anything else, no place for a daughter and a son, not to mention a wife. "I can understand why she snapped," Dorothy said. "I mean, think of how dull, no matter where. No one can live like that, in a fishbowl."

I sat and listened. The heat was god-awful. I had on the yellow nightgown. I had never worn it before; it seemed silly in the winter and when the weather turned warmer I entirely forgot. It was only while packing, reaching into an out-of-the-way drawer for my athletic socks, that I came upon it, crumpled into a silk ball, cocoon-like. I packed it who knows why; it was hot, as I have said, the night balmy in the way summer nights can be in places near Rochester, as if all the melted snow has been absorbed into the air, so heavy with it that your weight feels tripled. No matter. We fanned ourselves outside the strange tent and drank old-fashioneds from a thermos that smelled of chicken soup. Dorothy talked. She wore her bathing suit — the style popular at the time, polka-dotted, with a ruffled skirt — and her hair, that horse-brown color that is not at all ordinary, she had combed into a tight bun. I could see her through the just dark. I watched her hands, punctuating.

I do not entirely remember what happened next, how it came that the two of us, me in my yellow silk, Dorothy in her bathing suit, wandered around the edge of the lake in the moon shadow of Mt. Rattlesnake. There was a tension about the evening, something awkward in the weather, as if a thunderstorm might erupt at any moment or lightning tear across the sky. Swallows behaved as bats, swooping about our heads, and frenzied balls of mosquitoes bred over the shallower parts of the lake water. At some point Dorothy took my hand to stress something, and she did not let go.

Before I continue I should say that this was a time when women had clear boundaries, and even in discussion the boundaries were observed. Dorothy had already broken down those boundaries between the two of us, and I believed her holding my hand as we walked the lakeshore trail was just a natural extension of all those afternoons together, lying jagged on her Persian rug. I don't know. I can tell you that the fireflies were thick and that the only sound we could hear across the lake was the sound of fish jumping. My silk nightgown felt light against my skin, damp from the humidity. It was not a weekend; there were no other campers. We were, quite truthfully, alone. Because of this, perhaps, we drew close, aware, as one becomes in certain moments, of the brevity of life.

After some time Dorothy stopped and turned toward me. "Marion," she said, and put her hands on my shoulders. Her hair, as I have told you, was pulled back tightly, and when she smiled her whole face seemed to lean into her mouth or radiate out from it in a way remarkable. Only her eyes were sad.

"You are my best friend," she said.

You are too young to understand what this once meant between women. No matter. I can tell you that there will be times when you have to choose between beginning again in a cold and lonely place or making do with whatever fragile shelter you have already built. I understood this, and knew that after that night I would never have another friend like Dorothy, nor would I return to her house in the late afternoon or lean against her, back to back, to wish for spring. When she tried to kiss me I turned away. "I'm sorry," is what I said.

I slept that night outside and she slept in the tent. The flags hung limply. The next morning we woke before sunrise and climbed Mt. Rattlesnake. The top of the mountain was a collection of rocks, some moss covered, some bare. From there we looked down at our tent, a miniature in the distance, and saw clearly the path we walked the night before.

Dorothy held the urn up high intending to scatter her moth-

er's ashes into the wind, but there was no wind and so the
ashes simply fell into a heap on the rock on which we were
standing. The two of us used branches to scrape them over
the edge and then sat and watched the sun ascend.

"I'm afraid she would have been displeased with me," Dorothy said after some time. "I'm afraid she would have been
horribly displeased. They all are, aren't they? Horribly displeased."

"I don't know," I said, and took her hand in mine. "No,"
I said.

•

Dorothy died several years after we moved to Norfolk. I got
the news over the telephone. We had lost touch, but that was
not so unusual in those days when a woman stayed in a place
only until her husband's next transfer. She had sent me Christmas cards, of course, and a longer note when she heard about
your sister's birth. I still felt close to her in a way I've felt with
no friend since, though after that excursion we saw each other
rarely. Still, I waved whenever I drove down Country Club
Road and passed her Tudor, forgetting that her windows were
overgrown, imagining that she might be looking out, seeing
me.

When Rick called, we were packing for Durham, getting
things organized for the movers the next day. I had been
feeling the nostalgia I have always felt on those eves of leaving.
When I hung up the phone, I went back to what I had been
doing, rolling china into sheaves of newspaper, marking card-
board boxes *den, kitchen*. I did not think of Dorothy. Instead,
I thought of the next neighborhood, the next house: how I
would paint the living-room walls, paper the bedrooms; how
I would knock on the front doors of the houses on our new
street, introducing myself, introducing you and your sister,
accepting when the ones at home invited us in for tea and
cookies. It felt somehow impossible to think of anything else,
to think of the way she must have looked, so indiscreet, so

inelegant, slumped against the steering wheel of that automobile going nowhere, idling in the garage over the long weekend Rick had chosen to take the boys camping. Instead, I pictured her in her coffin, pictured her in a yellow silk nightgown, because she always said things like silky nightgowns helped to chase away the blowzy feeling that came with every blue hour, when no man or beast, she said, should be left to swim alone.

ST.
Aldo in N.Y
1954?

Portrait by Saul Steinberg.

A Self-Interview

Aldo Buzzi

Mr. Buzzi, you were born in the north of Italy, in Como . . .

Yes, behind the Duomo. My last name, Buzzi, in order to be pronounced correctly by Americans, should be written thus: "Bootzie." My paternal grandparents were the Büzz (Buzzis) of Sondrio, a town even closer to the Alps than Como, and perhaps they were distant relatives of Butz, the dark-brown poodle (*Canis aquaticus*) that accompanied Schopenhauer on his daily walk. Heinzen, Kunzen, Utzen and Butzen, in the dialect of lower Swabia, are the equivalent of Tom, Dick and Harry, or as we Italians say, Tizio, Caio and Sempronio (and Mevio) or, as Dante says, Donna Berta and Ser Martino.

Before moving to Sondrio the Büzz lived in Rodero, in the Brianza (also in Lombardy), where I can trace them back to Giacomo Antonio de Buzzi, born in 1651.

What did my ancestors do in the time of the Crusades? I don't know, and that is the only difference between us common people and the nobility. But certainly they, too, existed

and perhaps allowed others to go, and they stayed home,
perhaps studying.

Do you still have relatives in Sondrio?

Yes, Dora . . . my second cousin . . . She is a pianist, a
piano teacher, she teaches the young Sondrians to play the
piano. Her older sister had tiny feet, not like the Chinese
women of long ago but still so small that often she couldn't
find shoes in her size (this gave her a touch of pride), I think
sometimes she must have had to buy children's shoes.

Sondrio is called Sundri by its inhabitants, who have the
good fortune to breathe mountain air on their streets. If, as
I'm walking through Sondrio, breathing the good mountain
air, I hear coming through a window the sound of a piano,
I think that the pianist is probably one of my second cousin
Dora's students. I stop, listen, and if I recognize the piece I
am even more certain that it is.

This happens . . . once every . . . twenty years . . . or so.

A hunting dog (*Canis sagax*) — belonging to my father, who
was a hunter — a female, named Diana, was my first childhood
friend. She would have defended me even against a lion.

Diana would sit on the lawn with her front paws spread
like a pyramid and her tail wrapped around her body and her
eyes staring at me intensely, waiting for me to say something
in the slobbery language of children and dogs. She understood
me and she spoke to me: when she moved her tail, beating
it against the ground, she was telling me that Paulìn, my
father, was coming.

I was sitting on the lawn, too, on a rug surrounded by a
wooden fence, painted blue, the color for boys. The lawn
where we were sitting was on Mount Olimpino, also in Como
. . . The name of the street, like so many other names, has
gone right out of my *cabeza*, my poor head. Maybe it's just
as well to forget, little by little, what is not essential.

My father was a chemist. He went from one industrial plant
to another. After a few years we changed city, school, language
. . . Not outside Italy, but from Lombardy to Tuscany to
Piedmont. With a red pencil a Lombard teacher corrected,

on papers, completely correct Tuscan expressions. Useless to get upset.

At the end of his wanderings Papa started a laboratory on an old street in the center of Milan. The most precious object in the laboratory was a spool of platinum wire, locked up in a cabinet. I never liked chemistry — perhaps because it was my father's work and sons want to be different — but that spool attracted me hugely, for its value, its mysterious weight, the oddly poor color of the platinum, so different from that of silver and gold.

Do you still have that spool?

It was during the war: of the spool, of the whole laboratory, of the whole house nothing remained. So ended my father's career.

Your mother . . .

My mother was German. She had come very young with her family to Prato, in Tuscany, and had studied painting in Florence, with a fine teacher. Her name was Käthe (Katherine), a name too difficult for her Italian relatives, who called her Ketty. Some small paintings of hers keep me company at home, although it's painful to recall that while she was alive she was not appreciated as she deserved. Who knows where they will be in a few years, I wonder, if they still exist — in what houses, entrusted to whose hands. Best not to think about it.

One painting shows the window of the room in Via Santo Garovaglio, in Como, where I was born, open onto the looming face of the mountain of Brunate, in shadow, where some black swallows are flying.

She said she didn't know perspective, and she made some mistakes in perspective similar to those of Bonnard, whom she didn't know. Another picture shows the toy corner of the children's room. There is some toy furniture made by Papa, who had a carpenter's bench in the basement: chest of drawers, sideboard and dining table, chairs, stove with little aluminum pots, bed. This miniature apartment, illuminated from above

by the dim light from the window, was inhabited by teddy
bears of velvet and sawdust, the work of Käthe.

All the paintings were small, probably in order not to spend
too much. Sometimes, if there was a frame smaller than the
picture, she cut the picture to make it fit.

The only works she succeeded in selling were some minia-
tures. She did the first one as a trial: a portrait of Princess
Maria Jose of Belgium as a child, painted on a thin slice of
elephant tusk. With this she went to an antique dealer who
gave her photographs of some customers. She did the minia-
tures beautifully—a laborious burden on the eyesight, and
certainly the antique dealer paid very little. Still, when she
returned home with her reward she was pleased.

The only painter who came (and very rarely) to our house
was Costanza, a chemist friend of Paolino, my father. Costanza
was an amateur artist of little merit, but he found a way to
devote himself to painting and to dress like a painter. Very shy
and modest, he talked about painting with Käthe and praised
her pictures. He was interested above all in a portrait of his friend
Paolino done in the evening while he was reading, with a cigar
stub in his mouth, in profile, exactly like Piero della Francesca's
Duke of Urbino, and illuminated by the reddish light of the
lamp shade. Was the red too bright? Costanza talked about
these problems during dinner, which he appreciated as much
as painting. Around eleven he would ceremoniously take his
leave, and he would not reappear for several years.

Who are your favorite writers?

All of them, sort of—the good ones. They change with the
passage of time.

*Do you prefer to live in the city or the country, or by the
sea?*

I prefer a house in the city, surrounded by a garden which
on one side faces the main street and on the other the sea or
the country. It's a house that doesn't exist. It (the house)
should also look out on a solitary meadow where a donkey,

a calf and also a chicken are feeding. Plus a dog, a cat and a couple of blackbirds.

Would you like to raise animals?

No. I would like to live near many animals. To welcome them, offer them tasty bites, see them live to old age, to a natural death. To see a calf chewing its cud sets my soul at ease. That is, it would set my soul at ease if I could see it. The last calf I saw was at the butcher.

Are you a good cook?

Yes, but now, after so many years, I would like someone to cook for me, by surprise. Not a cook, but one of those blessed women who exist now only in the country, with four petticoats and three aprons; and while she works, while she's making the tagliatelle, I can sit there watching her as if she were a calf chewing its cud, with a glass of port beside me and the bottle, too, as a guarantee of the future.

What is your most successful dish?

I find that . . . the apron, as it is worn in the north, is very becoming to women, I can look at it, as at a calf chewing its cud, without getting tired.

What is your favorite dish?

All of them, sort of—the good ones. They change with the passage of time. Once, in the United States, while sitting in the kitchen in front of an electric oven with the light on, and watching, for lack of a calf chewing its cud, some scallops, which, dusted with bread crumbs and black pepper, were cooking on a lightly buttered tray, I said—that is, my host said—"The oven is your television."

It was indeed a show, because the poor mollusks, owing to the extremely high heat, were making little settling move-

ments, as if at the point of taking on the gastronomically most
perfect form they regained, for just a moment, life.

"The fact is," I said, "that I have a weakness for scallops."

"The fact," my host responded, "is that you have a weakness
for almost everything."

*Do you remember the first piece you published? When
was it?*

It was a marvelous night . . .

A night?

One of those nights that exist perhaps only when we are
young . . . That's not me, obviously. It's Fyodor Mikhailovich
. . . . The beginning of "White Nights." . . . The first piece
I published? Yes, I remember . . . "When the Panther Roars."
It came out in *Il Selvaggio*, a literary journal. Then I included
it, with some changes, in my first book, and then, still correct-
ing and cutting, in another book. Because I've written several
books, always writing the same things.

*So, according to you, a written work never reaches its defini-
tive form?*

A writer (with exceptions, like Carlo Emilio Gadda) continually corrects his works. If Dante had lived twenty years more
The Divine Comedy would be different.

Is there such a thing as inspiration?

There are the Muses, and without their help it is useless to try
to write, nothing good will come out. Comforts, conveniences,
even a beautiful view keep the Muses away. When Goethe
was writing he deliberately sat in an uncomfortable chair, as
he explained to Eckermann. If a writer says to me, "I'm going
to Capri to write my novel," I'm dubious; that is, it seems

unlikely that that novel (if it's ever written) will be a good novel. I think you can see very easily if a work has been written with the help of the Muses or not.

Are you working now on something new?

I am trying to free myself from the roar of the panther; I wish the calf would come forward to replace the panther.

Do you have regrets?

Of course. For example, not having read many books that I ought to have read. One of the many is *The Man without Qualities*. Perhaps at the beginning there is something that curbs the desire to go forward. Or one has read something about the author that makes him unsympathetic. Anyway, as I usually do when I break off my reading of a book, I went to the end of the first volume, which I was reading:

"He was surprised by the entrance of the servant, who, with the solemn expression of one who has arisen early, had come to wake him. He took a bath, allowed his body some hurried but vigorous gymnastic exercises, and went to the station."

An echo of this fascinating finale at the station, which invites the reader to take up the book again, appears in a page of Delfini's "Diaries." But the Italian writer, because of his incurable indecisiveness, has gone even further than Musil:

"I took a shower bath. I washed a handkerchief and a small towel. Then I packed my suitcase with the intention of leaving. At the station, however, *je me suis découragé*. I went and got a shave and then returned home."

Are there other books you regret not having read?

The endless *Rāmāyana,* the most famous Indian text, which is composed of 24,000 dystichs, and is one of the most glorious (it seems) masterpieces of human genius; and — also in India — the *Mahābhārata* and the *Rig Veda;* and, moving on to Japan, to China . . . *Je me suis découragé.* Of the most famous Arab poet, Amr'ul Quais, I have read only these three lines, noted down years ago on a scrap of paper: "Her hand is gentle and her delicate fingers are like the insects that climb on the sands of Zhibi or toothpicks made of ishil wood."

I felt some consolation in reading, in Gide's Diary (in his library he had a shelf devoted to books he had not finished reading), of a dialogue between him and Valéry during a meeting at French Radio at which they were consultants. Someone mentioned the *Iliad.* Valéry says under his breath to Gide: "Do you know anything more boring than the *Iliad*?" "Yes," Gide replies, "the *Chanson de Roland.*"

You asked me who are my favorite writers. It would be easier to tell you who are my least favorite. I am happy to be almost always in agreement with the judgments expressed by Nabokov in *Strong Opinions,* which I've just finished reading. Here is the list, I hope complete, which should help to modify certain classifications:

"Second-rate and ephemeral the works of several puffed-up writers—such as Camus, Lorca, Kazantzakis, etc. . . . *Ulysses* towers over the rest of Joyce's writings, and, in comparison to its noble originality and unique lucidity of thought and style, the unfortunate *Finnegans Wake* is nothing but a formless and dull mass of phony folklore, a cold pudding of a book, a persistent snore in the next room . . . . Brecht, Faulkner, Camus, many others, mean absolutely nothing to me . . . . *Doctor Zhivago* . . . I regard as a sorry thing: clumsy, trivial and melodramatic . . . . [There are] some others—such as Ilya Ehrenburg, Bertrand Russell and Jean-Paul Sartre—with whom I would not consent to participate in any festival or conference whatsoever . . . . Since the days when such formidable mediocrities as Galsworthy, Dreiser, a person called Tagore, another called Maksim Gorky, a third called Romain Rolland used to be accepted as geniuses . . ."

Doesn't that seem to you a bit excessive?

No, some of his other opinions I don't share, but these, yes. After giving his opinion of *Finnegans Wake*, Nabokov, who knew the milieu, wrote: "I know I am going to be excommunicated for this pronouncement."

What in your view is the ideal novel?

Today, at my age, it seems to me the ideal model for the novel is the novel that Proust wished to write (and did): "A novel full of passion and meditation and landscapes." The illustrious Charles Robert Darwin had a different model in mind. "A novel," he wrote in his autobiography, "is a work of the first rank only when it has some character whom one can love, and if this character is a beautiful woman, so much the better." Above all, he thought a novel should have a happy ending. "There should be a law," he said, "prohibiting them from having unhappy endings." No one excommunicated him.

I know you were at the Linguists' Club, in London.

Yes, one of the many English schools for foreigners. The place itself was very beautiful: a white neoclassical villa, pleasingly run-down, with a nice garden, in Kensington. (The villa isn't there anymore, it was leveled by bulldozers, which unfortunately work even in London.) I was no longer a boy, but, for that very reason, to sit in a classroom with a professor at the front and fellow students, men and women, many of them young, beside me was a wonderful adventure, which I recommend to everyone, including you.

One must have the time.

One must find the time. I also gave some Italian lessons to English people who were preparing for a trip to Italy, and earned a few pounds, which I spent at The Tun of Port, an elegant restaurant a few steps from the club (it's no longer there, either), where the meal ended unfailingly with blue Stilton, oat biscuits and a glass of port—a wine that many years later became my favorite—served by the young proprietor himself, who was very elegant, always courteous and smiling. He was one of those young Londoners who in the time of Stevenson gathered at the Haunt of the Bohemian Cigar, on Rupert Street, Soho. His mother, who must have had a lot of money, had financed that gastronomic venture which was destined to come to a bad end precisely because of the ideal way it was run. As he poured the port into my glass, I saw the immaculate shirt cuff, which, coming out of the sleeve of his Savile Row jacket, displayed an aristocratic gold cuff link. Making the comfort of the neighborhood complete, there was, near the club, and I hope it's still there, a luxurious old public toilet (as to dimensions: a small villa), with the noble sign "Gentlemen." On foggy nights I would see Sherlock Holmes come staggering out the door, under the blue light of a gas lamp, followed by Dr. Watson.

Does one learn English well in those schools?

Not very. To learn it well one has to be the only foreigner in the midst of English people. But what can I say? I spent at the Linguists' Club one of the coldest winters of my life but I have a wonderful memory of it, a great nostalgia.

Is there any other country that you feel a special nostalgia for?

Yes, there is, it's Yugoslavia, where I was for quite a while, for work. It was soon after the war. We often cursed the backwardness, the dirt, the incredible slowness of everything. And yet . . . for the first time I saw Cyrillic characters . . . the icons . . . Russia . . . In Belgrade I usually ate at the Metropole restaurant. Here and there sat some *segnorine*, generally rather pretty girls, in little hats and not at all vulgar, looking for someone to sit at their tables. The waiters brought big tureens of steaming soups, *ciorbe*, a bit too fatty but good. *Bez maste*! Without fat! was one of the first expressions to learn. Veal, chicken, pork soups; big oval-bottomed plates with delicious boiled beef swimming in an excellent broth, flavored with horseradish. The customers smoked and drank rakiya continually. In one corner a duo (violin and piano) played gypsy music. I still remember a few words from the menu, which was our grammar book: *kuvana govedina sa renom*, boiled beef with horseradish . . .

It's not easy to communicate in those countries.

True, but in the end one succeeds. The maître d' of the Metropole, who wore in a dignified manner a Dostoyevskian tailcoat, greenish-black, knew a few words of French and even fewer of Italian, only enough to communicate, in approximate fashion, with the Italian customers. When someone, picking out on the menu the word *spaghetti,* said "spaghetti," the maître d' wrote down the order with a flourish and, with a connoisseur's smile, added, "*à la Dante.*"

One day I went up to Cetinje, once the capital of Montenegro — the country of our Queen Elena (Jela), "raven-haired," as Babel says — at the end of a long road that wound through the wild mountains of the lower Adriatic, where the air smelled of aromatic grasses, rocks, sheep and goats warmed by the sun.

There was a little Grand Hotel, the former haunt of diplomats from Great Britain, France, Austria-Hungary, and Russia accredited to the court of King Nicholas (or Danilo?) and sent to that isolated post probably as a punishment — as with us they were sent to Sardinia — while in reality it was a prize. The cook, who was very clean, like the cooks in the French restaurants in Petersburg in the time of Gogol, was taking out of the oven a cake made with wild strawberries. Have you ever tried that cake? He brought it to the table himself: a fine cook, and modest. Today the great chefs have their toques and white uniforms made by famous tailors, their wives circulate in the dining room, dressed similarly. . . . I prefer a modest trattoria, maybe with a paper tablecloth, where while eating I can glimpse the cook at work, amid the steam of the kitchen, in an ordinary apron, and on his head an ordinary toque, which has to serve only the purpose for which it was created, that is, to keep the cook's hair from ending up in the customer's soup, an accident that waiters sometimes react to with amusing remarks. The hair in the soup has had the honor of being

cited by Kafka, I don't know if from his own experience. But
Kafka was able to describe even things that he hadn't seen,
like the Brooklyn Bridge, which he described very well, although
he had never been to America. I myself have crossed that bridge
on foot, something that not many Americans have done.

*Are you pleased that your book has been published in
America?*

Very. It's something that when I began writing would have
seemed to me impossible. America at that time was a very
distant country, unreachable. Luckily it is no longer that way.

How did you eat there?

No problem. But I would like to suggest to Americans not
to leave anything on their plates when they eat (they all do
it, for them it's a sign of good breeding), that is, to take or
be served a reasonable portion and to eat it all, even cleaning
their plate with a piece of bread, a delicious bite whose existence will otherwise be unknown. It would mean saving mountains of food and garbage every day.

That seems a sensible suggestion.

Yes.

When did you go to America for the first time?

In 1952, on a most beautiful airplane, the Constellation.
The woman who sat next to me on the plane was an Italian-
American doctor—I remember her hair, which was red but
tinted yellow to make a pale chestnut color. Her father, she
told me, had discovered an excellent, green Sicilian olive oil,
on Mott Street, in New York. She talked to me about America
for a long time. "Lindbergh," she said, "when traveling by
plane would go tourist class and put his hat over his face. He
lived in Hana, in Hawaii, he washed his own laundry and
made his own bed and cooked for himself. For nourishment,

during the great flight, a packet of sandwiches was enough for him." She ended with an anecdote: "Someone said to the American comic Jack Benny, 'When you die, you have to leave your money here, you can't take it with you,' and he replied, 'Then death doesn't interest me.'"

She added a last recommendation: "After the Vikings and Columbus," she said, "infinite numbers of people have still discovered America."

"It's true," I said.

"Don't join the group. Take my father for an example, who discovered not America but Sicilian olive oil on Mott Street."

So when the airplane, with a light shake, touched down on Jack Benny Land (or Vine Land, as the Vikings called it), I knew, in a certain sense, how to behave.

Did you look for that olive oil?

No, because my friend used a very good oil from Provence, golden-yellow in color, sold in the most expensive stores, in elegant little bottles hardly bigger than a perfume bottle, and perfect on Boston lettuce: oil, salt and a few drops of water.

I see that cooking still interests you . . .

Really . . . nothing interests me anymore.

I can't believe that. Listen . . . a last question. Is there something that you would have liked to do in your life and didn't?

There must be, certainly. That's the final question in almost all interviews. Anyway, to end in a slightly different way, more down-to-earth, as Donna Berta and Ser Martino would, or Heinzen, Kunzen, Utzen and Butzen, allow me not to answer the question.

All right. Then we'll end with the olive oil?

Yes.

—translated from the Italian
by Ann Goldstein

John Updike

Two Cunts in Paris

Although stone nudes are everywhere — some crammed
two to a column, supple caryatids,
and others mooning in the Tuileries —
the part that makes them women is the last
revelation allowed to art; the male
equipment, less concealable, is seen
since ancient items: a triune bunch of fruit.

Courbet's oil, *L'Origine du monde,* was owned
by Madame Jacques Lacan and through some tax
shenanigans became the Musée d'Orsay's.
Go see it there. Beneath the pubic bush —
a matted Rorschach blot — between blanched thighs
of a fat and bridal docility,
a curved and rosy closure says, *"Ici!"*

We sense a voyeur's boast. The *Ding an sich,*
self-knowledgeless, a centimeter long
as sculpted, in *terre cuite,* in fine detail
of labia and perineum, exists
in the Musée des Arts Décoratifs,
by Claudion (Claude Michel *dit.*) A girl
all young and naked, with perfected limbs

and bundled, banded hair, uplifts her legs
to hold upon her ankles a tousled dog
yapping in an excitement forever frozen:
caught in the impeccably molded clay
his canine agitation and the girl's,
the dark slits of her smile and half-shut eyes
one with the eyelike slot she lets us see.

Called *La Gimblette* ("ring-biscuit" — a low pun?),
this piece of the eternal feminine,
a doll of femaleness whose vulval facts
are set in place with a watchmaker's care,
provides a measure of how far art falls
of a Creator's providence, which gives
His creatures, all, the homely means to spawn.

Michael Blumenthal

Falling Asleep at the Erotic *Mozi*

Budapest, January 1995

Because I want to watch them do what I would like to do
if I were free, and because it is late and I am tired
and out for what I say is my nightly walk, I stop
at the Erotic *Mozi* on Hegedus Gyula Street, and slide past
the 30-minute, 60-minute, 90-minute videos, the promises
of bondage and rectal penetration, of threesomes and
twosomes and sums of all colors and kinds: the Black man
doing it to the white girls, the white girls to each other,
a world of cocks, cunts, sphincters and easy riders,
and pay my 140 forints at the register, pushing my way
into the small, dark theater where men mostly older than
   I am
are sitting in raincoats and mufflers, in sweaters and T-
shirts, chewing and pondering, watching and fidgeting
over the dirty talk (mostly in German), the thrusts
and counterthrusts punctuated by the periodic squirtings
of seed, occasionally landing on a stray cheek,
a breast, a shoulder, a thigh, rubbed like a salve
into the skin of their targets, sometimes licked
from their fingers, until slowly I find myself,
like an old champion back at Wimbledon after twenty-
   five years,
dozing off, then waking again, comparing my backhand
to the younger competitors', checking the spectators
for someone I might have loved, and, since everything
becomes metaphor in the end, I enact here, too,
the metaphoric whole: I slide back into my seat.
I hunger. I fidget. I dream. I fall asleep.

Maura Stanton

The Last Judgment

In Bible Class I stared at a colored print
Of Michelangelo's *The Last Judgment*.
I looked at the swirling bodies drawn up
To God's throne, or tossed down to Hell
As if a tornado were churning over the earth
Pulling reluctant corpses from their graves,
And felt terror at the sight of helpless men.
I could read fear or torment in every back
Or creased stomach, in round, molded calves,
In muscular arms thrown over anguished faces.
I saw how the body could fly without wings.
Nothing seemed to matter — not age or strength.
The good looked just like the bad, who were falling.

Years later, in the Sistine Chapel, I studied
The smoke-darkened fresco on the altar wall —
I felt dizzy when I looked up at the ceiling
Where the guide was pointing now to the Creation.
I could only stare at the triumphant angels
Who blew long golden horns until their cheeks
Puffed and swelled in the great final effort.
I hadn't eaten for hours. I crouched down
In the crowd, rocking on my heels to keep myself
From fainting and saw not art but a hundred legs,
Trousered, nyloned, hairy, tanned or veined,
Shaped like the legs on the wall, everyone straining
Up on tiptoe to see over someone's head
As if they were flying up to the throne, or returning.

Terese Svoboda

Old God

Ah, to be old and rage uncontrollably,
to command the sun and moon to stop
and yet be treated like a dog,
house training at ten and two
or we'll weight your walker. Flatline

the sun goes daily, and the dog
howls anyway. I read where men's bodies
can be made twenty years younger,
only men's—we're so simple. I totter
toward a diamond of yellow light,

where the same geese snatch bread
ad nauseam. No one wants to see
them past their prime—they fly elsewhere
for their duplicate unsexed deaths.
Why feed them? I parade,

leg by leg, back to my barracks,
my rage rising over a horizon
of sleeping nieces. Weep, wombs,
for what you hold is
not yourself, over and over.

Kenneth Koch

My Olivetti Speaks

Birds don't sing, they explain. Only human beings sing.

If half the poets in the world stopped writing, there would still be the same amount of poetry.

If ninety-nine percent of the poets in the world stopped writing poetry, there would still be the same amount of poetry. Going beyond ninety-nine percent might limit production.

The very existence of poetry should make us laugh. What is that all about? What is it for?

Oxford and Cambridge, two great English universities, are based on poetry. If poetry vanished, they would fall down.

Olive likes poetry but Popeye doesn't. Popeye says, "Swee'pea is poetry for me." Popeye is making a familiar mistake. Human beings and poems are entirely different things. But, claims Popeye, Swee'pea is not a human being. He am a cartoon. It may be that Swee'pea is a poem but he is not exactly written. He is a calligramme without words. It is quite possible to like such kinds of poems but I prefer the others, the regular ones, written out.

In the old days a good place to publish a poem was the *Partisan Review*. Heady—among those thick, heavy pages—one felt ranked by the rankers, a part of the move, a part of the proof—toward what? of what? To find out, you had to read countless *Partisan Reviews*. Then you would see what it was. You could be as serious as Delmore Schwartz, as serious as anyone who ever lived. He consistently turned down my poems. I loved that magazine. It weighed an intellectual ton. What would a poem of mine have been doing inside it anyway? How could it have fitted into that heavy and amazing vision of contemporary life?

Sex is to poetry as sex is to everything else. It forgives it but it also forgets it even while it is planning it.

"I don't like it but I know it is a great poem." I feel the same way about you.

"Poetry is making a comeback." But why is it always bad poetry, or a false idea about poetry, that is making a comeback? I don't think good poetry has ever made a comeback, or ever will. That's one reason it is necessary to keep on writing it.

A dog barks in rhyme but the rhyme is never planned by the dog. This is not a value judgment in any way but it may be an introduction to the consideration of the aesthetic pleasures of being and not being a dog.

Rhyme was very good. Then rhyme was very bad. Then it was forbidden. Then, leader of a rebellion, it came back. Now it has grown old and mellowed, no longer smokes cigars, is less militant, seems to be sinking into acceptance of parliamentary democracy (to a degree!), and a poet can use it or not, pretty much as he or she chooses. However, anyone who uses it has to be careful, extra-careful, he doesn't get shot. No old-fashioned communism, if you please! Use it and get out. Use it and run. Probably more quickly than anything else, rhyme can show how self-uninformed you are.

On the island of rhymesters, anyone who is any good is king. It's a rare talent. Statues of Byron, Ariosto, Petrarch, and Herrick on the coast are misleading. In the interior, there are no statues at all.

A short life and one hundred good poems. A long life and two good poems. No one has ever had to make this choice.

Here is someone talking about poetry. The only people who listen are those who don't know anything about poetry and those who do.

Shakespeare was the last great poet of the Middle Ages. Keats was the first great poet of Modern Times. Each of us alive now is both desirous of, and afraid of, being the last.

I bring fresh showers for thirsting flowers. Poetry sometimes seems part of an enormous game of Fill in the Blanks. Let every emotion, idea, sensation be covered (filled in) and may none escape. When we have totally completed this board, when all is color, line and shading, no blank spaces at all, we may, then, see what this great solved jigsaw puzzle means. (I already have one idea: the refreshment of childhood grossly modified by social and historical change.) The Last Judgment is nothing compared to what then we shall see! Otherwise (if there is no puzzle of this sort) why is Shelley disguising himself as a cloud? Wouldn't that be a waste of time?

The awakening of sexual feelings in a hedgehog is a poetic subject possibly not yet covered. This doesn't imply, however, that we should concentrate our efforts on covering it, though someone may, and if he is as good a poet as Ronsard, and has a thriving tradition behind him, he may do it well.

The last century was full of music, as this one has been full of painting. Poetry, complexly amused, has been content to take second place in both.

Byron was so unlikely ever to write a sonnet that people in his time used to say, when they were skeptical about a thing, "Oh, sure, like Byron's sonnet!" A seemingly impossible wind-fall, any staggeringly unlikely event was called a "Byron's sonnet." When someone proposed removing all the Carpaccio paintings from Venice, the witty Doge Meduno Rabanatti is reported to have said, "Certainly! as soon as we get Byron's sonnet in exchange." Byron, according to one story, hearing of this conversation, immediately sat down and wrote a sonnet, which—since he loved the Carpaccios and wanted them to stay—he then just as immediately tore up.

Nostalgia for old poetry is like nostalgia for Ancient Egypt— one is hardly lamenting one's own youth. Imagine an Egyptian youth and that he speaks to you. Who is that lovely young woman by his side? No one you have ever hurt with your fear or your false promises, that's sure. Dissolution may not be so bad, if only it didn't need to be preceded by death, as it isn't in poetry.

A glass breaks when someone sings a high note, and when someone makes a great breakthrough in a poem there is a stranger in the mirror.

To read a poem we sit down; to look at a painting we stand up. Art is always saying hello and poetry is always saying good-bye. It says Your dreams are leaving town, and not even Byron can prevent it, nor any other Lord.

To look at a painting we stand up because of our voracity. We don't want anyone else getting it before us, not the slightest part. We are quickly satisfied, however, given how strong this voracity is. We soon move away. Reading a poem we don't mind interruptions. That poem will still be there when we come back. But someone reading over our shoulder is not what we want. It's time to leave!

I will live in that little house with you and write poetry! This statement, taken in isolation from all others, and from all the rest of reality, is wonderful and touching to think about.

Yes! I will write too! Already the situation is less "ideal." This means two quiet places and two typewriters. And as for the house —

Five great poets writing about five different things constitute a Renaissance. Five great poets writing about the same thing constitute a "school" (une école).

A mermaid who recites poetry is a lost mermaid.

A curious thing about the wind is that one can't tell if its music is ever the same, because one never hears the beginning.

Write poetry as if you were in love. If you are always in love you will not always write the same poem. If you are never in love, you may.

The relation of emotion to poetry is like that of squirrels to a tree. You don't live in what you never have to leave.

"The most modern person in Europe is you Pope Pius the Tenth," Apollinaire wrote in 1913. Being modern was equivalent to being surprising — for about twenty years (1908–1928).

To be ahead of everything and still to be behind in love — a predicament poets may imagine they are in.

That person in the corner has published poems! — A marvel for youth.

My brother-in-law here is a poet. — Leap out the door. Though the brother-in-law may be a much better poet than that one in the corner. Or they may be the same person.

This poem is worth more than these emeralds and diamonds. How can that possibly be? There is no monetary value to a poem. To this one there is: I set the price myself.

I know for sure that I am not a calligramme. When I look at my arm or my hands or my legs, there are no comments, they aren't formed by letters of words. From birth to death I remain unexplained — at least in that manner.

The first poem one writes is usually not the worst. It is not like one's first kiss or one's first time driving a car but more like one's first success.

Ice is like prose; fire is like poetry. But neither melts nor goes out. Ideally (or unideally, some would say) they generally ignore each other's existence.

Rhyme is like a ball that bounces not in the same place but at least in another place where it can bounce.

Poets who write every day also write every year, which is the important thing for poetry.

Poets are the unacknowledged impersonators of the greatest unborn actors of their time.

The Romantic movement left, when it departed, a tremendous gap in poetry which could be filled by criticism and by literary theory but which would be better left alone.

Rome inspired architects and sculptors and painters; the Lake Country inspired poets. Milton inspired Keats. Perugino taught Raphael. Blake gave ideas to Yeats. Sciascia read *Chroniques italiennes* once every year. Byron learned something from Pope. Even the most unsentimental person is glad to see his home country again.

A tapestry is not like a lot of little poems woven together but like one big poem being taken apart.

Starting off as an Irish poet, one has a temperamental and geographical advantage. Starting off as a French poet, one incites an overwhelming curiosity as to what can be done. Starting off as an American poet, one begins to develop a kind of self-consciousness that may quickly lead to genius or to nothing.

Would that he had blotted a thousand! "Perfection" is wonderful in poetry but Shakespeare is good enough — one reads on!

There are three Testaments and one is illegible.

The iris is a flower that is past meridian, a ghost come bearing you a villanelle.

What is the matter with having a subject? Wittgenstein says there are no subjects in the world; a subject is a limitation of the world. In fact our subject is all around us like a mail-order winter that we accidentally sent in a request for when it seemed it would always be spring.

Eve was the first animal. Therefore she could not have been Eve, and Adam could not have written poetry. Adam could not write poetry unless there was a human Eve. Thousands of years later, there was: Eve de Montmorency. But she didn't encourage the production of poetry. She said I'll kill anyone who writes me a poem. I like life to be real! Inspired, all the same, a few poets began writing "free verse" (and it was pretty good) which she was unable to recognize as poetry. Meanwhile, back in the Garden of Eden, Eve woke up. She was a fox no more, but a woman, and a ravishing one! Adam saw her and became terribly excited. Without willing to or wishing to at all (for who could know the consequences) he fell to one knee before her, held out his hands and recited: Roses are red, violets are blue. Yes, what's the rest? Eve said. I don't know, Adam said. I'm not yet fully a poet. That's as far as I've got. So far so good, Eve said, and she loved him with a new ardor that night. From their union were born Abel and Cain, who

178

represented two dissenting schools of criticism: Abel, the "inspirational," let-your-self-go, just SAY it, let it all hang out, or blossom! Lyrical School; Cain, the party of more rigorously crafted delight, a sylvan Valéry: *l'inspiration n'est pour rien, le travail, en poésie, est tout!* They fought and killed each other many times, while Eve brought forth more children in sorrow, and Adam, his body aching, tilled the land.

Once I taught polar bears to write poetry. After class each week (it was once a week) I came home to bed. The work was extremely tiring. The bears tried to maul me and for months refused to write a single word. If refused is the right term to use for creatures who had no idea what I was doing and what I wanted them to do. One day, however, it was in early April, when the snow had begun to melt and the cities were full of bright visions on windowglass, the bears grew quieter and I believed that I had begun to get through to them. One female bear came up to me and placed her left paw on top of my head. Her mouth was open and her very red tongue was hanging out. I realized that she, and the other bears, must be thirsty, so I procured for them several barrels of water. They drank it thirstily and looked up at me from time to time gratefully but even then they wrote no poems. They never did write a word. Still I don't think this teaching was a waste of time, and I'm planning on continuing it in the future if I find I have the necessary strength. For hard and exhausting it is to attempt something one knows it is impossible to do — but what if one day these bears actually started to write? I think we would all put down our Stefan George and our Yeats and pay attention! What wonders might be disclosed! what dreams of bears!

Reading is done in the immediate past, writing in the immediate future.

The world never tires of bad poetry, and for this reason we have come to this garden, which is in another world.

I don't think one can avoid irrationality when one is young if one is planning to enjoy it when one is old. For this reason a poet's life may be called "precarious."

Similarity of sound is similarity of adventure. If you believe that, you are a musician.

Poetry, which is written while no one is looking, is meant to be looked at for all time.

ROUND

What was the need like driving rain
That struck the house and pelted the garden
So poorly planned? What was the creature
That needed to hide from the stunning torrent
Among the piers of the stone foundation
Under the house

That groaned in the wind? The seedlings floated
And spun in furrows that turned to runnels
Of muddy water while the dry one watched   *the hidden*
Apart from the ones that lived inside.   *others*
The house *was* pounded and stung by the wind   *wall*
That flailed the siding

And pried at the roof. Though the beams looked sound
The rooms all shook. Who were the ones
Shaken inside and the one that hid
Among the stones in the noisy storm *squall storm*   *all through the storm*
While their failed garden melted to ruin? —
What was the need?

Sturdy and stained

The whole

A manuscript page of the poem "Round."

Robert Pinsky

The Art of Poetry LXXVI

When Robert Pinsky was named Poet Laureate of the United States earlier this year, it felt deeply appropriate. To an unusual degree, Pinsky has mulled, both on the page and off, over the relationship between American civic and private life. Although far from jingoistic, he's an unabashed patriot who embodies many of our more attractive national traits: ingenuity, open-mindedness, a certain stalwart optimism. His second volume is called An Explanation of America, *and where Pinsky once helped poets make sense of their country, it's safe to guess that he'll now prove just as good at spurring the country to take stock of its verse; the art couldn't find a more effective advocate. Among the endeavors he's undertaken is his "say a poem" project, whose purpose, Pinsky writes, "is to create an audio and video archive of perhaps a hundred or a hundred-*

and-fifty Americans each choosing and reading aloud a favorite poem. The archive would be a record, at the end of the century, of what we choose, and what we do with our voices and faces, when asked to say aloud a poem we love."

Pinsky's *resume reads like a literary version of the American success story. Born in 1940 in Long Branch, New Jersey into a family he describes as lower-middle class, he went to Rutgers and then, in 1965, won a Stegner Fellowship to Stanford, where he studied with Yvor Winters. Since 1966, he has taught continuously: at the University of Chicago, Wellesley, Har-vard, U.C.–Berkeley, and, for the past nine years, at Boston University.* He was the poetry editor of The New Republic *from 1978–1987, and now fills the same position at the on-line magazine* Slate. *His books of poetry are* Sadness And Happi-ness *(1975),* An Explanation of America *(1980),* History of My Heart *(1984),* The Want Bone *(1990) and* The Figured Wheel: New and Collected Poems 1966–1996. *In addition, he cotranslated Czeslaw Milosz's* The Separate Notebooks *(1984) and in 1995 produced an acclaimed translation of Dante's* Inferno. *Pinsky has also been active as a critic, publishing* Landor's Poetry *(1968),* The Situation of Poetry *(1977) and* Poetry and the World *(1988). Over the years, he has garnered many prizes and awards, including the William Carlos Wil-liams Award, the Landon Prize in Translation, the Los Angeles Times Book Award, the Shelley Memorial Award and the Am-bassador Prize. He's also been nominated once for the National Book Critics Circle Award in Criticism and once for the Pulitzer Prize in Poetry.*

In person, Pinsky is relaxed, amusing, effortlessly charas-matic, but also poised, alert and robust beyond his years. He commands a strong, resonant voice, which he deploys to equal effect whether reciting a passage of George Herbert or spinning an old-time Long Branch yarn. From the Metaphysical poets to New Jersey boardwalks, his conversation ranges easily and unaffectedly between subjects high and low. One senses that Pinsky feels nearly as at home in the garage where he gets his

Chrysler convertible fixed as in the halls of academe — or, for
that matter, of Congress. He's the refreshing opposite of ivory-
towered, and, for a poet, uncommonly extroverted.

This interview took place in August 1995 on the campus
of Skidmore College, where Pinsky was taking part in the New
York State Writers' Institute. When we entered the apartment
in which Pinsky was staying, a saxophone stood on the floor.
Our first question was obvious.

INTERVIEWER
You play the sax?

ROBERT PINSKY
I was playing it five minutes ago, to relax before you arrived.
I keep the horn out, the way you see it now, and blow it from
time to time. In high school, I was ambitious about it, and
I played a little in college. Then I took it up again a few years
ago — after maybe a thirty-year gap!

INTERVIEWER
Is this the same saxophone as in high school?

PINSKY
No, in the old days I had a great horn, a Buescher Aristo-
crat — I like the name — that I paid for with money earned
playing high-school dances, bar mitzvahs and so forth. When
I went to California, I left the Buescher in my parents' house,
and in their characteristic way they lost track of it. Maybe it
was sold, maybe it was stolen or given away. I must have been
twenty-five or -six when that happened, and it provided an
excuse to stop playing all those years. Then a few years ago,
I went out in a trance and bought this Grassi, an Italian copy
of the Selmer Mark VI.

INTERVIEWER
A midlife crisis?

PINSKY

I think my first experience of art, or the joy in making art, was playing the horn at some high-school dance or bar mitzvah or wedding, looking at a roomful of people moving their bodies around in time to what I was doing. There was a piano player, a bass player, a drummer, and my breath making the melody. The audience may not have been thinking, My God, that kid is the best saxophone player I've ever heard; I'm *positive* they weren't. But we were making music, and the fact that it was my breath making a party out of things was miraculous to me, a physical pleasure. So maybe the horn, this fumbling after a kind of melodic grace and ease I know I'll never have, stands for a rededication to art itself—with that eager, amateur's love.

INTERVIEWER

Can you relate the two arts?

PINSKY

There's a lot of cant about poetry and jazz. And yet there *is* something there in the idea of surprise and variation, a fairly regular structure of harmony or rhythm—the left margin, say—and all the things you can do inside it or against it. There are passages, like the last two stanzas of "Ginza Samba," where I try to make the consonants and vowels approach a bebop sort of rhythm.

In *Poetry and the World*, I wrote: "Poetry is the most bodily of the arts." A couple of friends who read it in draft said, "Well, Robert, you know . . . *dancing* is probably more bodily than poetry." But I stubbornly left the passage that way without quite having worked out why I wanted to say it like that. Sometimes the ideas that mean the most to you will feel true long before you can quite formulate them or justify them. After a while, I realized that for me the medium of poetry is the column of breath rising from the diaphragm to be shaped into meaning sounds inside the mouth. That is, poetry's medium is the individual chest and throat and mouth of whoever undertakes to say the poem—a body, and not necessarily the body of the artist or an expert as in dance.

In jazz, as in poetry, there is always that play between what's regular and what's wild. That has always appealed to me.

INTERVIEWER

In one of your essays, you quote Housman's wonderful statement that he knows a line of poetry has popped into his head when his hair bristles and he cuts himself shaving. Is that the kind of thing you mean by the body of the audience?

PINSKY

Well, there is certainly a physical sensation that even subvocalized reading of some particular Yeats or Stevens or Dickinson poem can give me, just the imagination of the sounds. This sensation is as unmistakably physical as humming or imagining a tune.

INTERVIEWER

But it's pretty rare to see a poetry-reading audience responding with their bodies as if it were a rock concert, isn't it? Would that be something you'd welcome?

PINSKY

Well, the point isn't performance. Poetry is a vocal art for me—but not necessarily a performative one. It might be reading to oneself or recalling some lines by memory. That physical tingle, that powerful, audible experience of poetry, has come to me not with poets projecting their own work powerfully to an audience, or with the John-Gielgud-reading-Shakespeare-sonnets records that friends have played for me on their stereos. It tends to be more intimate, less planned, than that. One is alone, or maybe with a friend or two.

Or it might even be in actual school. In my classes, I ask the students to find a poem they like and to get it by heart. To see someone in their late teens or early twenties, often by gender or ethnicity different from the author, shaping his or her mouth around those sounds created by somebody who is perhaps long dead, or perhaps thousands of miles away, and the students bringing their own experience to it, changing it with their own sensibility, so that they're both possessed and possessing—those moments have been very moving to me. Though the vocal performance may be crude, that crudeness just throws the essence of the poetry into higher relief. Whereas the effective personality of a poet giving a reading or the rich expert tones of an actor reading "When to the sessions of sweet silent thought" might muffle that essence by encasing it within the other art of performance.

INTERVIEWER

To quote from your essay "Some Passages of Isaiah": "Grandpa Dave stood for the immense beauty and power of idolatry, the adoration of all that can be made and enjoyed by the human body." Do you feel that your acute focus on *making* in poetry reflects a need to continue the family line of utility, to shape something that is actual and worldly? Was your fear of poetry straying over into hoity-toity abstractions fostered by your upbringing?

PINSKY

I'm far from immune to the American, perhaps historically male, prejudice toward practical and physical competence; I hope I've also considered that prejudice enough to have some distance from it. I come from a class that is lower-middle and retail-oriented, and when I was quite young, we were more or less poor, so pragmatism had considerable urgency or necessity.

Both my grandfathers lived within a few blocks of us. One had a bar and had bootlegged during Prohibition; the other was a window washer, a part-time tailor and tinkerer. In an American way, and in line with your question, it is the bootlegger I have written about most. Dave, my father's father, had a certain swagger, glamour and capacity for violence. I once spoke with a huge old Irish guy who said, "More than once

I seen your grandfather jump over the bar and knock a guy out." There's something particularly thrilling and anomalous about that in relation to Jewish life; in Isaac Babel's stories of Odessa gangsters there are issues and patterns I recognize. I guess violence is one side of that practical, physical skill. But my other grandfather, Morris, could fix clocks and motors; he courted his wife by dazzling her with a motorcycle. (She was married to someone else at the time.) He tuned up his own car, replaced the brake linings and so forth.

INTERVIEWER

Do you consider that background an advantage to you as a writer?

PINSKY

I certainly wish I had those skills! — and I don't. But there is a spirit there that I feel grateful toward, and some loyalty. Both grandfathers partook of the pleasures of the marketplace, a term that maybe connotes capitalism. But there's a more ancient sense of the marketplace or *agora,* that's very attractive to me: the public space. It's the place where people see each other, where they venture out of the family — the shared home away from the hearth. From one point of view, the *Odyssey* is a great hymn not just to coming home but to cruising the sea, risking Poseidon to see what deals you can make, what you can achieve or learn. I think that the laboring, mercantile, small-town, lower-middle class has a lot of respect not only for gain, but for *exchange.* To see someone, nod to that person and think, as you say hello, Oh yes, that's an Odiotti. His father had the paint store — or was it his uncle? And he knows vaguely that I must be an Eisenberg or a Pinsky, and that I might have something to do with the bar. We exchange recognition. That's all part of a certain marketplace fabric that includes a lower-class work ethic, a neighborhood sense of worth, a shrewd practicality. And yes, I suppose there is something in my work as a writer that extends that ethic or reacts against it.

You've also shown an affection for the language of trade, notably in your poem "Shirt."

PINSKY

I grew up with respect for the skills and the knowledge of people who knew how to do things. The tenants in our building and in the rooming houses on either side of us were housepainters, railroad workers, masons and so forth. In the summer, horse trainers and one or two jockeys. My father was an optician, and there was a whole technical jargon that went with that job.

I suppose I'm the kind of writer who has respect, and maybe some nostalgia, for practical knowledge of the world — for that earthly competence. But it's important to recognize that there's a boring cult of competence in American life and literature — especially competence in basic, even primitive skills. There's a certain amount of baloney, for instance, about fishing and hunting, which is not to say that those things cannot be written about well, also. The baloney and something truly distinguished are not always easy to separate in Hemingway. And *Moby-Dick* can be read as the world's best how-to book.

INTERVIEWER

In your essay "American Poetry and American Life," you salute what you term our poetry's *heteroglossia,* its force of contrast between high and low diction. Do you try in your own work to include as many levels of speech as possible?

PINSKY

I would like to keep and somehow unify all the different kinds of experience, and therefore all the different kinds of language, I've ever known. I grew up in a neighborhood that you might call — as my mother did, complaining endlessly about having to live there — a slum. It was not monochromatic. There was a lot of variety culturally, ethnically, in class and in kind of education. People spoke with various accents. Ideally, I'd like to write a poetry that pretends neither that I've been a professor all my life, nor that I'm still a streetboy. A poetry that doesn't pretend that I've never watched television, and that doesn't pretend, either, that I've never been to graduate school.

I love the way some poems—not only poems by Williams, but by Dickinson or Ben Jonson, too—constantly modulate precise answers to the questions, "Who says this?" or "Who's talking?" In a satisfying work of art, the answer can change from second to second: the voice proclaiming "That is no country for old men" is subtly different from the one that notices "What is past, or passing, or to come." The idiom is always flexing, responding like the line in an oscilloscope. It's not just the plain style, or the grand style or the Eurekan style, but, as with the human face in conversation, at once always changing and always itself.

For me, writing has a lot to do with collision and departure. In the anonymous lyric "Western wind, when will thou blow, / The small rain down can rain? / Christ! That my love were in my arms / And I in my bed again," I love that movement when the poet exclaims, "Christ!" because you haven't been at "Christ!"—you've been addressing the wind, asking it a question. You're thinking about a "small rain," and the last thing that would follow a small rain might seem to be Christ. The change from imploring the wind to saying "Christ!" is a gesture of impatience and exaltation. For me that movement, like when an ice skater suddenly changes directions, has a lot to do with what poetry is.

My favorite parts of language may be those places where the distinction between high and low breaks down, because *high* and *low* are unsatisfactory, tentative gestures toward describing the flow of language. Is *strewn* a high word or low? It's a word roofers use, after all. I've spoken elsewhere about going to the hardware store and overhearing a salesman say, "You could buy one of these whirling things to distribute the fertilizer, or you can just strew it broadcast." It was the first time I realized that the word *broadcast* wasn't coined during the Industrial Revolution, or for Marconi. Farmers walk through the fields with a sack slung over one shoulder, and they broadcast. Obscenities are low by most standards, but *fuck,* which is a very old word, perhaps contains a quality of loftiness by virtue of being archaic. One of the most exciting phenomena in language — it happens often in Williams and in Stevens — is when you lose the sense of what's high and what's low. Is *mullion* the mullion of Sir Kenneth Clark talking about a church, or is it the mullion of a carpenter saying, "Shit, the mullion is too short. We're going to have to go back and cut some more"?

INTERVIEWER

It sounds as if etymology is often a point of departure for you. Will you suddenly wonder what the etymology of *fuck* or *mullion* is, and then go look it up? Do you go so far as to browse in etymological dictionaries?

PINSKY

When I was a kid I read the dictionary as an absorbing book, sometimes browsing in it for hours. There's a lot you can learn from it besides the meanings of words, like why we eat *venison* and not *deer.* It's the same reason we eat *pork* and not *pig,* or *beef* instead of *cow:* because the food names are the French words, brought over by the Normans. The Saxon who took care of the animal called it a *sheep;* after it had been slaughtered, cut up and presented to a Norman lord, it was called *mutton,* because *mouton* was what the people in the big house ate. Then there are surprises in the dictionary, too, like *atonement,* which sounds nearly as Latinate as *prevaricate.* But *atonement,* as it turns out, comes from "at one"; it means "at one-ment." That's interesting.

INTERVIEWER

Two quotes: you say in the first line of "Long Branch, New Jersey" that "Everything is regional," and then in *Poetry and the World* that "to make one's native place illustrious is an acceptable ancient form of claiming personal significance."

Do you feel lucky to come from a place that can be described —
as you yourself do — as a microcosm?

PINSKY

In principle, I don't believe any one person's experience is
rich or poor in itself: we are all in history, and we are in it
at the shopping mall exactly as much as or as little as when
we are in Tuscany. The mall and Florence, equally, are out-
comes of history, and the challenge to our historical perception
is merely more egregious in some places than others.

But it's true that Long Branch has considerable historical
interest — right on its surface, in a way. You could argue that
Long Branch is where the modern idea of celebrity was born,
in the last few decades of the nineteenth century. The town,
fairly close to New York by boat or road, was a more raffish
resort than Newport and Saratoga Springs, where the social
elite went. Long Branch was full of patent-medicine tycoons
and theater people, in those days before money and entertainment conferred the kind of status they do today. President
Grant loved Long Branch, which suited his rough style. Diamond Jim Brady vacationed there with Lillian Russell: a sport-
ier, lower, more raw and less European elite than at Newport,
a social level which you could say evolved a hundred years
later, with "high society" dead and gone, into its successor in
People magazine. Winslow Homer drew illustrations of people
summering in Long Branch for *Harper's*; in the Boston Museum of Fine Arts, there's his great painting of women on the
bluffs, called "Long Branch, New Jersey."

INTERVIEWER

How conscious were you of all that when you lived there?

PINSKY

Hardly at all! Or not until the seventh or eighth grade,
when I'm happy to say we did a unit on Long Branch history,
using Judge Alton Evans's WPA book *Entertaining a Nation*.
And I suppose people did talk about some of it. The downtown
hotel was called the Garfield-Grant.

But there are other kinds of history, too, in odd survivals
that one isn't aware are survivals at the time. I grew up in an
old part of Long Branch, near Flanagan's Field, where the
circus was held. Every summer, elephants, clowns and girls
in tights standing on horses paraded right by my house. There
were lions in wheeled cages. My friends and I would work for
tickets, doing things like setting up chairs, which was tantaliz-
ingly close to the mythology of running away with the circus.
Once, when I was snooping around in an alley between tents,
I ran into a bunch of midgets. One had bleached, slicked-down
yellow hair and was immaculately dressed in a suit, like a little
boy going to his first communion. He looked at me gawking
and said, "*Who* let these fucking *son* of a bitch, *god*damn
cocksucking *kids* in here. Get your *god*damn fucking asses
out of here!" — really virtuoso cussing, but in a high-pitched
voice. I can still feel the goosebumps.

And the midget, the vanished tradition of show people,
the carny and circus jargon, the European roots and gypsy
slang, Barnum — that man cussing me out was the fading voice
of all that history. A few years later, everyone was watching
television.

INTERVIEWER

Did you have a religious upbringing?

PINSKY

In a way. My parents were nominally Orthodox Jews, but
they were of a very assimilated, secular generation, definitely
not the black suit and sidelocks idea. My father was a locally
famous jock and Best Looking Boy in his high-school year-
book — he was described as the "Adonis of the basketball
court," and a few years ago I actually met the reporter who
wrote that line, Herb "Hub" Kamm. Both my parents were
quite good dancers. They didn't go to synagogue except on
High Holidays, and sometimes not even then.

On the other hand, we did keep kosher; I didn't taste ham
until I was in college. A hamburger and a milkshake together

seemed like some bizarre sexual practice. They sent me to Hebrew school when I was eleven, but I knew that even on the more religious side of the family, my mother's, her brother hadn't been bar mitzvahed. The conflict, ambiguity and compromise went back before their generation.

INTERVIEWER

And what was your reaction to that kind of conflict and ambiguity?

PINSKY

Restless, I suppose. The Jewish service and the rituals of Jewish life seem designed to insulate, to define one away from the majority culture. And the majority culture is so attractive. It was the fifties, with American baseball in its golden age, and rock 'n' roll in its formative, glorious early years. I was born in a good year, just the right age for Jackie Robinson and for Elvis Presley. Across the street from our synagogue was a Catholic church; in my memory, beautifully dressed people, including girls my own age, would come and go, two or three shifts sometimes, while we were in there praying away at our three-hour service.

I've never met a Jew who had the experience Joyce describes in *A Portrait of the Artist as a Young Man*, that crisis of faith. My Catholic friends have told me about having such crises. But how can you have one in Judaism? Being Jewish isn't a *faith*, is it? It's a condition, like having a certain eye color, or a principle of life, like gravity, or a loyalty, as to one's family. The comparison with Christianity seems only approximate to me. As I get it, Judaism as a religion is quite vague about the afterlife. Even the concept of sin is more like a merit/demerit system, where you get *mitzvoth* for performing good deeds and lose them for bad ones. But you never know exactly where you stand, and I don't think there's any category like grace.

Although there's no crisis of faith to be had, there *is* a crisis of seduction, because the rituals and customs tend to pull you away from that sweet predominant secular culture, and from the religious majority with its Christmas and Easter, its baseball, its movies, its everything. Terms like *assimilation,* or saying you're second or third generation, don't catch the subtlety of this richly absorbing conflict, the crisis of attraction toward the sweets, the question of idolatry.

My grandfather, the one I associate with "idolatry" in the passage you've quoted, sneered at religion, but when his young wife — my father's mother — died during childbirth, he went to synagogue five days á week, early in the morning, to say Kaddish for her: I picture him as a young gangster, wearing two-tone shoes, going amongst religious men who probably had as intense a dislike for him as he had for them, to chant the prayer for the dead. And when he died, my father astonished me by doing the same, getting up before dawn to say Kaddish for Dave. When I asked him why he, who never went to synagogue, would do such a thing for a man who celebrated Christmas, who had a Christian wife, my father answered, "Because he did it for my mother." So to that extent, or in some idiosyncratic way along those lines, yes, I had a religious upbringing.

INTERVIEWER

After you left Long Branch, you went to Rutgers and then Stanford. Did anyone at those schools leave a lasting impression?

PINSKY

I've had at least two truly great teachers, Francis Fergusson at Rutgers and Yvor Winters at Stanford. I suppose I feel that Fergusson taught me literature and Winters taught me poetry. From Fergusson I learned ways to think about movies, paintings and poems as kinds of action — *action* meaning a movement of the soul. The work of art, especially one that has duration like a play or a spoken poem, is not a bag of meanings or images or a pile of beautiful phrases; it is an action, something that happens. I learned that when I was in my late teens from Fergusson and it still serves me. It is the basis of everything I do in writing. And maybe even music. Musicians say about a good solo, "He was really going somewhere."

INTERVIEWER

What do you mean by Winters teaching you poetry, as opposed to literature?

PINSKY

I learned an immense amount from him, especially about the English sixteenth and seventeenth centuries, and through those poets about how one writes in lines, and about poetic styles. It was the way I imagine conservatory. I arrived at Stanford with a typescript volume of what I then called my poems. My plan was to show these to Winters—I knew very little about him—and he'd be so dazzled by what a great genius I was that he'd give me some extra academic credit for that typescript. I imagined that he'd take the poems home with him, and the next day I'd get a phone call saying, "You're just a crazy genius." So I went into his office and told him I'd like to get credit for these poems I'd written. He grunted, and while I was standing in front of him, he began thumbing through the poems. After maybe three or four minutes, he looked up and said, "Well, there may be some gift here, but it's impossible to tell, because you simply don't know how to write."

I congratulate myself retrospectively for not acting on my first impulse, which was to snatch my poems back, say "Fuck you," and slam out of there. Then Winters asked me, "What poetry have you read?" I replied, "Well, I've read everything by Eliot, Yeats, Frost and Williams." When Winters asked what I had read before the twentieth century, I said I'd read some Donne and Marvell, by which I meant the poems by them that were in anthologies. "What else?" Winters prodded. "I don't know. I've read Shakespeare, naturally." Winters said, "No one who's only read that much can write a good poem." Somehow, I felt all at once that he was right, or at least that he knew things I needed. "What am I supposed to do, take a class with you?" I asked. He said, "Well, my History of the

Lyric class isn't offered this quarter, and that's the prerequisite to my other classes." And I replied, immediately won over, along the lines of, "You don't understand. I need to be a great poet, my education's in danger here," and so forth—a really ludicrous turnabout from my initial, thin arrogance.

He looked amused and, I believe in retrospect, as if he sensed some genuine mania that appealed to him. Anyway, remarkably, he handed me a copy of the syllabus to his History of the Lyric course—and offered to do the course with me individually! He did this, I think, on the basis of my intensity, not my poems. But I worked hard at learning "how to write" and the next year he awarded me a Stegner Fellowship. Albert Guerard used to say, "Pinsky went from 'doesn't know how to write' to 'one of the fine, promising young poets' in six months." That's not praising me; it's a satirical, yet somewhat admiring, acknowledgment by Albert of Winters's susceptibility to his students.

Winters claimed to have read every poem by every poet of any distinction who ever wrote in English; he challenged those of us who disagreed with him to do the same. He certainly seemed able to respond to anything anybody ever alluded to. Winters resurrected Fulke Greville, a really great poet, I am convinced; and some of the poems he pointed to, like Herbert's "Church Monuments" and Jonson's "To Heaven," were influential to many of us who studied with him, like Thom Gunn, Bob Hass, Donald Justice, Phil Levine, James McMichael, John Peck.

INTERVIEWER

Some of Winters's favorite poems seem to have found their way into your own work, as for instance your "Poem with Refrains," with its gobbets of Fulke Greville.

PINSKY

Yes, "Absence my presence is, strangeness my grace. / With them that walk against me is my sun." That's Greville, and he is unsurpassed at lines of that kind. What Winters showed me about the English poets of that period gave me an inkling of the level of the art, the quality of seriousness, the principles of musical language that one might hope to attain. I feel that those couple of years when I read poetry intensely with him have served me well, and I'm grateful for that.

INTERVIEWER

Do you think teaching is a good profession for a poet?

PINSKY

I think that I and poets of my generation have found it so. But nowadays . . . I'm not sure. We benefited from a brief golden age of a kind. I was a student just after a period when the academic world was suspicious of, and not particularly hospitable toward writers. Winters liked to tell a story about himself, that when he first began publishing his bold, brilliant essays about American literature, the department chairman called him in and said his work was a disgrace to the department because it was criticism, as distinct from real scholarship, and criticism and scholarship did not mix. (Whereas nowadays every professor is "a critic" or "a critical theorist," a leftover from those days.) In his twenties, Winters had written that W.C. Williams was a great writer, that Wallace Stevens was a great writer—and I think this was before Stevens had even published a book. This kind of thing was scandalous. Scholarship was historical, theoretical and philological; it had no room for attention to literature as art, and certainly none for contemporary literature.

Then there was a phase during the fifties and sixties when— partly due to the influence and prestige of Eliot and Pound as critics, and partly, I suspect, because the academic profession was suddenly infiltrated by people from a lower social class than their predecessors—a kind of loosening-up occurred. Literary art had a superficial cachet, too. There were cultural factors I don't fully understand that encouraged a cult around Hemingway and a cult around Frost, even a cult (now largely forgotten) around Sandburg. Critics without Ph.D.s, like Fergusson and Blackmur, found places in universities. And professors were persuaded that there was a lot for them to learn from literature, or they were persuaded to behave as if they believed this. When I was in college, acknowledged great writers were still around: Faulkner, Hemingway, Williams, Stevens, Moore, Frost, Eliot, Pound, all were alive.

That turns out to have been a brief interregnum, coinciding with the period when creative writing became institutionalized. Now, times have changed again. Once again, the academic study of literature is historical, theoretical, cultural and philological; once again, on the whole, it has relatively little interest in literature as art, or in contemporary literature.

So in a way we've returned to the norm. For the students I teach in the B.U. creative writing program, the academic world is a less welcoming haven than it was for people in my generation. For me, teaching has been a good profession. I get to talk to students who are intensely concerned with exactly the things I care about. The work is appealing, and I have earned my bread by it. I think teaching can be a noble profession, and I feel impatient when people condescend to it.

INTERVIEWER

A significant strain in your work is didactic, and I don't mean in the pejorative sense. For instance, the title of one of your books is *An Explanation of America*.

PINSKY

Advice and instruction have always fascinated me, partly because of their pathos — so little is transmitted in any given instance of advice or pedagogy. On the one hand, there's the idea of the quest, that wisdom-seeking is noble. On the other, the figure of the advisor or schoolmaster is nearly always comic; even Aristotle becomes comic once he is the schoolmaster to Alexander. I think of *An Explanation of America* not as didactic, itself, but as a weird experiment in that vulnerable enterprise of explaining or instructing. And of thinking about the future, straining to imagine it.

INTERVIEWER
If I understand correctly, you have taught at schools for the deaf and blind in Illinois.

PINSKY

I made three visits of a few days each to schools for the deaf and blind in Jacksonville, Illinois. We talked about poetry a bit, and the kids read their poems to me. That is, they signed and vocalized, reading their work from traditional writing or from Braille. Sometimes I could understand the vocalizing and sometimes I couldn't; a teacher interpreted for me when necessary. The kids were very enthusiastic. They sort of yelled and babbled to each other in Sign a lot, in a raucous, bouncy manner, exactly as other rambunctious kids that age yell and babble vocally. I asked the teacher whether she had to shush them, and she said, "All the time." She put her finger to her lips and said, "I have to do *this*. If there's too much signing going on, then they're not concentrating."

At the request or assignment of the teacher, I wrote a poem about visiting them and read it aloud to them, with Sign interpretation. I'm here to tell you that a deaf audience is a great audience, because man are they *watching!* Their faces become very animated — the faces you might dream of eliciting in response to a poem. I really liked working with those students, and with the blind kids, though given my emphasis on sound I had been nervous about dealing with deaf students. Far from contradicting my idea of the body as the medium of poetry, that experience helped crystallize my thinking. All the mysteries of consciousness flower in the body; this was manifest in the way the kids moved as they recited their poems, and in the way the others responded while watching. It was a more intense version — different at the blind school, but occurring there too — of something I had noticed in my own classes when people recite from memory. The attention becomes palpable, entranced by a physical charm.

INTERVIEWER

To what extent do you focus on prosody and other technical matters when you teach?

PINSKY

I don't give lectures on prosody. I believe in examples. When a student asks, "What's a good book about traditional iambic verse?" I always respond, *"The Collected Poems of Ben Jonson."* "What's a really excellent book about free verse?" *"The Collected Poems of William Carlos Williams."* "What's a good book about writing short lines in ballad meter?" *"The Collected Poems of Emily Dickinson."* I agree with Yeats when he says, "Nor is there singing school but studying / Monuments of its own magnificence." Craft is something that you learn by studying models. A good teacher can tell you what to look for, point things out.

INTERVIEWER

You recently put together your own collected poems. In doing so, did you discern a particular line of development? Have you come to see your older poetry in a new light?

PINSKY

I was pleased to find more continuity than I had expected—more I think than critics of my work, even friendly ones, had suggested. *An Explanation of America* and "Essay on Psychiatrists" contain not only thematic material and preoccupations that pop up again in recent poems, but also a certain kind of movement, a nervous or syncopated movement.

INTERVIEWER

Has your work become more experimental, or less so?

PINSKY

I don't know if that would be the term. When you're learning an art, you want to blow the riffs that epitomize it. You want to make the sound that says very clearly, "This is funky blues." The most natural place to show virtuosity is right down the middle of the art. But there's a counter-impulse, which is to test or stretch the limits of where the art can go. Maybe both attractions operate all through a life's work.

You try to avoid the clichés of the avant-garde, or go beyond them, just as you do the clichés of the middlebrow.

INTERVIEWER
Your collected poems is called *The Figured Wheel,* the computer game you wrote is called *Mindwheel,* and the work you recently chose to translate, Dante's *Inferno,* progresses through circles. Am I right in guessing that the circle is your favorite geometric metaphor?

PINSKY
There is something about the circle: each thing reflected by an opposite, and also on a continuum with that opposite — everything contained by a cycle, with each small arc implying the whole. That notion probably governs my response to your previous question, too: one cycles through a life's work, maybe journeying far away from the Ithaca of overt lyricism, and then back to it.

Louise Glück wrote something about me that I like, that the poems are less about the particular history in them than what lies behind the history: "chaos, eternity." That's the circle.

INTERVIEWER
One clear trend in your work is the increasing fascination with religion and religious imagery.

PINSKY
The making of religion, and the construction of its cultural realities, fascinate me. My mother's mental illness and her scorn, at times, for everything the world believes may have made me especially sensitive to the phenomenon of belief, the discovery of meaning. I've expressed this by saying that for a person who practices some particular religion, creation is a major episode in the career of God, whereas for me, God is a major episode in the career of creation.

I'm reluctant to pretend to religion as worship, as a human

activity and theater of the soul for me in the communal, traditional way that many people practice it. But it's tremendously
interesting to me as a fact. That's maybe a digressive way of
saying that the religious images, names and phenomena in
the later poems aren't so different from the cultural materials
in the earlier poems. The later poems express, in a way that
comes closer to the autobiographical core, some of the same
concerns. Always the question, "This is believed, this has credit
among people. What is it to me?"

To approach it a different way, maybe in some part of my
mind I was asking myself, "What is your subject? Your subject
is culture. But that seems a little cold—what does it mean?
Your subject is making, or the marketplace, the place where
people normally come together." And in the market square,
facing the plaza, there is always a place of worship. If not
such a place *for* me, still such a place *to* me. For me, religion
is an aspect of the addiction to creativity of the human animal,
the making predilection of the human heart.

INTERVIEWER

You call "Desecration of the Gravestone of Rose P." an
antiphony with George Herbert's "Church Monuments";
"Shirt" can perhaps also be described as an antiphony, with
Hart Crane and, again, Herbert coming through. Do these
poems betoken a special indebtedness?

PINSKY

For twenty years or more before I wrote those poems, I
would feel in my emotional life, from time to time, like Lao-
coön going down. Often I was rescued from that sensation by
certain machines made out of words (as Williams calls them):
poems that gave me moral or intellectual courage; a few hundred lines, by a few poets including those you mention, served
as a kind of spiritual amulet. Certain of my recent poems
acknowledge that shield or rescue in a way I never directly
had in writing before.

My grandmother's grave—she was the one who had the

gangster husband and died very young, when my father was small—is in the Jewish cemetery in Long Branch, where my other grandparents are also buried. Rose's grave is particularly beautiful. The young hoodlum-bootlegger who was her husband paid to have the stone carved in the image of a tree with its branches lopped off, to symbolize the life cut off too soon. Rose was a celebrated beauty, as confirmed by an oval portrait of her, a daguerreotype under glass that is set into the gravestone.

At some point in the seventies, someone went into the Jewish cemetery in Long Branch and desecrated many of the graves with hammers and crow bars. Somebody struck Rose's portrait, probably with a hammer, leaving just a light fleck in the glass, but not seriously defacing the photograph. That fact, that mixed pathos and strangeness, was cooking in my head for fifteen years before I wrote the poem. Also in my head was Herbert's "Church Monuments," a poem I have by heart: "While that my soul repairs to her devotion, / Here I entomb my flesh, that it betimes / May take acquaintance of this heap of dust, / To which the blast of death's incessant motion, / Fed with exhalation of our crimes, / Drives all at last. / Therefore I gladly trust / / My body to this school. . . ."

The Christian feeling of the poem is for me both beautiful and incongruous, or maybe, more precisely, it makes me aware of my own incongruity to it. And the vandalization, in its contempt for that flesh, those earthly remains, those lovingly graven images, seemed an odd echo of the Christian feeling, also evoking my simultaneous immersion and remove in relation to religions.

I imagined that the crime had been committed by boys in their teens or early twenties, since we males at around that age perpetrate—in our society, anyway—most of the violence, bad driving and general bodily degradation. It's as if we should take males from fifteen to twenty-four and send them to Mars. We wouldn't have any problems with crime, nor even need traffic lights; we'd all just be sensible about things. Of course, the desecration may have been done by old ladies—who knows? But I imagined it as carried out by teenage boys and chose to pretend that those boys somehow knew "Church Monuments." It's crazy, but somehow the act of imagining myself as one of them merged with imagining the Christian sensibility of George Herbert.

After all, their crime oddly accords with the poem. Herbert says of earth and dust that "These laugh at jet and marble put for signs, / / To sever the good fellowship of dust, / And spoil the meeting. What shall point out them, / When they shall bow, and kneel, and fall down flat / To kiss those heaps which now they have in trust?" That is a brilliant image, because the stone that over the centuries tilts — in a kind of mocking slow-motion — then falls flat onto the grave, resembles the distraught mourner who falls down flat onto the grave, to kiss the beloved dust. Well, that's what these guys did by knocking the stones over. From a Hindu time perspective, they weren't doing anything that Herbert doesn't say is inevitable anyway — the boys were just telling me that my grandmother's portrait is dust. In any case, all of that got swirled together, and instead of some more linear narrative, it became an amalgam. In some ways, the nosegay principle applies, the poem sweetening the stench of desecration; in other ways, the nosegay becomes part of the pestilence, or maybe even the other way around.

INTERVIEWER

In your most recent poems — "Avenue," for example — you seem particularly fascinated with cities.

PINSKY

I went through a period when I had a lot of dreams about a city like the ones in the movies of my childhood: a guy in a trench coat walking by a railing, looking down at the Seine or the Thames or the East River. It felt like the city you see in the background of an R. Crumb or Bill Griffith drawing, combined with the atmosphere of foreign intrigue from a movie like *The Third Man*. That's the ambience of those dreams.

By meditating on my dreams in a sort of unreflecting, touris-

tic way, but also mulling consciously over the relationship
between the words *civic, city* and *civilization*, I generated the
poems. The urban atmosphere seems to me like a smoke or
mist yet also a clay I'm trying to shape into an image that will
tell you what I'm feeling, what I'm thinking about.

INTERVIEWER

Do you think your fascination with observing communities
has been fueled and inflected by working on Dante? The *Inferno*
is, of course, a type of community, albeit a very twisted one.

PINSKY

Just as I don't see how anybody writing in English who tries
to give a character a moment of eloquent self-expression can
avoid being influenced by Shakespeare, I don't see how any
writer can write about groups of people in a large, constructed
setting without being influenced by Dante. By looking at a
group of people and their architectural context, seeing individuals emerge from a kind of cinematic vista, and perhaps having
a conversation with one of them, you will be imitating the
Comedia even if you've never read a line of it — that's the way
cultural powers work. Even the writer who has never read much
literature will, out of the very cultural air he breathes, inherit
literary gestures. That's why naive writers sometimes use *thee,
thy* and *thine;* they're in thrall to literature because they've
read almost no literature.

But nobody can read so much, or study so many monuments
of magnificence, as to escape a force field as powerful as
Dante's. So yes, one might find poems of mine that suggest
something in the *Inferno*. But with a work of such magnitude,
one that has affected so many other works for so long, it is hard
to know if the act of creating an English version is necessarily
involved. Dante is like the sun or the ocean: his presence is
no surprise.

INTERVIEWER

Was your interest in taking on all of the *Inferno* sparked
by your original assignment for the Ecco Press translation?

PINSKY

Shortly after Dan Halpern assigned me Canto XXVIII, I started doing Canto I just to see what it was like. Then Dan assigned me Canto XX as well, because somebody else in the project hadn't been able to do it. After finishing Canto I, which I began just to have something to do, I began Canto II in the same aimless spirit; and I was well into Canto III, as well as having finished XX and XXVIII, before I began consciously to reason with myself—figuring that there were thirty-four cantos in the *Inferno*, and five out of thirty-four is more than one seventh . . . and so forth.

INTERVIEWER

So you strayed from the straight path.

PINSKY

Yes—lost in a forest of translator's problems. I started doing it before I could acknowledge to myself that I actually was. And it was a matter of art, not one of scholarship or having a strong opinion about the work's meaning or style. I was working on it because I could, the way you get an idea for a poem and are grateful to be working on it. You do it because you can, keeping on because it would be hard to stop. I would sneak away from other demands to work on it, sometimes staying up too late at night.

I need some such task in order to concentrate. Compared to a lot of my friends, I don't have a scholarly mind; I don't assimilate information easily and don't use a library well. But I enjoy things like whittling, fixing machines, drawing, puzzles, playing games.

I think one of the strongest human cravings is for difficulty; we are selected by evolution to be creatures that like dealing with various problems of a certain kind. The formal challenge of terza rima was like the carrot or sugar cube before the donkey.

INTERVIEWER

Are you tempted to tackle *Purgatory* and *Paradise?*

PINSKY

Of course. If I were a scholarly translator, there's no question that I'd go on to the other books—it'd seem an obligation. But I'd have to want to write them the way I want to write a poem, and so far that hasn't happened. Also, there are technical problems. The language of the *Inferno* is, well, low. When Dante says that he couldn't tell whether a certain shade was a cleric or a layman, couldn't see his tonsure because his head was covered in shit—that's how he says it, he uses *merde*, the Italian word that corresponds to shit. That's because the language of hell is low. By the time he gets to *Paradiso*, though, it's lofty, practically Greek and Latin, which is a disadvantage for a translator. If you can use low language like *shit* and *fart*, you can also get away with a certain amount of elevation, a slightly archaic or formal quality to the idiom—which I consider desirable for this poem—because you have the counterbalance of the low words, a kind of ballast-idiom. But if everything is up high, it's much harder to create a credible idiom. My goal in the *Inferno* was to shape an idiom that reads as though rapidly, that feels sufficiently close to American English for pleasurable reading, with a kind of onward momentum—yet gives some sense that the poem was written a long time ago, and with a certain formal gravity. It would be harder to do all that in a loftier language.

Going on would present a separate problem, like writing another poem, and I don't know whether that's a poem I want to write.

INTERVIEWER

What did you do to get that archaic feeling into the *Inferno?*

PINSKY

Formal might be a better term. There are little turns of phrase, small syntactical things you can do, liberties you can allow yourself, vocabulary that will give just a slightly written or period quality to your language.

Opening at random in the *Inferno*, the first sentence I see has Virgil speaking to Pier della Vigna in the Wood of the Suicides. Virgil says, "Had he been able to credit or comprehend / Before, O Wounded spirit . . ." Well, "had he been able to credit or comprehend" is subjunctive and rather formal, especially for dialogue. That's syntactical, apart from the somewhat old-fashioned use of "credit." Then we get, "What he had witnessed only in my verses, / His hand would never have performed this deed / Against you." Here, "verses" and "deed" are a bit archaic. My idea is that on the one hand it should feel fairly natural, yet a dead Roman epic poet should not address the soul of a suicide, in a poem this old, in a perfectly familiar manner: "If he could understand a thing he'd only seen, before, when he was reading my poetry." No.

INTERVIEWER

Walter Savage Landor—about whom you wrote your first critical book—lived, like Dante, in Florence for a time. Did the coincidence of writing about a second Florentine, years later, strike you as one of those cyclical occurrences you're so attuned to?

PINSKY

It pleases me to think about, which I did especially when talking to Mike Mazur about his illustrations, and about certain passages. But the main work of mine that adumbrated the *Inferno* is *Mindwheel*. A lot of the totem objects and settings in the computer game are in the shapes of reels and disks and spirals, and the structure of the game itself is more or less circular, with a lot of loops along the way. The character who sets things in motion is called Dr. Virgil.

I worked on *Mindwheel* with programmers who read a lot of science fiction and fantasy—bright people, but not very literary. After reading reviews of the game in a computer magazine, one of them said, "I've got to read this Dante's *Inferno*— everybody keeps comparing it to *Mindwheel*." I had raided some of the imagery in a carefree way, never imagining that I'd someday attempt the translation. A great freedom when writing for the software audience is that you can loot all of Western literature quite shamelessly and blatantly. It's like having a supercharger with extra muscles that you don't really have, because for the audience it's all new.

INTERVIEWER

In *Poetry and the World,* you describe poets as having characteristic turns of energy. What would you say yours is?

PINSKY

We've talked about how much I like circles; we could have added that I have to keep myself from using the various concessives as my normal mode of transition. *But*, *though*, *yet* and *on the other hand* are natural turns for me. So, maybe a kind of circling back, a belief, sometimes despairing, that everything comes out the same in the end. The most negative aspects of my childhood made me feel that there was no meaning in the world. It was a household with an insane mother. To take a minor example, when my family had something called dinner, it never happened at the same time of day. It might happen at five in the afternoon, or at eleven at night — or it might not happen at all, because of squabbling or distraction or an eccentricity so profound it is hard to describe credibly. The notion of meaning or significance that actually rests somewhere is almost exotic to me. There is a bleakly fatalistic kind of circle. The more positive aspect of that same figure is the understanding that any given night or day will pass, the sun will rise and set again, winter or distress will end.

INTERVIEWER

Is your adult writing life more routine than your childhood culinary life was?

PINSKY

It's one of my peculiarities that I hate to concede having any routines at all. I panic at questions like, "When do you get up in the morning?" or "What do you have for breakfast?" I write with a felt-tip or fountain pen, and I write with a computer. Sometimes I write in the morning, sometimes in the afternoon, sometimes late at night. Sometimes my handwriting is rather neat, sometimes sloppy. Often, the characters are very small, but not always. Having been a poor student in high school, I am always amazed that I can get anything done, and I almost have to sneak up on myself to do it, to feel I'm playing hooky: "It's between times—I'm not supposed to write now."

INTERVIEWER

Do you revise much?

PINSKY

I revise a lot, especially the last five to fifteen percent. I generate writing fairly easily; a schpritz of words or images is not hard to create. I can say a paragraph, or even talk a page, without much trouble. But the conversion to something that feels right or distinguished often takes a lot of effort.

INTERVIEWER

It sounds as if you do a lot of polishing with the assistance of friends, through the mail and on the phone.

PINSKY

At times it verges on collaboration. When I lived in California, there were a lot of heavy FedEx and phone bills. There have been times when Frank Bidart and I have actually written together on the phone. Consultation with poet friends like Frank, Tom Sleigh, Thom Gunn, Bob Hass, Seamus Heaney, Jim McMichael, David Ferry, Louise Glück and Alan Williamson—to give a partial list—has been important to me; it's hard to imagine where I'd be without it.

INTERVIEWER

Do you think of your collaborative group as a kind of *agora*?

It's a pleasing idea, yes, because a lot of my thinking has involved the relationship between what's inside me and communal life. Working on the *Inferno* with Frank, we spent many hours on each canto. We'd schedule a phone date and Frank would prepare for it by comparing my draft of a canto to three or four other translations. Wherever he found a passage or phrase he thought was clearer or more energetic in someone else's version, he'd explain to me what I had to improve. That was collaboration indeed, demanding a great deal of labor and patience. Sometimes he had to bear with my groans and protests. When you unstitch a rhyme word in terza rima it *hurts* — it's worse than knitting.

It was also a great pleasure, reading such a poem with such a friend. The sentences became a sort of tunnel through which we walked, and upon which we turned our searchlights, saying, "Oh, look how this fits together here. Look at the surface there — it needs to be worked to flow into that other branch back a way." We walked the delicate yet mighty labyrinth of a great work together.

When people ask you what you do, what do you tell them?

You mean like to the guy sitting next to me on the airplane? "Teacher," usually. Sometimes I say, "Writer," but that often leads to "What do you write?" There might be less reluctance to answer "Poet" in Mexico or Poland, say, but in this country the word *poet* leaves a kind of social blank. It's not that people are hostile or contemptuous — the term just doesn't have any meaning. Socially, it's not a category, for reasons that in fact I like, reasons that can make me quite proud of this country. We don't have certain aristocratic, established social criteria that are involved with art as firmly as in many cultures. There are corners of the United States where this is less true: at Harvard or Princeton, a notion that mingles money, social class, intellectual pursuits and arts like poetry and music into a matrix of social superiority may be quite strong, but in the country at large that notion is pretty diluted. There's relatively little snob value to poetry here. I can see plenty of cause to celebrate that fact, as well as cause to lament it.

Generally, I welcome the relative absence of that connection between social status and art. But on the other hand, the substitute of being hip or sophisticated or avant-garde — a fashion awareness, basically — is maybe worse than the old snobbery, which had at least a pretense of civic meaning, a pretense of public or communal presence for art. When I started out, when I inspected great poetry, I found that a lot of it was in the civic realm, a communal focus like that of Greek tragedy. I don't know why eloquence and civic life in the U.S. have diverged so sharply in my lifetime, but in my mind it's related to a nervousness about fashion, a nervousness that has maybe displaced the European or Anglophile nervousness about class. It almost seems that "sophistication" has replaced "class" in our manners.

What does that mean for art? You could argue that American poetry was a lot better off when Edgar Guest and Bliss Carman were figures of some respect, or when Hallmark greeting cards were in verse. At some moment, people got just sophisticated enough to know that Rod McKuen and Kahlil Gibran were corn — but not sophisticated enough to relish Milton or Hart Crane. Maybe we would benefit from more of a continuum all through the culture and fewer sealed compartments. Our national genius is polyglot, syncretic, culturally diverse, rebellious toward any would-be presiding aristocratic center. As Whitman more or less says, we're always contending with fragmentation. So our national thirst for art, which is immense, never calls itself by name.

As a kind of contrast, I heard an interesting thing, possibly true, about Bengal. As I heard the story, a referendum proposal to build a new railroad line was headed for defeat until its advocates put forward the argument that the new railway would give workers another hour or two every evening to paint and write poetry; apparently every Bengali is in self-image a painter or poet—or both. So the tide was reversed and the referendum passed.

And that arc of the circle, too, has its appeal and its absurdity—different from our own, it would seem. And yet there are times, in a town like Berkeley or Boston at least, when the guy trimming your trees or the woman at the tax-preparation place asks you what you do, and if you say, "I'm a poet," the answer comes back, "Oh really—so am I!"

—**Ben Downing**
Daniel Kunitz

The Mansion on the Hill

Rick Moody

The Chicken Mask was sorrowful, Sis. The Chicken Mask
was supposed to hustle business; it was supposed to invite the
customer to gorge him or herself within our establishment;
it was supposed to be endearing and funny; it was supposed
to be an accurate representation of the featured item on our
menu. But, Sis, in a practical setting, in test markets—like
right out in front of the restaurant—the Chicken Mask had
a plaintive aspect, a blue quality (it was stifling, too, even
in cold weather), so that I'd be walking down Main, by the
waterfront, after you were gone, back and forth in front of Hot
Bird (Bucket of Drumsticks, $2.99), wearing out my imitation
basketball sneakers from Wal-Mart, pudgy in my black jogging
suit, lurching along in the sandwich board, and the kids would
hustle up to me, tugging on the wrists of their harried, under-
financed moms. The kids would get bored with me almost
immediately. They knew the routine. Their eyes would narrow, and all at once there were no secrets here in our town
of service-economy franchising: *I was the guy working nine
to five in a Chicken Mask*, even though I'd had a pretty good
education in business administration, even though I was more

or less presentable and well-spoken, even though I came from a good family. I made light of it, Sis, I extemporized about Hot Bird, in remarks designed by virtue of my studies in business tactics to drive whole families in for the new *low-fat roasters*, a meal option that was steeper, in terms of price, but tasty nonetheless. (And I ought to have known, because I ate from the menu every day. Even the coleslaw.)

Here's what I'd say, in my Chicken Mask. Here was my pitch: *Feeling a little peckish? Try Hot Bird!* or *Don't be chicken, try Hot Bird!* The mothers would laugh their nervous adding-machine laughs (those laughs that are next door over from a sob), and they would lead the kids off. Twenty yards away, though, the boys and girls would still be staring disdainfully at me, gaping backward while I rubbed my hands raw in the cold, while I breathed the synthetic rubber interior of the Chicken Mask—that fragrance of rubber balls from gym classes lost, that bouquet of the gloves Mom used for the dishes, that perfume of simpler times—while I looked for my next shill. I lost almost ninety days to the demoralization of the Chicken Mask, to its grim, existential emptiness, until I couldn't take it anymore. Which happened to be the day when Alexandra McKinnon (remember her? from Sunday school?) turned the corner with her boy Zack—he has to be seven or eight now—oblivious while upon her daily rounds, oblivious and fresh from a Hallmark store. It was nearly Valentine's Day. They didn't know it was me in there, of course, inside the Chicken Mask. They didn't know I was *the chicken from the basement, the chicken of darkest nightmares*, or, more truthfully, they didn't know I was a guy with some pretty conflicted attitudes about things. That's how I managed to apprehend Zack, leaping out from the in-door of Cohen's Pharmacy, laying ahold of him a little too roughly, by the hem of his pillowy, orange ski jacket. Little Zack was laughing, at first, until, in a voice racked by loss, I worked my hard sell on him, declaiming stentoriously that *Death Comes to All*. That's exactly what I said, just as persuasively as I had once hawked *White meat breasts, eight pieces, just $4.59!* Loud enough that he'd be sure to know what I meant. His look was interrogative, quizzical. So I repeated myself. *Death Comes to Everybody, Zachary.* My voice was urgent now. My eyes bulged from the eyeholes of my standard-issue Chicken Mask. I was even crying a little bit. Saline rivulets tracked down my neck. Zack was terrified.

What I got next certainly wasn't the kind of flirtatious attention I had always hoped for from his mom. Alex began drumming on me with balled fists. I guess she'd been standing off to the side of the action previously, believing that I was a reliable paid employee of Hot Bird. But now she was all over me, bruising me with wild swings, cursing, until she'd pulled the Chicken Mask from my head — half expecting, I'm sure, to find me scarred or hydrocephalic or otherwise disabled. Her denunciations let up a little once she was in possession of the facts. It was me, her old Sunday school pal, Andrew Wakefield. Not at the top of my game.

I don't really want to include here the kind of scene I made, once unmasked. Alex was exasperated with me, but gentle anyhow. I think she probably knew I was in the middle of a rough patch. People knew. The people leaning out of the storefronts probably knew. But, if things weren't already bad enough, I remembered right then — God, this is horrible — that Alex's mom had driven into Lake Sacandaga about five years before. Jumped the guardrail and plunged right off that bridge there. In December. In heavy snow. In a Ford Explorer. That was the end of her. *Listen, Alex*, I said, *I'm confused, I have problems and I don't know what's come over me and I hope you can understand, and I hope you'll let me make it up to you. I can't lose this job. Honest to God.* Fortunately, just then, Zack became interested in the Chicken Mask. He swiped the mask from his mom — she'd been holding it at arm's length, like a soiled rag — and he pulled it down over his head and started making simulated automatic-weapons noises in the directions of local passersby. This took the heat off. We had a laugh, Alex and I, and soon the three of us had repaired to Hot Bird itself (it closed four months later, like most of the businesses on that block) for coffee and biscuits and the chef's special spicy wings, which, because of my position, were on the house.

Alex was actually waving a spicy wing when she offered her life-altering opinion that I was too smart to be working for Hot Bird, especially if I was going to brutalize little kids with the creepy facts of the hereafter. What I should do, Alex said, was get into something positive instead. She happened to know a girl—it was her cousin, Glenda—who managed a business over in Albany, the Mansion on the Hill, a big area employer, and why didn't I call Glenda and use Alex's name, and maybe they would have something in accounting or valet parking or flower delivery, *yada yada yada,* you know, some job that had as little public contact as possible, something that paid better than minimum wage, because minimum wage, Alex said, wasn't enough for a guy of twenty-nine. After these remonstrances she actually hauled me over to the pay phone at Hot Bird (people are so generous sometimes), while my barely alert boss Antonio slumbered at the register with no idea what was going on, without a clue that he was about to lose his most conscientious chicken impersonator. All because I couldn't stop myself from talking about death.

Alex dialed up the Mansion on the Hill (while Zack, at the table, donned my mask all over again), penetrating deep into the switchboard by virtue of her relation to a Mansion on the Hill management-level employee, and was soon actually talking to her cousin: *Glenda, I got a friend here who's going through some rough stuff in his family, if you know what I mean, yeah, down on his luck in the job department too, but he's a nice bright guy anyhow. I pretty much wanted to smooch him throughout confirmation classes, and he went to . . . Hey, where did you go to school again? Went to SUNY and has a degree in business administration, knows a lot about product positioning or whatever, I don't know, new housing starts, yada yada yada, and I think you really ought to . . .*

Glenda's sigh was audible from several feet away, I swear, through the perfect medium of digital telecommunications, but you can't blame Glenda for that. People protect themselves from bad luck, right? Still, Alex wouldn't let her cousin refuse, wouldn't hear of it, *You absolutely gotta meet him, Glenda, he's a doll, he's a dream boat,* and Glenda gave in, and that's the end of this part of the story, about how I happened to end up working out on Wolf Road at the capital region's finest wedding- and party-planning business. Except that before the Hot Bird recedes into the mists of time, I should report to you that I swiped the Chicken Mask, Sis. They had three or four of them. You'd be surprised how easy it is to come by a Chicken Mask.

Politically, here's what was happening in the front office of my new employer: Denise Gulch, the Mansion on the Hill staff writer, had left her husband and her kids and her steady job, because of a wedding, because of the language of the vows — that soufflé of exaggerated language — vows which, for quality-control purposes, were being broadcast over a discreet speaker in the executive suite. Denise was so moved by a recitation of Paul Stookey's "Wedding Song" taking place during the course of the Neuhaus ceremony ("Whenever two or more of you / Are gathered in His name, / There is love, / There is love . . .") that she slipped into the Rip Van Winkle Room disguised as a latecomer. Immediately, in the electrifying atmosphere of matrimony, she began trying to seduce one of the ushers (Nicky Weir, a part-time Mansion employee who was acquainted with the groom). I figure this flirtation had been taking place for some time, but that's not what everyone told me. What I heard was that seconds after meeting one another — the bride hadn't even recessed yet — Denise and Nicky were secreted in a nearby broom closet, while the office phones bounced to voice mail, and were peeling back the layers of our Mansion dress code, until, at day's end, scantily clad and intoxicated by rhetoric and desire, they stole a limousine and left town without collecting severance. Denise was even fully vested in the pension plan.

All this could only happen at a place called the Mansion on the Hill, a place of fluffy endings: the right candidate for the job walks through the door at the eleventh hour, the check clears that didn't exist minutes before, government agencies agree to waive mountains of red tape, the sky clears, the snow ends, and stony women like Denise Gulch succumb to torrents of generosity, throwing half-dollars to children as they embark on new lives.

The real reason I got the job is that they were shorthanded, and because Alex's cousin, my new boss, was a little difficult. But things were starting to look up anyway. If Glenda's personal demeanor at the interview wasn't exactly warm (she took a personal call in the middle that lasted twenty-eight minutes, and later she asked me, while reapplying lip liner, if I wore cologne) at least she was willing to hire me — as long as I agreed to renounce any personal grooming habits that inclined in the direction of Old Spice, Hai Karate or CK1. I would have spit-polished her pumps just to have my own desk (on which I put a yellowed picture of you when you were a kid, holding up the bass that you caught fly-fishing and also a picture of the four of us: Mom and Dad and you and me) and a Rolodex and unlimited access to stamps, mailing bags and paper clips.

Let me take a moment to describe our core business at the Mansion on the Hill. We were in the business of helping people celebrate the best days of their lives. We were in the business of spreading joy, by any means necessary. We were in the business of paring away the calluses of woe and grief to reveal the bright light of commitment. We were in the business of producing flawless memories. We had seven auditoriums, or *marriage suites,* as we liked to call them, each with a slightly different flavor and decorating vocabulary. For example, there was the *Chestnut Suite,* the least expensive of our rental suites, which had lightweight aluminum folding chairs (with polyurethane padding) and a very basic altar table, which had the unfortunate pink and lavender floral wallpaper and which seated about 125 comfortably; then there was the *Hudson Suite*, which had some teak in it and a lot of panelling and a classic iron altar table and some rather large standing tables at the rear, and the reception area in Hudson was clothed all in vinyl, instead of the paper coverings that they used in Chestnut (the basic decorating scheme there in the Hudson

Suite was meant to suggest the sea vessels that once sailed through our municipal port); then there was the *Rip Van Winkle Room*, with its abundance of draperies, its silk curtains, its matching maroon settings of inexpensive linen, and the *Adirondack Suite,* the *Ticonderoga Room,* the *Valentine Room* (a sort of giant powder puff), and of course the *Niagara Hall*, which was grand and reserved, with its separate kitchen and its enormous fireplace and white-gloved staff, for the sons and daughters of those Victorians of Saratoga County who came upstate for the summer during the racing season, the children of contemporary robber barons, the children whose noses were always straight and whose luck was always good.

We had our own on-site boutique for wedding gowns and tuxedo rentals and fittings—hell, we'd even clean and store your garments for you while you were away on your honeymoon—and we had a travel agency who subcontracted for us, as we also had wedding consultants, jewelers, videographers, still photographers (both the arty ones who specialized in photos of your toenail polish on the day of the wedding and the conventional photographers who barked directions at the assembled family far into the night), nannies, priests, ministers, shamans, polarity therapists, a really maniacal florist called Bruce, a wide array of deejays—guys and gals equipped to spin Christian-only selections, Tex-Mex, music from Hindi films and the occasional death-metal wedding medley—and we could get actual musicians, if you preferred. We'd even had Dick Roseman's combo, The Sons of Liberty, do a medley of "My Funny Valentine," "In-a-Gadda-Da-Vida," "I Will Always Love You" and "Smells Like Teen Spirit," without a rest between selections. (It was gratifying for me to watch the old folks shake it up to contemporary numbers.) We had a three-story, fifteen-hundred slip parking facility on site, convenient access to I-87, I-90 and the Taconic, and a staff of 175 full- and part-time employees on twenty-four hour call. We had everything from publicists to dicers of crudités to public orators (need a brush-up for that toast?)—all for the purpose of making your wedding the high watermark of your American life. We had done up to fifteen weddings in a single day (it was a Saturday in February, 1991, during the Gulf

War) and, since the Mansion on the Hill first threw open its door for a gala double wedding (the Gifford twins, from Balston Spa, who married Shaun and Maurice Wickett) in June of 1987, we had performed, up to the time of my first day there, 1,963 weddings, many of them memorable, life-affirming, even spectacular ceremonies. We had never had an incidence of serious violence.

This was the raw data that Glenda gave me, anyway, Sis. The arrangement of the facts is my own, and in truth, the arrangement of facts constitutes the job I was engaged to perform at the Mansion on the Hill. Because Glenda Manzini (in 1990 she married Dave Manzini, a developer from Schenectady), couldn't really have hated her job any more than she did. Glenda Manzini, whose marriage (her second) was apparently not the most loving ever in upstate history (although she's not alone; I estimate an even thousand divorces resulting from the conjugal rites successfully consummated so far at my place of business), was a cynic, a skeptic, a woman of little faith when it came to the institution through which she made her living. She occasionally referred to the wedding party as *the cattle*; she occasionally referred to the brides as *the hookers* and to herself, manager of the Mansion on the Hill, as *the Madame*, as in, *The Madame, Andrew, would like it if you would get the hell out of her office so that she can tabulate these receipts*, or, *Please tell the Hatfields and the McCoys that the Madame cannot untangle their differences for them, although the Madame does know the names of some first-rate couples counselors*. In the absence of an enthusiasm for our product line or for business writing in general, Glenda Manzini hired me to tackle some of her responsibilities for her. I gave the facts the best possible spin. Glenda, as you probably have guessed, was good with numbers. With the profits and losses. Glenda was good at additional charges. Glenda was good at doubling the price on a floral arrangement, for example, because the Vietnamese poppies absolutely had to be on the tables, because they were so . . . *je ne sais quoi*. Glenda was good at double-booking a particular suite and then auctioning the space to the higher bidder. Glenda was good at quoting a figure for a band and then adding instruments so that the price increased astronomically. One time she padded a quartet with two vocalists, an eight-piece horn section, an African drumming ensemble, a dijeridoo and a harmonium.

The other thing I should probably be up-front about is that Glenda Manzini was a total knockout. A bombshell. A vision of celestial loveliness. I hate to go on about it, but there was that single strand of Glenda's amber hair always falling over her eyes—no matter how many times she tried to secure it; there was her near constant attention to her makeup; there was her total command of business issues and her complete unsentimentality. Or maybe it was her stockings, always in black, with a really provocative seam following the aerodynamically sleek lines of her calf. Or maybe it was her barely concealed sadness. I'd never met anyone quite as uncomfortable as Glenda, but this didn't bother me at first. My life had changed since the Chicken Mask.

Meanwhile, it goes without saying that the Mansion on the Hill wasn't a mansion at all. It was a homely cinder-block edifice formerly occupied by the Colonie Athletic Club. A trucking operation used the space before that. And the Mansion wasn't on any hill, either, because geologically speaking we're in a valley here. We're part of some recent glacial scouring.

On my first day, Glenda made every effort to insure that my work environment would be as unpleasant as possible. I'd barely set down my extra-large coffee with two half-and-halfs and five sugars and my assortment of cream-filled donuts (I was hoping these would please my new teammates) when Glenda bodychecked me, tipped me over into my reclining desk chair, with several huge stacks of file material.

—Andy, listen up. In April we have an Orthodox Jewish ceremony taking place at 3 P.M. in Niagara while at the same time there are going to be some very faithful Islamic-Americans next door in Ticonderoga. I don't want these two groups to come in contact with one another at any time, understand? I don't want any kind of diplomatic incident. It's your

job to figure out how to persuade one of these groups to be
first out of the gate, at noon, and it's your job to make them
think that they're really lucky to have the opportunity. And
Andy? The el-Mohammed wedding, the Muslim wedding,
needs prayer mats. See if you can get some from the discount
stores. Don't waste a lot of money on this.

This is a good indication of Glenda's management style.
Some other procedural tidbits: she frequently assigned a dozen
rewrites on her correspondence. She had a violent dislike for
semicolons. I was to double-space twice underneath the date
on her letters, before typing the salutation, on pain of death.
I was never, ever to use one of those cursive word-processing
fonts. I was to bring her coffee first thing in the morning,
without speaking to her until she had entirely finished a second
cup and also a pair of ibuprofen tablets, preferably the elon-
gated, easy-to-swallow variety. I was never to ask her about
her weekend or her evening or anything else, including her
holidays, unless she asked me first. If her door was closed, I
was not to open it. And if I ever reversed the digits in a phone
number when taking a message for her, I could count on my
pink slip that very afternoon.

Right away, that first A.M., after this litany of scares, after
Glenda retreated into her chronically underheated lair, there
was a swell of sympathetic mumbles from my coworkers, who
numbered, in the front office, about a dozen. They were offering condolences. They had seen the likes of me come and
go. Glenda, however, who keenly appreciated the element of
surprise as a way of insuring discipline, was not quite done.
She reappeared suddenly by my desk—as if by secret entrance—with a half-dozen additional commands. I was to find
a new sign for her private parking space, I was to find a new
floral wholesaler for the next fiscal quarter, I was to *refill her
prescription for birth-control pills*. This last request was spooky
enough, but it wasn't the end of the discussion. From there
Glenda starting getting personal:

—Oh, by the way, Andy? (she liked diminutives) What's
all the family trouble, anyway? The stuff Alex was talking
about when she called?

She picked up the photo of you, Sis, the one I had brought with me. The bass at the end of your fishing rod was so outsized that it seemed impossible that you could hold it up. You looked really happy. Glenda picked up the photo as though she hadn't already done her research, as if she had left something to chance. Which just didn't happen during her regime at the Mansion on the Hill.

— Dead sister, said I. And then, completing my betrayal of you, I filled out the narrative, so that anyone who wished could hear about it, and then we could move onto other subjects, like Worcester's really great semipro hockey team.

— Crashed her car. Actually, it was my car. Mercury Sable. Don't know why I said it was her car. It was mine. She was on her way to her rehearsal dinner. She had an accident.

Sis, have I mentioned that I have a lot of questions I've been meaning to ask? Have I asked, for example, why you were taking the windy country road along our side of the great river, when the four-lanes along the west side were faster, more direct and, in heavy rain, less dangerous? Have I asked why you were driving at all? Why I was not driving you to the rehearsal dinner instead? Have I asked why your car was in the shop for muffler repair on such an important day? Have I asked why you were late? Have I asked why you were lubricating your nerves *before* the dinner? Have I asked if four G&Ts, as you called them, before your own rehearsal dinner, were not maybe in excess of what was needed? Have I asked if there was a reason for you to be so tense on the eve of your wedding? Did you feel you had to go through with it? That there was no alternative? If so, why? If he was the wrong guy, why were you marrying him? Were there planning issues that were not properly addressed? Were there things between you two, as between all the betrothed, that we didn't know? Were there specific questions you wanted to ask, of which you were afraid? Have I given the text of my toast, Sis, as I had imagined it, beginning with a plangent evocation of the years before your birth, when I ruled our house like a tyrant, and how with earsplitting cries I resisted your infancy, until I learned to love

the way your baby hair, your flaxen mop, fell into curls? Have
I mentioned that it was especially satisfying to wind your hair
around my stubby fingers as you lay sleeping? Have I made
clear that I wrote out this toast and that it took me several
weeks to get it how I wanted it and that I was in fact going
over these words again when the call from Dad came announc-
ing your death? Have I mentioned — and I'm sorry to be hurtful
on this point — that Dad's drinking has gotten worse since you
left this world? Have I mentioned that his allusions to the
costly unfinished business of his life have become more fre-
quent? Have I mentioned that Mom, already overtaxed with
her own body count, with her dead parents and dead siblings,
has gotten more and more frail? Have I mentioned that I have
some news about Brice, your intended? That his tune has
changed slightly since your memorial service? Have I mentioned that I was out at the crime scene the next day? The
day after you died? Have I mentioned that in my dreams I
am often at the crime scene now? Have I wondered aloud to
you about that swerve of blacktop right there, knowing that
others may lose their lives as you did? Can't we straighten
out that road somehow? Isn't there one road crew that the
governor, in his quest for jobs, jobs, jobs, can send down there
to make this sort of thing unlikely? Have I perhaps clued you
in about how I go there often now, to look for signs of further
tragedy? Have I mentioned to you that in some countries DWI
is punishable by death, and that when Antonio at Hot Bird
first explained this dark irony to me, I imagined taking his
throat in my hands and squeezing the air out of him once
and for all? Sis, have I told you of driving aimlessly in the
mountains, listening to talk radio, searching for the one bit
of cheap, commercially interrupted persuasion that will let
me put these memories of you back in the canister where you
now at least partially reside so that I can live out my dim,
narrow life? Have I mentioned that I expect death around
every turn, that every blue sky has a safe sailing out of it, that
every bus runs me over, that every low, mean syllable uttered
in my direction seems to intimate the violence of murder,
that every family seems like an opportunity for ruin and every

marriage a ceremony into which calamity will fall and hearts will be broken and lives destroyed and people branded by the mortifications of love? Is it all right if I ask you all of this?

Still, in spite of these personal issues, I was probably a model employee for Glenda Manzini. For example, I managed to sort out the politics concerning the Jewish wedding and the Islamic wedding (both slated for the first weekend of April), and I did so by appealing to certain aspects of light in our valley at the base of the Adirondacks. Certain kinds of light make for very appealing weddings here in our valley, I told one of these families. In late winter, in the early morning, you begin to feel an excitement at the appearance of the sun. Yes, I managed to solve that problem, and the next (the prayer mats) — because K-Mart, *where America shops,* had a special on bathmats that week, and I sent Dorcas Gilbey over to buy six dozen to use for the Muslim families. I solved these problems and then I solved others just as vexing. I had a special interest in the snags that arose on Fridays after 5 P.M. — the groom who on the day of the ceremony was trapped in a cabin east of Lake George and who had to snowshoe three miles out to the nearest telephone, or the father of the bride (it was the Lapsley wedding) who wanted to arrive at the ceremony by hydrofoil. Brinksmanship, in the world of nuptial planning, gave me a sense of well-being, and I tried to bury you in the rear of my life, in the back of that closet where I'd hidden my secondhand golf clubs and my ski boots and my Chicken Mask — never again to be seen by mortal man.

One of my front-office associates was a fine young woman by the name of Linda Pietrzsyk, who tried to comfort me during the early weeks of my job, after Glenda's periodic assaults. Don't ask how to pronounce Linda's surname. In order to pronounce it properly, you have to clear your throat aggressively. Linda Pietrzsyk didn't like her surname anymore than you or I, and she was apparently looking for a groom from whom she could borrow a better last name. That's what I found out after awhile. Many of the employees at the Mansion on the Hill had ulterior motives. This marital ferment, this loamy soil of romance, called to them somehow. When I'd been there a few months, I started to see other applicants go through the masticating action of an interview with Glenda Manzini. Glenda would be sure to ask, *Why do you want to work here?* and many of these qualified applicants had the same reply, *Because I think marriage is the most beautiful thing and I want to help make it possible for others.* Most of these applicants, if they were attractive and single and younger than Glenda, aggravated her thoroughly. They were shown the door. But occasionally a marital aspirant like Linda Pietrzsyk snuck through, in this case because Linda managed to conceal her throbbing, sentimental heart beneath a veneer of contemporary discontent.

We had Mondays and Tuesdays off, and one weekend a month. Most of our problem-solving fell on Saturdays, of course, but on that one Saturday off, Linda Pietrzsyk liked to bring friends to the Mansion on the Hill, to various celebrations. She liked to attend the weddings of strangers. This kind of entertainment wasn't discouraged by Glenda or by the owners of the Mansion, because everybody likes a party to be crowded. Any wedding that was too sparsely attended at the Mansion had a fine complement of *warm bodies,* as Glenda liked to call them, provided gratis. Sometimes we had to go to libraries or retirement centers to fill a quota, but we managed. These gate crashers were welcome to eat finger food at the reception and to drink champagne and other intoxicants (food and drink were billed to the client), but they had to make themselves scarce once the dining began in earnest. There was a window of opportunity here that was large enough for Linda and her friends.

She was tight with a spirited bunch of younger people. She was friends with kids who had outlandish wardrobes and styles of grooming, kids with pants that fit like bedsheets, kids with haircuts that were, at best, accidental. But Linda would dress them all up and make them presentable, and they would arrive in an ancient station wagon in order to crowd in at the back of a wedding. Where they stifled gasps of hilarity.

I don't know what Linda saw in me. I can't really imagine.

I wore the same sweaters and flannel slacks week in and week out. I liked classical music, Sis. I liked historical simulation festivals. And as you probably haven't forgotten (having tried a couple of times to fix me up—with Jess Carney and Sally Moffitt), the more tense I am, the worse is the impression I make on the fairer sex. Nevertheless, Linda Pietrzsyk decided that I had to be a part of her elite crew of wedding crashers, and so for a while I learned by immersion of the great rainbow of expressions of fealty.

Remember that footage, so often shown on contemporary reality-based programming during the dead first half-hour of prime time, of the guy who vomited at his own wedding? I was at that wedding. You know when he says, *Aw, Honey, I'm really sorry,* and leans over and flash floods this amber stuff on her train? You know, the shock of disgust as it crosses her face? The look of horror in the eyes of the minister? I saw it all. No one who was there thought it was funny, though, except Linda's friends. That's the truth. I thought it was really sad. But I was sitting next to a fellow *actually named Cheese* (when I asked which kind of cheese, he seemed perplexed), and Cheese looked as though he had a hernia or something, he thought this was so funny. Elsewhere in the Chestnut Suite there was a grievous silence.

Linda Pietrzsyk also liked to catalogue moments of spontaneous erotic delight on the premises, and these were legendary at the Mansion on the Hill. Even Glenda, who took a dim view of gossiping about business most of the time, liked to hear who was doing it with whom where. There was an implicit hierarchy in such stories. *Tales of the couple to be married caught in the act on Mansion premises were considered obvious and therefore uninspiring.* Tales of the best man and matron of honor going at it (as in the Clarke, Rosenberg, Irving, Ng, Fujitsu, Walters, Shapiro or Spangler ceremonies) were better, but not great. Stories in which parents of the couple to be married were caught—in, say, the laundry room, with the dad still wearing his dress shoes—were good (Smith, Elsworth, Waskiewicz), but not as good as tales of the parents of the couple to be married trading spouses, of which we had one

unconfirmed report (Hinkley) and of which no one could stop
talking for a week. Likewise, any story in which the bride or
the groom were caught *in flagrante* with someone other than
the person they were marrying was considered astounding (if
unfortunate). But we were after some even more unlikely tall
tales: any threesome or larger grouping involving the couple
to be married and someone from one of the other weddings
scheduled that day, in which the third party was unknown
until arriving at the Mansion on the Hill, and at which *a house
pet was present*. Glenda said that if you spotted one of these
tableaux you could have a month's worth of free groceries
from the catering department. Linda Pietrzsyk also spoke long-
ingly of the day when someone would arrive breathlessly in
the office with a narrative of a full-fledged orgiastic reception
in the Mansion on the Hill, the spontaneous, overwhelming
erotic celebration of love and marriage by an entire suite full
of Americans, tall and short, fat and thin, young and old.

In pursuit of these tales, with her friends Cheese, Chip,
Mick, Stig, Mark and Blair, Linda Pietrzsyk would quietly
appear at my side at a reception and give me the news—
*Behind the bandstand, behind that scrim, groom reaching
under his cousin's skirts.* We would sneak in for a look. But
we never interrupted anyone. And we never made them feel
ashamed.

You know how when you're getting to know a fellow employee, a fellow team member, you go through phases,
through cycles of intimacy and insight and respect and doubt
and disillusionment, where one impression gives way to another? (Do you know about this, Sis, and is this what happened
between you and Brice, so that you felt like you personally
had to have the four G&Ts on the way to the rehearsal dinner?
Am I right in thinking you couldn't go on with the wedding
and that this caused you to get all sloppy and to believe erron-
eously that you could operate heavy machinery?) Linda Pietrzsyk was a stylish, Skidmore-educated girl with ivory skin and
an adorable bump in her nose; she was from an upper-middle-
class family out on Long Island somewhere; her father's peri-

odic drunkenness had not affected his ability to work; her
mother stayed married to him according to some mesmerism
of devotion; her brothers had good posture and excelled in
contact sports; in short, there were no big problems in Linda's
case. Still, she pretended to be a desperate, marriage-obsessed
kid, without a clear idea about what she wanted to do with
her life or what the hell was going to happen next week. She
was smarter than me — she could do the crossword puzzle in
three minutes flat and she knew all about current events —
but she was always talking about *catching a rich financier with
a wild streak and extorting a retainer from him,* until I wanted
to shake her. There's usually another layer underneath these
things. In Linda's case it started to become clear at Patti Wackerman's wedding.

The reception area in the Ticonderoga Room — where walls
slid back from the altar to reveal the tables and the dance
floor — was decorated in branches of forsythia and wisteria and
other flowering vines and shrubs. It was spring. Linda was
standing against a piece of white wicker latticework that I had
borrowed from the florist in town (in return for promotional
considerations), and sprigs of flowering trees garlanded it,
garlanded the spot where Linda was standing. Pale colors ha-
loed her.

— Right behind this screen, she said, when I swept up beside
her and tapped her playfully on the shoulder, — check it out.
There's a couple falling in love once and for all. You can see
it in their eyes.

I was sipping a Canadian spring water in a piece of company
stemware. I reacted to Linda's news nonchalantly. I didn't
think much of it. Yet I happened to notice that Linda's expression was conspiratorial, impish, as well as a little beatific.
Linda often covered her mouth with her hand when she'd said
something riotous, as if to conceal unsightly dental work (on
the contrary, her teeth were perfect), as if she'd been treated
badly one too many times, as if the immensity of joy were
embarrassing to her somehow. As she spoke of the couple in
question her hand fluttered up to her mouth. Her slender
fingertips probed delicately at her upper lip. My thoughts

came in torrents: *Where are Stig and Cheese and Blair? Why am I suddenly alone with this fellow employee? Is the couple Linda is speaking about part of the wedding party today? How many points will she get for the first sighting of their extra-marital grappling?*

Since it was my policy to investigate any and all such phenomena, I glanced desultorily around the screen and, seeing nothing out of the ordinary, slipped further into the shadows where the margins of Ticonderoga led toward the central catering staging area. There was, of course, no such couple behind the screen, or rather Linda (who was soon beside me) and myself *were the couple* and we were mottled by insufficient light, dappled by it, by lavender-tinted spots hung that morning by the lighting designers, and by reflections of a mirrored *disco ball* that speckled the dance floor.

—I don't see anything, I said.

—Kiss me, Linda Pietrzyk said. Her fingers closed lightly around the bulky part of my arm. There was an unfamiliar warmth in me. The band struck up some fast number. I think it was "It's Raining Men" or maybe it was that song entitled "We Are Family," which played so often at the Mansion on the Hill in the course of a weekend. Whichever, it was really loud. The horn players were getting into it. A trombonist yanked his slide back and forth.

—Excuse me? I said.

—Kiss me, Andrew, she said. —I want to kiss you.

Locating in myself a long-dormant impulsiveness, I reached down for Linda's bangs, and with my clumsy hands I tried to push back her blond and strawberry-blond curlicues, and then, with a hitch in my motion, in a stop-time sequence of jerks, I embraced her. Her eyes, like neon, were illumined.

—Why don't you tell me how you feel about me? Linda Pietrzyk said. I was speechless, Sis. I didn't know what to say. And she went on. There was something about me, something warm and friendly about me, I wasn't fortified, she said; I wasn't cold, I was just a good guy who actually cared about other people *and you know how few of those there are.* (I think these were her words.) She wanted to spend more time with me, she wanted to get to know me better, she wanted to give the roulette wheel a decisive spin: she repeated all this twice in slightly different ways with different modifiers. It made me sweat. The only way I could think to get her to quit talking was to kiss her in earnest, my lips brushing by hers the way the sun passes around and through the interstices of falling leaves on an October afternoon. I hadn't kissed anyone in a long time. Her mouth tasted like cherry soda, like barbecue, like fresh hay, and because of these startling tastes, I retreated. To arm's length.

Sis, was I scared. What was this rank taste of wet campfire and bone fragments that I'd had in my mouth since we scattered you over the Hudson? Did I come through this set of coincidences, these quotidian interventions by God, to work in a place where everything seemed to be about *love*, only to find that I couldn't ever be a part of that grand word? How could I kiss anyone when I felt so awkward? What happened to me, what happened to all of us, to the texture of our lives, when you left us here?

I tried to ask Linda why she was doing what she was doing— behind the screen of wisteria and forsythia. I fumbled badly for these words. I believed she was trying to have a laugh on me. So she could go back and tell Cheese and Mick about it. So she could go gossip about me in the office, about what a jerk that Wakefield was. *Man, Andrew Wakefield thinks there's something worth hoping for in this world*. I thought she was joking, and I was through being the joke, being the Chicken Mask, being the harlequin.

—I'm not doing anything to you, Andrew, Linda said.
—I'm expressing myself. It's supposed to be a good thing.

Reaching, she laid a palm flush against my face.

—I know you aren't . . .
—So what's the problem?

I was ambitious to reassure. If I could have stayed the hand that fluttered up to cover her mouth, so that she could laugh unreservedly, so that her laughter peeled out in the Ticonderoga Room . . . But I just wasn't up to it yet. I got out of there. I danced across the floor at the Wackerman wedding—

I was a party of one — and the Wackermans and the Delgados and their kin probably thought I was singing along with "Desperado" by the Eagles (it was the anthem of the new Mr. and Mrs. Fritz Wackerman), but really I was talking to myself, *about work,* about how Mike Tombello's best man wanted to give his toast while doing flips on a trampoline, about how Jenny Parmenter wanted live goats bleating in the Mansion parking lot, as a fertility symbol, as she sped away, in her Rolls Cornische, to the Thousand Islands. Boy, I always hated the Eagles.

Okay, to get back to Glenda Manzini. Linda Pietrzsyk didn't write me off after our failed embraces, but she sure gave me more room. She was out the door at 5:01 for several weeks, without asking after me, without a kind word for anyone, and I didn't blame her. But in the end who else was there to talk to? To Marie O'Neill, the accountant? To Paul Avakian, the human resources and insurance guy and petty-cash manager? To Rachel Levy, the head chef? Maybe it was more than this. Maybe the bond that forms between people doesn't get unmade so easily. Maybe it leaves its mark for a long time. Soon Linda and I ate our bagged lunches together again, trading varieties of puddings, often in total silence; at least this was the habit until we found a new area of common interest in our reservations about Glenda Manzini's management techniques. This happened to be when Glenda took a week off. What a miracle. I'd been employed at the Mansion six months. The staff was in a fine mood about Glenda's hiatus. There was a carnival atmosphere. Dorcas Gilbey had been stockpiling leftover ales for an office shindig featuring dancing and the recitation of really bad marital vows we'd heard. Linda and I went along with the festivities, but we were also formulating a strategy.

What we wanted to know was how Glenda became so unreservedly cruel. We wanted the inside story on her personal life. We wanted the skinny. How do you produce an individual like Glenda? What is the mass-production technique? We waited until Tuesday, after the afternoon beer-tasting party.

We were staying late, we claimed, in order to separate out the green M&Ms for the marriage of U.V.M. tight end Brad Doelp who had requested bowls of M&Ms at his reception, *excluding any and all green candies.* When our fellow employees were gone, right at five, we broke into Glenda's office.

Sis, we really broke in. Glenda kept her office locked when she wasn't in it. It was a matter of principle. I had to use my Discover card on the lock. I punished that credit card. But we got the tumblers to tumble, and once we were inside, we started poking around. First of all, Glenda Manzini was a tidy person, which I can admire from an organizational point of view, but it was almost like her office was empty. The pens and pencils were lined up. The in and out boxes were swept clean of any stray dust particle, any scrap of trash. There wasn't a rogue paper clip behind the desk or in the bottom of her spotless waste basket. She kept her rubber bands banded together with rubber bands. The files in her filing cabinets were orderly, subdivided to avoid bowing, the old faxes were photocopied so that they wouldn't disintegrate. The photos on the walls (Mansion weddings past), were nondescript and pedestrian. There was nothing intimate about the decoration at all. I knew about most of this stuff from the moments when she ordered me into that cubicle to shout me down, but this was different. Now we were getting a sustained look at Glenda's personal effects.

Linda took particular delight in Glenda's cassette player (it was atop one of the black filing cabinets)—a cassette player that none of us had ever heard play, not even once. Linda admired the selection of recordings there. A complete set of cut-out budget series: *Greatest Hits of Baroque, Greatest Hits of Swing, Greatest Hits of Broadway, Greatest Hits of Disco* and so forth. Just as she was about to pronounce Glenda a rank philistine where music was concerned, Linda located there, in a shattered case, a copy of *Greatest Hits of the Blues.*

We devoured the green M&Ms while we were busy with our reconnaissance. And I kept reminding Linda not to get any of the green dye on anything. I repeatedly checked surfaces for fingerprints. I even overturned Linda's hands (it made me happy while doing it), to make sure they were free of emerald smudges. Because if Glenda found out we were in her office, we'd both be submitting applications at the Hot Bird of Troy. Nonetheless, Linda carelessly put down her handful of M&Ms, on top of a filing cabinet, to look over the track listings for *Greatest Hits of the Blues*. This budget anthology was released the year Linda was born, in 1974. Coincidentally, the year you too were born, Sis. I remember driving with you to the tunes of Lightnin' Hopkins or Howlin' Wolf. I remember your preference for the most bereaved of acoustic blues, the most ramshackle of musics. What better soundtrack for the Adirondacks? For our meandering drives in the mountains, into Corinth or around Lake Luzerne? What more lonesome sound for a state park the size of Rhode Island where wolves and bears still come to hunt? Linda cranked the greatest hits of heartbreak and we sat down on the carpeted floor to listen. I missed you.

I pulled open that bottom file drawer by chance. I wanted to rest my arm on something. There was a powerful allure in the moment. I wasn't going to kiss Linda, and probably her desperate effort to find somebody to liberate her from her foreshortened economic prospects and her unpronounceable surname wouldn't come to much, but she was a good friend. Maybe a better friend than I was admitting to myself. It was in this expansive mood that I opened the file drawer at the bottom of one stack (the *J* through *P* stack), otherwise empty, to find that it was full of a half-dozen, maybe even more, of those circular packages *of birth-control pills,* the color-coated pills, you know, those multihued pills and placebos that are a journey through the amorous calendars of women. All unused. Not a one of them even opened. Not a one of the white, yellow, brown or green pills liberated from its package.

—Must be chilly in Schenectady, Linda mumbled.

Was there another way to read the strange bottom drawer? Was there a way to look at it beyond or outside of my exhausting tendency to discover only facts that would prop up darker prognostications? The file drawer contained the pills, it contained a bottle of vodka, it contained a cache of family

pictures and missives the likes of which were never displayed
or mentioned or even alluded to by Glenda. Even I, for all
my resentments, wasn't up to reading the letters. But what
of these carefully arranged packages of photo snapshots of the
Manzini family? (Glenda's son from her first marriage, in his
early teens, in a torn and grass-stained football uniform, and
mother and second husband and son in front of some bleach-
ers, et cetera.) Was the drawer really what it seemed to be,
a repository for mementos of love that Glenda had now hidden
away, secreted, shunted off into mini-storage? What was the
lesson of those secrets? Merely that concealed behind rage (and
behind grief) is *the ambition to love*?

—Somebody's having an affair, Linda said. —The hubby
is coming home late. He's fabricating late evenings at the
office. He's taking some desktop meetings with his secretary.
He's leaving Glenda alone with the kids. Why else be so cold?

—Or Glenda's carrying on, said I.

—Or she's polygamous, Linda said, —and this is a completely separate family she's keeping across town somewhere
without telling anyone.

—Or this is the boy she gave up for adoption and this is
the record of her meeting with his folks. And she never told
Dave about it.

—Whichever it is, Linda said, —it's *bad*.

We turned our attention to the vodka. Sis, I know I've
said that I don't touch the stuff anymore—because of your
example—but Linda egged me on. We were listening to music
of the delta, to its simple unadorned grief, and I felt that
Muddy Waters's loss was my kind of loss, the kind you don't
shake easily, the kind that comes back like a seasonal flu, and
soon we were passing the bottle of vodka back and forth.
Beautiful, sad Glenda Manzini understood the blues and I
understood the blues and you understood them and Linda
understood them and maybe everybody understood them—
in spite of what ethno-musicologists sometimes tell us about
the cultural singularity of that music. Linda started to dance
a little, there in Glenda Manzini's office, swiveling absently,
her arms like asps, snaking to and fro, her wrists adorned in

black bangles. Linda had a spell on her, in Glenda's anaerobic and cryogenically frigid office. Linda plucked off her beige pumps and circled around Glenda's desk, as if casting out its manifold demons. I couldn't take my eyes off of her. She forgot who I was and drifted with the lamentations of Robert Johnson (hellhound on his trail), and I could have followed her there, where she cast off Long Island and Skidmore and became a naiad, a true resident of the Mansion on the Hill, that paradise, but when the song was over the eeriness of our communion was suddenly alarming. I was sneaking around my boss's office. I was drinking her vodka. All at once it was time to go home.

We began straightening everything we had moved — we were really responsible about it — and Linda gathered up the dozen or so green M&Ms she'd left on the filing cabinet — excepting the one she inadvertently fired out the back end of her fist, which skittered from a three-drawer file down a whole step to the surface of a two-drawer stack, before hopping and skipping over a cassette box, before free-falling behind the cabinets, where it came to rest, at last, six inches from the northeast corner of the office, beside a small coffee-stained patch of wall-to-wall. I returned the vodka to its drawer of shame, I tidied up the stacks of *Brides* magazines, I locked Glenda's office door and I went back to being the employee of the month. (My framed picture hung over the water fountain between the rest rooms. I wore a bow tie. I smiled broadly and my teeth looked straight and my hair was combed. I couldn't be stopped.)

My ambition has always been to own my own small business. I like the flexibility of small-capitalization companies; I like small businesses at the moment at which they prepare to franchise. That's why I took the job at Hot Bird — I saw Hot Birds in every town in America, I saw Hot Birds as numerous as post offices or ATMs. I like small businesses at the moment at which they really define a market with respect to a certain need, when they begin to sell their products to the world. And my success as a team player at the Mansion on the Hill was the result of these ambitions. This is why I came to feel, after a time, that I could do Glenda Manzini's job myself. Since I'm a little young, it's obvious that I couldn't *replace* Glenda—I think her instincts were really great with respect to the service we were providing to the Capital Region—but I saw the Mansion on the Hill stretching its influence into population centers throughout the northeast. I mean, why wasn't there a Mansion on the Hill in Westchester? Down in Mamaroneck? Why wasn't there a Mansion on the Hill in the golden corridor of Boston suburbs? Why no mainline Philly Mansion? Suffice to say, I saw myself, at some point in the future, having the same opportunity Glenda had. I saw myself cutting deals and whittling out discounts at other fine Mansion locations. I imagined making myself indispensable to a coalition of Mansion venture-capitalists and then I imagined using these associations to make a move into, say, the high-tech or bio-tech sectors of American industry.

The way I pursued this particular goal was that I started looking ahead at things like upcoming volume. I started using the graph features on my office software to make pie charts of ceremony densities, cost ratios and so forth, and I started wondering how we could pitch our service better, whether on the radio or in the press or through alternative marketing strategies (I came up with the strategy, for example, of getting various non-affiliated religions—small emergent spiritual movements—to consider us as a site for all their group wedding ceremonies). And as I started looking ahead, I started noticing who was coming through the doors in the next months. I became well versed in the social forces of our valley. I watched for when certain affluent families of the region might be needing our product. I would, if required, attempt cold-calling the attorney general of our state to persuade him of the splendor of the Niagara Hall when Diana, his daughter, finally gave the okey-dokey to her suitor, Ben.

I may well have succeeded in my plan for domination of the Mansion on the Hill brand, if it were not for the fact that as I was examining the volume projections for November (one Monday night), the ceremonies taking place in a mere three months, I noticed that Sarah Wilton of Corinth was marrying one Brice McCann in the Rip Van Winkle Room. Just before Thanksgiving. There were no particular notes or annotations to the name on the calendar, and thus Glenda wasn't focusing much on the ceremony. But something bothered me. That name.

Your Brice McCann, Sis. Your intended. Getting married almost a year to the day after your rehearsal-dinner-that-never-was. Getting married before even having completed his requisite year of grief, before we'd even made it through the anniversary with its floodwaters. Who knew how long he'd waited before beginning his seduction of Sarah Wilton? Was it even certain that he had waited until you were gone? Maybe he was faithless; maybe he was a two-timer. I had started reading Glenda's calendar to get ahead in business, Sis, but as soon as I learned of Brice, I became cavalier about work. My work suffered. My relations with other members of the staff suffered. I kept to myself. I went back to riding the bus to work instead of accepting rides. I stopped visiting fellow workers. I found myself whispering of plots and machinations; I found myself making connections between things that probably weren't connected and planning involved scenarios of revenge. I knew the day would come when he would be on the premises, when Brice would be settling various accounts, going over various numbers, signing off on the pâté selection and the set list of the R&B band, and I waited for him—to be certain of the truth.

Sis, you became engaged too quickly. There had been that other guy, Mark, and you had been engaged to him, too, and that arrangement fell apart kind of fast—I think you were engaged at Labor Day and broken up by M.L.K.'s birthday—and then, within weeks, there was this Brice. There's a point I want to make here. I'm trying to be gentle, but I have to get this across. Brice wore a beret. *The guy wore a beret.* He was supposedly a great cook, he would bandy about names of exotic mushrooms, but I never saw him boil an egg when I was visiting you. It was always you who did the cooking. It's true that certain males of the species, the kind who linger at the table after dinner waiting for their helpmeet to do the washing up, the kind who preside over carving of viands and otherwise disdain food-related chores, the kind who claim to be effective only at the preparation of breakfast, these guys are Pleistocene brutes who don't belong in the Information Age with its emerging markets and global economies. But, Sis, I think the other extreme is just as bad. The sensitive, New Age, beret-wearing guys who buy premium mustards and free-range chickens and grow their own basil and then let you cook while they're in the other room perusing magazines devoted to the artistic posings of Asian teenagers. Our family comes from upstate New York and we don't eat enough vegetables and our marriages are full of hardships and sorrows, Sis, and when I saw Brice coming down the corridor of the Mansion on the Hill, with his prematurely gray hair slicked back with the aid of some all-natural mousse, wearing a gray, suede bomber jacket and cowboy boots into which were tucked the cuffs of his black designer jeans, carrying his personal digital assistant and his cell phone and the other accoutrements of his dwindling massage-therapy business, he was the enemy of my state. In his wake, I was happy to note, there was a sort of honeyed cologne. Patchouli, I'm guessing. It would definitely drive Glenda Manzini nuts.

We had a small conference room at the Mansion, just around the corner from Glenda's office. I had selected some of the furnishings there myself, from a discount furniture outlet at the mall. Brice and his fiancée, Sarah Wilton, would of course be repairing to this conference room with Glenda to do some pricing. I had the foresight, therefore, to jog into that space and turn on the speaker phone over by the coffee machine, and to place a planter of silk flowers in front of it and dial my own extension so that I could teleconference this conversation. I had a remote headset I liked to wear around, Sis, during inventorying and bill tabulation — it helped with the neck strain and tension headaches that I'm always suffering with — so I affixed this headset and went back to filing, down the hall, while the remote edition of Brice and Sarah's conference with Glenda was broadcast into my skull.

I figure my expression was ashen. I suppose that Dorcas Gilbey, when she flagged me down with some receipts that she had forgotten to file, was unused to my mechanistic expression and to my curt, unfriendly replies to her questions. I waved her off, clamping the headset tighter against my ear. Unfortunately, the signal broke up. It was muffled. I hurriedly returned to my desk and tried to get the forwarded call to transmit properly to my handset. I even tried to amplify it through the speaker-phone feature, to no avail. Brice had always affected a soft-spoken demeanor while he was busy extorting things from people like you, Sis. He was too quiet — the better to conceal his tactics. And thus, in order to hear him, I had to sneak around the corner from the conference room and eavesdrop in the old-fashioned way.

—We wanted to dialogue with you (Brice was explaining to Glenda), because we wanted to make sure that you were thinking creatively along the same lines we are. We want to make sure you're comfortable with our plans. As married people, as committed people, we want this ceremony to make others feel good about themselves, as we're feeling good about ourselves. We want to have an ecstatic celebration here, a healing celebration that will bind up the hurt any marriages in the room might be suffering. I know you know how the ecstasy of marriage occasions a grieving process for many persons, Mrs. Manzini. Sarah and I both feel this in our hearts, that celebrations often have grief as a part of their wonder, and we want to enact all these things, all these feelings, to bring them out where we can look at them, and then we want to purge them triumphantly. We want people to come out of this wedding feeling good about themselves, as we'll be feeling good about ourselves. We want to give our families a big collective hug, because we're all human and we all have feelings and we all have to grieve and yearn and we need rituals for this.

There was a long silence from Glenda Manzini.

Then she said:

—Can we cut to the chase?

One thing I always loved about the Mansion on the Hill was its emptiness, its vacancy. Sure, the Niagara Room, when filled with five-thousand-dollar gowns and heirloom tuxedos, when serenaded by Toots Wilcox's big band, was a great place, a sort of gold standard of reception halls, but as much as I always loved both the celebrations and the network of relationships and associations that went with our business at the Mansion, I always felt best in the *empty* halls of the Mansion on the Hill, cleansed of their accumulation of sentiment, utterly silent, patiently awaiting the possibility of matrimony. It was onto this clean slate that I had routinely projected my foolish hopes. But after Brice strutted through my place of employment, after his marriage began to overshadow every other, I found instead a different message inscribed on these walls: *Every death implies a guilty party*.

Or to put it another way, there was a network of sub-basements in the Mansion on the Hill through which each suite was connected to another. These tunnels were well-traveled by certain alcoholic janitorial guys whom I knew well enough. I'd had my reasons to adventure there before, but now I used every opportunity to pace these corridors. I still performed the parts of my job that would assure that I got paid and that I invested regularly in my 401K plan, but I felt more comfortable in the emptiness of the Mansion's suites and basements, thinking about how I was going to extract my recompense, while Brice and Sarah dithered over the cost of their justice of the peace and their photographer and their *Champlain Pentecostal Singers*.

I had told Linda Pietrzsyk about Brice's reappearance. I had told her about you, Sis. I had remarked about your fractures and your loss of blood and your hypothermia and the results of your post-mortem blood-alcohol test; I suppose that I'd begun to tell her all kinds of things, in outbursts of candor that were followed by equal and opposite remoteness. Linda saw me, over the course of those weeks, lurking, going from Ticonderoga to Rip Van Winkle to Chestnut, slipping in and out of infernal sub-basements of conjecture that other people find grimy and uncomfortable, when I should have been overseeing the unloading of floral arrangements at the loading dock or arranging for Glenda's chiropractic appointments. Linda saw me lurking around, *asked what was wrong and told me that it would be better after the anniversary, after that day had come and gone,* and I felt the discourses of apology and subsequent gratitude forming epiglottally in me, but instead I told her to get lost, to leave the dead to bury the dead.

After a long excruciating interval, the day of Sarah Danforth Wilton's marriage to Brice Paul McCann arrived. It was a day of chill mists, Sis, and you had now been gone just over one year. I had passed through the anniversary trembling, in front of the television, watching the Home Shopping Network, impulsively pricing cubic zirconium rings, as though one of these would have been the ring you might have worn at your ceremony. You were a fine sister, but you changed your mind all the time, and I had no idea if these things I'd attributed to you in the last year were features of the *you* I once knew, or whether, in death, you had become the property of your mourners, so that we made of you a puppet.

On the anniversary, I watched a videotape of your bridal shower, and Mom was there, and she looked really proud, and Dad drifted into the center of the frame at one point, and mumbled a strange *harrumph* that had to do with interloping at an assembly of such beautiful women (I was allowed on the scene only to do the videotaping), and you were very pleased as you opened your gifts. At one point you leaned over to Mom, and stage-whispered—so that even I could hear—*that your car was a real lemon and that you had to take it to the shop and you didn't have time and it was a total hassle and did she think that I would lend you the Sable without giving you a hard time?* My Sable, my car. Sure. If I had it to do again, I would never have given you a hard time even once.

The vows at the Mansion on the Hill seemed to be the part of the ceremony where most of the tinkering took place. I think if Glenda had been able to find a way to charge a premium on vow alteration, we could have found a really excellent revenue stream at the Mansion on the Hill. If the sweet instant of commitment is so singular, why does it seem to have so many different articulations? People used all sorts of things in their vows. Conchita Bosworth used the songs of Dan Fogelberg when it came to the exchange of rings; a futon-store owner from Queensbury, Reggie West, managed to work in material from a number of sitcoms. After a while, you'd heard it all, the rhetoric of desire, the incantation of commitment rendered as awkwardly as possible; you heard the purple metaphors, the hackneyed lines, until it was all like legal language, as in any business transaction.

It was the language of Brice McCann's vows that brought this story to its conclusion. I arrived at the wedding late. I took a cab across the Hudson, from the hill in Troy where I lived in my convenience apartment. What trees there were in the system of pavement cloverleafs where Route Seven met the interstate were bare, disconsolate. The road was full of potholes. The lanes choked with old, shuddering sedans. The parking valets at the Mansion, a group of pot-smoking teens who seemed to enjoy creating a facsimile of politeness that involved both effrontery and subservience, opened the door of the cab for me and greeted me according to their standard line, *Where's the party?* The parking lot was full. We had seven weddings going on at once. Everyone was working. Glenda was working, Linda was working, Dorcas was working. All my teammates were working, sprinting from suite to suite, micro-managing. The whole of the Capital Region must have been at the Mansion that Saturday to witness the blossoming of families, Sis, or, in the case of Brice's wedding, to witness the way in which a vow of faithfulness less than a year old, a promise of the future, can be traded in so quickly; how marriage is just a shrink-wrapped sale item, mass-produced in bulk. You can pick one up anywhere these days, at a mall, on layaway. If it doesn't fit, exchange it.

I walked the main hallway slowly, peeking in and out of the various suites. In the *Chestnut Suite* it was the Polanskis, poor but generous—their daughter Denise intended to have and to hold an Italian fellow, A.L. DiPietro, also completely penniless, and the Polanskis were paying for the entire cere-

mony and rehearsal dinner and inviting the DiPietros to stay
with them for the week. They had brought their own floral
displays, personally assembled by the arthritic Mrs. Polanski.
The room had a dignified simplicity. Next, in the *Hudson
Suite*, in keeping with its naval flavor, cadet Bobby Moore
and his high-school sweetheart Mandy Sutherland were tying
the knot, at the pleasure of Bobby's dad, who had been a
tugboat captain in New York Harbor; in the *Adirondack Suite*,
two of the venerable old families of the Lake George region —
the Millers (owners of the Lake George Cabins) and the Went-
worths (they had the Quality Inn franchise) commingled their
resort-dependent fates; in the *Valentine Room*, Sis, two
women (named Sal and Martine, but that's all I should say
about them, for reasons of privacy) were to be married by a
renegade Episcopal minister called Jack Valance — they had
sewn their own gowns to match the cadmium red decor of
that interior; *Ticonderoga* had the wedding of Glen Dunbar
and Louise Glazer, a marriage not memorable in any way at
all, and in the *Niagara Hall* two of Saratoga's great eighteenth-
century racing dynasties, the Vanderbilt and Pierrepont families, were about to settle long-standing differences. Love was
everywhere in the air.

I walked through all these ceremonies, Sis, before I could
bring myself to go over to the *Rip Van Winkle Room*. My steps
were reluctant. My observations: the proportions of sniffling at
each ceremony were about equal and the audiences were about
equal and levels of whimsy and seriousness were about the
same wherever you went. The emotions careened, high and
low, across the whole spectrum of possible feelings. The music
might be different from case to case — stately baroque anthems
or klezmer rave-ups — but the intent was the same. By 3:00 P.M.,
I no longer knew what marriage meant, really, except that
the celebration of it seemed built into every life I knew but
my own.

The doors of the Rip Van Winkle Room were open, as
distinct from the other suites, and I tiptoed through them
and closed these great carved doors behind myself. I slipped

into the bride's side. The light was dim, Sis. The light was deep in the ultraviolet spectrum, as when we used to go, as kids, to the exhibitions at the Hall of Science and Industry. There seemed to be some kind of mummery, some kind of expressive dance, taking place at the altar. The Champlain Pentecostal Singers were wailing eerily. As I searched the room for familiar faces, I noticed them everywhere. Just a couple of rows away Alex McKinnon and her boy Zack were squished into a row and were fidgeting desperately. Had they known Brice? Had they known you? Maybe they counted themselves close friends of Sarah Wilton. Zack actually turned and waved and seemed to mouth something to me, but I couldn't make it out. On the groom's side, I saw Linda Pietrzsyk, though she ought to have been working in the office, fielding calls, and she was surrounded by Cheese, Chip, Mick, Mark, Stig, Blair and a half-dozen other delinquents from her peer group. Like some collective organism of mirth and irony, they convulsed over the proceedings, over the scarlet tights and boas and dance belts of the modern dancers capering at the altar. A row beyond these Skidmore halfwits — though she never sat in at any ceremony — was Glenda Manzini herself, and she seemed to be sobbing uncontrollably, a handkerchief like a veil across her face. Where was her husband? And her boy? Then, to my amazement, Sis, when I looked back at the S.R.O. audience beyond the last aisle over on the groom's side, *I saw Mom and Dad*. What were they doing there? And how had they known? I had done everything to keep the wedding from them. I had hoarded these bad feelings. Dad's face was gray with remorse, as though he could have done something to stop the proceedings, and Mom held tight to his side, wearing dark glasses of a perfect opacity. At once, I got up from the row where I'd parked myself and climbed over the exasperated families seated next to me, jostling their knees. As I went, I became aware of Brice McCann's soft, insinuating voice ricocheting, in Dolby surround-sound, from one wall of the Rip Van Winkle Room to the next. The room was appropriately named, it seemed to me then. We were all sleepers who dreamed a reverie of marriage, not one of us had waked to see the bondage, the violence, the excess of its cabalistic prayers and rituals. Marriage was oneiric. Not one of us was willing to pronounce the truth of its dream language of slavery and submission and transmission of property, and Brice's vow, *to have and to hold Sarah Wilton, till death did them part, forsaking all others,* seemed to me like the pitch of a used-car dealer or insurance salesman, and these words rang out in the room, likewise Sarah's uncertain and breathy reply, and I rushed at the center aisle, pushing away cretinous guests and cherubic newborns toward my parents, to embrace them as these words fell, these words with their intimations of mortality, *to tell my parents I should never have let you drive that night, Sis. How could I have let you drive? How could I have been so stupid? My tires were bald—I couldn't afford better. My car was a death trap; and I was its proper driver, bent on my long, complicated program of failure, my program of futures abandoned, of half-baked ideas, of big plans that came to nought, of cheap talk and lies, of drinking binges, petty theft; my car was made for my own death, Sis, the inevitable and welcome end to the kind of shame and regret I had brought upon everyone close to me, you especially, who must have wept inwardly, in your bosom, when you felt compelled to ask me to read a poem on your special day, before you totaled my car, on that curve, running up over the bream, shrieking, flipping the vehicle, skidding thirty feet on the roof, hitting the granite outcropping there, plunging out of the seat (why no seat belt?), snapping your neck, ejecting through the windshield, catching part of yourself there, tumbling over the hood, breaking both legs, puncturing your lung, losing an eye, shattering your wrist, bleeding, coming to rest at last in a pile of mouldering leaves, where rain fell upon you, until, unconsciously, you died.*

Yet, as I called out to Mom and Dad, the McCann-Wilton wedding party suddenly scattered, the vows were through, the music was overwhelming, the bride and groom were married; there were Celtic pipes, and voices all in harmony—it was a dirge, it was jig, it was a chant of religious ecstasy—and I couldn't tell what was wedding and what was funeral, whether

there was an end to one and a beginning to the other, and
there were shouts of joy and confetti in the air, and beating
of breasts and the procession of pink-cheeked teenagers, two
by two, all living the dream of American marriages with cars
and children and small businesses and pension plans and so-
cial-security checks and grandchildren, and I couldn't get close
to my parents in the throng; in fact, I couldn't be sure if it
had been them standing there at all, in that fantastic crowd,
that crowd of dreams, and I realized I was alone at Brice
McCann's wedding, alone among people who would have been
just as happy not to have me there, as I had often been alone,
even in fondest company, even among those who cared for
me. I should have stayed home and watched television.

This didn't stop me, though. I made my way to the reception. I shoveled down the chicken satay and shrimp with green
curry, along with the proud families of Sarah Wilton and Brice
McCann. Linda Pietrzsyk appeared by my side, as when we
had kissed in the Ticonderoga Suite. She asked if I was feeling
all right.

—Sure, I said.

—Don't you think I should drive you home?

—There's someone I want to talk to, I said. —Then I'd be
happy to go.

And Linda asked:

—What's in the bag?

She was referring to my Wal-Mart shopping bag, Sis. I think
the Wal-Mart policy which asserts that *employees are not to
let a customer pass without asking if this customer needs help*
is incredibly enlightened. I think the way to a devoted customer is through his or her dignity. In the shopping bag, I
was carrying the wedding gift I had brought for Brice McCann
and Sarah Wilton. I didn't know if I should reveal this gift
to Linda, because I didn't know if she would understand, but
I told her anyhow. *Is this what it's like to discover, all at once,
that you are sharing your life?*

—Oh, that's some of my sister.

—Andrew, Linda said, and then she apparently didn't know
how to continue. Her voice, in a pair of false starts, oscillated

with worry. Her smile was grim. —Maybe this would be a good time to leave.

But I didn't leave, Sis. I brought out the most dangerous weapon in my arsenal, the pinnacle of my nefarious plans for this event, also stored in my Wal-Mart bag. The Chicken Mask. That's right, Sis. I had been saving it ever since my days at Hot Bird, and as Brice had yet to understand that I had crashed his wedding for a specific reason, I slipped this mask over my neatly parted hair, and over the collar of the wash-and-wear suit that I had bought that week for this occasion. I must say, in the mirrored reception area in the Rip Van Winkle Room, I was one elegant chicken. I immediately began to search the premises for the groom, and it was difficult to find him at first, since there were any number of like-minded beret-wearing motivational speakers slouching against pillars and counters. At last, though, I espied him preening in the middle of a small group of maidens, over by the electric fountain we had installed for the ceremony. He was laughing good-naturedly. When he first saw me, in the Chicken Mask, working my way toward him, I'm sure he saw me as an omen for his new union. *Terrific! We've got a chicken at the ceremony! Poultry is always reassuring at wedding time!* Linda was trailing me across the room. Trying to distract me. I had to be short with her. I told her to go find herself a husband.

I worked my way into McCann's limber and witty reception chatter and mimed a certain Chicken-style affability. Then, when one of those disagreeable conversational silences overtook the group, I ventured a question of your intended:

—So, Brice, how do you think your last fiancée, Eileen, would be reacting to your first-class nuptial ceremony today? Would she have liked it?

There was a confused hush, as the three or four of the secretarial beauties of his circle considered the best way to respond to this thorny question.

—Well, since she's passed away, I think she would probably be smiling down on us from above. I've felt her presence throughout the decision to marry Sarah, and I think Eileen knows that I'll never forget her. That I'll always love her.

—Oh, is that right? I said, —because the funny thing is I happen to have her *with me here,* and . . .

Then I opened up the small box of you (you were in a Tiffany jewelry box that I had spirited out of Mom's jewelry cache because I liked its pale teal shade: the color of rigor mortis as I imagined it) held it up toward Brice and then tossed some of it. I'm sure you know, Sis, that chips of bone tend to be heavier and therefore to fall more quickly to the ground, while the rest of the ashes make a sort of cloud when you throw them, when you cast them aloft. Under the circumstances, this cloud seemed to have a character, a personality. *Thus, you darted and feinted around Brice's head,* Sis, so that he began coughing and wiping the corners of his eyes, dusty with your remains. His consorts were hacking as well, among them Sarah Wilton, his troth. How had I missed her before? She was radiant like a woman whose prayers have been answered, who sees the promise of things to come, who sees uncertainties and contingencies diminished, and yet she was rushing away from me, astonished, as were the others. I realized I had caused a commotion. Still, I gave chase, Sis, and I overcame your Brice McCann, where he blockaded himself on the far side of a table full of spring rolls. Though I have never been a fighting guy, I gave him an elbow in the nose, as if I were a Chicken and this elbow my wing. I'm sure I mashed some cartilage. He got a little nosebleed. I think I may have broken the Mansion's unbroken streak of peaceful weddings.

At this point, of course, a pair of beefy Mansion employees (the McCarthy brothers, Tom and Eric) arrived on the scene and pulled me off of Brice McCann. They also tore the Chicken Mask from me. And they never returned this piece of my property afterwards. At the moment of unmasking, Brice reacted with mock astonishment. But how could he have failed to guess? That I would wait for my chance, however many years it took?

—Andy?

I said nothing, Sis. Your ghost had been in the cloud that wreathed him; your ghost had swooped out of the little box that I'd held, and now, at last, you were released from your disconsolate march on the surface of the earth, your march of unfinished business, your march of fixed ideas and obsessions unslaked by death. I would be happy if you were at peace now, Sis, and I would be happy if I were at peace; I would be happy if the thunderclouds and lightning of Brice and Sarah's wedding would yield to some warm autumn day in which you had good weather for your flight up through the heavens.

Out in the foyer, where the guests from the Valentine Room were promenading in some of the finest threads I had ever seen, Tom McCarthy told me that Glenda Manzini wanted to see me in her office — before I was removed from the Mansion on the Hill permanently. We walked against the flow of the crowd beginning to empty from each of the suites. Our trudge was long. When I arrived at Glenda's refrigerated chamber, she did an unprecedented thing, Sis, she closed the door. I had never before inhabited that space alone with her. She didn't invite me to sit. Her voice was raised from the outset. Pinched between thumb and forefinger (the shade of her nail polish, a dark maroon, is known in beauty circles, I believe, as *vamp*), as though it were an ounce of gold or a pellet of plutonium, she held a single green M&M.

—Can you explain this? she asked. —Can you tell me what this is?

—I think that's a green M&M, I said. —I think that's the traditional green color, as opposed to one of the new brighter shades they added in a recent campaign for market share.

—Andy, don't try to amuse me. What was this green M&M doing behind my filing cabinet?

—Well, I—

—I'm certain that I didn't leave a green M&M back there. I would never leave an M&M behind a filing cabinet. In fact, I would never allow a green M&M into this office in the first place.

—That was months ago.

—I've been holding on to it for months, Glenda said. —Do you think I'm stupid?

—On the contrary, I said.

—Do you think you can come in here and violate the privacy of my office?

—I think you're brilliant, I said. —And I think you're very sad. And I think you should surrender your job to someone who cares for the institution you're celebrating here.

Now that I had let go of you, Sis, now that I had begun to compose this narrative in which I relinquished the hem of your spectral bedsheet, I saw through the language of business, the rhetoric of hypocrisy. Why had she sent me out for those birth-control pills? Why did she make me schedule her chiropractic appointments? Because she could. *But what couldn't be controlled, what could never be controlled, was the outcome of devotion.* Glenda's expression, for the first time on record, was stunned. She launched into impassioned colloquy about how the Mansion on the Hill was supposed to be a *refuge,* and how, with my *antics,* as she called them, I had sullied the reputation of the Mansion and endangered its business plan, and how it was clear *that assaulting strangers while wearing a rubber mask is the kind of activity that proves you are an unstable person, and I just think, well, I don't see the point in discussing it with you anymore and I think you have some serious choices to make, Andy, if you want to be part of regular human society,* and so forth, which is just plain bunk, as far as I'm concerned. It's not as if Brice McCann were a *stranger* to me.

I'm always the object of tirades by my supervisors, for overstepping my position, for lying, for wanting too much — this is one of the deep receivables on the balance sheet of my life — and yet at the last second Glenda Manzini didn't fire me. According to shrewd managerial strategy, she simply waved toward the door. With the Mansion crowded to capacity now, with volume creeping upward in the coming months, they would need someone with my skills. To validate the cars in the parking lot, for example. Mark my words, Sis, parking validation will soon be as big in the Northeast as it is in the West.

When the McCarthys flung me through the main doors,

Linda Pietrzsyk was waiting. What unfathomable kindness. At the main entrance, on the way out, I passed through a gauntlet of rice-flingers. Bouquets drifted through the skies to the mademoiselles of the Capital. Garters fell into the hands of local bachelors. Then I was beyond all good news and seated in the passenger seat of Linda's battered Volkswagen. She was crying. We progressed slowly along back roads. I had been given chances and had squandered them. I had done my best to love, Sis. I had loved you, and you were gone. In Linda's car, at dusk, we sped along the very road where you took your final drive. Could Linda have known? Your true resting place is forested by white birches, they dot the length of that winding lane, the fingers of the dead reaching up through burdens of snow to impart much-needed instruction to the living. In intermittent afternoon light, in seizure-inducing light, unperturbed by the advances of merchandising, I composed a proposal.

Selected Notes from
Hampstead

Elias Canetti

In 1980, the year before Elias Canetti was awarded the Nobel Prize for literature, Susan Sontag wrote that the notebook was the perfect form for a writer like him — a man who was a student of everything rather than of anything in particular — for "it allows entries of all lengths and shapes and degrees of impatience and roughness." Canetti's published works are as various in their shapes as the entries in his notebooks. He originally intended his 1936 Auto-da-Fé *to be the first in a series of eight novels, each examining a monomaniac whose madness typified a facet of the modern era. But* Auto-da-Fé, *an epic about a reclusive scholar who is ultimately driven to immolate himself in his vast library, was to be the only book in that series. Canetti never wrote another novel. Twenty-five years passed before the publication of his next book, the monumental* Crowds and Power, *a pancultural study of the basic human urge for dominance. He did eventually return to his* monomaniacs in the 1974 volume Earwitness, *a collection of sketches of fifty different monomaniacal characters.*

Canetti's ability to immerse himself in multiple obsessions is partly explained by his manifold cultural and linguistic heritage. He was born in 1905 in Bulgaria of Sephardic Jewish parents; his father was of Turkish and his mother of Spanish descent; his first language was the Ladino dialect of the Sephardim, but he also learned Bulgarian as a child and became fluent in French, English and German, the language in which his parents communicated and in which he wrote all of his books. Canetti's family left Bulgaria when he was six, and he lived in Manchester, Vienna, Zurich and Frankfurt during his youth. In 1938, after the Anschluß, *he fled Austria, and eventually became a British citizen. Though he always was a reclusive figure, and especially so after winning the Nobel, Canetti revealed much about his childhood and his later life in several volumes of memoirs,* The Voices of Marrakesh, The Tongue Set Free, The Torch in My Ear, *and* The Play of the Eyes. *"My first memory is dipped in red," he writes in the opening line of* The Tongue Set Free, *characteristically conjoining beauty and violence. Throughout his work, Canetti's vision manages to be dark yet somehow optimistic. "There is almost nothing bad that I couldn't say about humans and humankind. And yet my pride in them is so great that there is only one thing I really hate: their enemy, death." Canetti died in 1994 at the age of 89, and his body is buried in Zurich alongside the grave of James Joyce.*

The following notebook entries, which range from the aphoristic to the novelistic, were written in Hampstead, England, during the middle of Canetti's life. Since they are being published posthumously, they have a rougher quality than those he edited himself. With that, however, we are granted a glimpse at the otherwise hidden messy desk of his writing process, a modicum of insight into the workings of the author's mind.

—Elizabeth Gaffney

He is a tall, powerful man, his face set in a kind of permanent astonishment, never revealing any other expression. He approaches everyone quite openly, shying away from no one. He greets everyone with a trusting handshake. His trusting nature is like a child's, but in this archetype of a man it is irresistible.

While getting to know him, many mistrust him and try to uncover all sorts of dark secrets. But this always proves his innocence and eventually embarrasses even the most evil-minded doubter.

People like talking to him because he doesn't remember anything. He is the least dangerous of all father confessors. He has no possessions, but he has everything he needs. Everyone wants to be alone with him, and in this way he gets clothed and taken care of. He accumulates nothing: since he doesn't see anything as belonging to him, he gives it all away.

A woman's attempt to bind him to her through an object of value. She brings him a beautiful gleaming ring, then she takes it way, bringing it back again every time she sees him. At last she thinks she can leave the ring with him. But on her next visit the ring has vanished. His household consists of the property of others. His benefactors are mindful of his minimal needs and keep things stored away for him.

Though he is often talked about, he never takes part in these discussions. To make him one's slave would be impossible since he obeys no one. At some point he must have learned speech; thus he cannot always have been without a memory. But since no one remembers this period, his background and his youth remain a mystery.

Animals approach him as if they were humans; it appears they get to know him.

He always sees the end in advance, so as not to begin anything.

How many people you have seen this week! The five historians from Berlin. The Italian actress from Australia. The young

Jew from New York who worships Isaac Babel. The publisher
with the most important voice in England. The mother of
the deceased Otter woman. The secret hairdresser from the
Abruzzi. Veza's weepy cavalier. The Chinese pianist and his
fiancée, the daughter of the famous violinist. Kafka, who came
from Frankfurt to ask for the hand of his cousin. It was a lot,
it was too much, and yet you were nearly smothered by yourself
alone.

Indignation at being admired. That long, scornful nose of
hers bounces men right off. She knows that she is beautiful
only when she looks somber. The tragic aspect of her face
would be likeable without that weapon of a nose on it.

I went home and found a fez. Whose had it been? I put
it on and went for a walk. Now everyone knew me. Soon I
was a celebrity. The fez cast its crimson dignity about me.
What was its purpose? There was general curiosity but never
disrespect: all my pursuers kept their distance. I was disin-
clined to take off the fez; without it, everyone would have
felt humiliated. I felt how I was exalting them all with my
fez. If I had foreseen the fateful consequences, I would not
have shown myself as much with it on.

The first several days I felt proud but calm. There was a
certain positive tension, but it was containable. I did, though,
note the anxious look an old woman gave me when her grand-
child, an impressionable little girl, pointed her finger toward
my fez and began to cry softly. I thought, she must *want* it,
but I didn't dare kneel down for her to play with it. I bowed
by head slightly, swaying the hat gently. At first the child was
silent, then she burst into tears. Her sobs were heartbreaking,
and I pulled away, embarrassed by the unseemly commotion
she was making. I saw groups of people whispering on the
other side of the square, but as I approached them they fell
stonily silent. A dog put its tail between its legs and slunk
away. A young woman fell to her knees in front of me and
begged the fez for its blessing. How could I have withheld

from her the very thing she so longed for? With a nod of my
head I granted her wish; she clasped my knees and fell into
a swoon. I was very moved, but got away somehow and left
her lying there in bliss. How little, how little a human being
needs. For him God can even take the form of a fez.

The day before yesterday, late: *Sonia*, a story reminiscent
of Grimmelshausen. The father, a Hungarian landowner in
Slovakia, the mother a Jew, three daughters (of whom I now
know Enid and Sonia). The father always in his library. His
talks with Sonia, the strongest daughter, during the second
half of the war, his certainty of coming catastrophe. He sent
two of his daughters to Budapest — Sonia studied agriculture
at the university in Altenburg. Her last visit to the estate: she
was never to return. Her parents' last postcard: "We are going
to Komorn in a truck." A student who she knows is half-Jewish
but who has false papers warns her she is in danger. Sonia
demands to see her own papers and she gets them: her Jewish
grandparents are there in bold underlining. The friendly student goes with her, first to Komorn, where she tries to get
news of her parents. She learns that the only man who can
tell her anything is the head of the local militia, a photographer. She tracks him down in his shop; he is in uniform. She
asks about her father. "Baron Weiss? Sure, I remember him,
he left four days ago." Not till much later does she learn what
happened. The photographer was responsible for selection for
transport. First the "intellectuals" were sorted out from the
"manual laborers"; the latter were to be sent back home since
there were no trains or trucks around. But first the Jews in
the group were separated out; they would not be sent home.
Her mother was with the Jews. Her father said, "Then I am
going too." "By all means, if you like," said the photographer,
and made note of the Baron Weiss, the only non-Jew to go
along of his own free will, so to speak. But then the women
were separated from the men immediately. Her father ended
up at Flossenburg, doing hard labor; he was killed there in
December 1944. Her mother was sent to Ravensbrück; she
was too weak to work. She died on January 12, 1945.

Sonia and the student left the photographer and started off for Budapest. In the next town there was a great hue and cry; she had strange premonitions and nearly fainted, without knowing why; then she heard that they were having a "Jew drive." She wanted to look among the people for her parents, but the student pulled her away: "Your parents have been gone four days." Sonia knew this, but the thought that she had somehow passed her parents by as they were being taken away never left her. The student accompanied her as far as Budapest and brought her to her sisters.

Later she heard about a position as chambermaid to the Archduchess Stephanie, the widow of Crown Prince Rudolf (she had married a Lonyai and now, age eighty, lived in the Orosvar Castle). "Her Royal Highness" wanted to emigrate to Switzerland and wanted a chambermaid who spoke languages to take along. Sonia made herself known to her, but the old lady didn't understand why she wanted the position. Sonia confided in her and found empathy: "She was not an anti-Semite." A week later Sonia started work; most of the castle was occupied by German soldiers, and she had to pass the sentry point. "That's sure no chambermaid." She pretended not to know German and got through. She was gradually trained in her duties by the archduchess, but already by the fifth day she had been entrusted with her mistress's wig; from then on she was indispensable. They were busy making preparations for the journey to Switzerland when the old lady had a stroke, and that was the end of travel plans. A German staff medical officer visited her "Highness"; he went up to Sonia and declared, "You're no maid! Who are you? I want to help you!"

Sonia trusted him and told him her whole story. He told her that she was the subject of talk among the German soldiers in the castle, that they thought she was a Jew in hiding. He could help her only if he could say she was his lover. She agreed to this. He behaved honorably; in the course of the next week he confessed to her that he loved her. He was around fifty, married, he had children but his wife did not understand him. When the Russians came, the Germans vacated the cas-

tle; he wanted to stay for her sake, if she would agree to marry
him later. They discussed the idea at length and came to the
decision that he could not stay. He left, and she stayed behind,
in great consternation.

As the Russians approached, a priest (a Benedictine who
happened to be at the castle) gathered all the women and
girls, to wall them in (and thus protect them from the Russian
soldiers). But Sonia had to stay with the archduchess. The
Russians arrived, and on hearing that an old princess was living
in the castle, they wanted to have a look at her. They were
expected any minute in the old lady's sickroom, and to save
Sonia the priest hit upon the idea of having her hide in the
old lady's bed. Still clothed she crawled under the covers and
squeezed up against the wall. Now came the parade of Russians; one after the other they filed politely by the bed of
the "princess" and looked at her curiously. While they were
plundering all over the castle, here in the room of the "princess" they touched nothing. The priest received them all and
did the honors, so to speak. They did not touch him; it was
simply not true that the Russians were after aristocrats, priests
or other Hungarians. They were looking only for German soldiers and, when they were drunk, for women.

After they had left the sickroom, she thought she was saved.
But when night came, she heard a drunken Russian in the
courtyard below. He was yelling that he knew the chambermaid was there, hiding in the bed of the "princess." He came
upstairs, she squeezed more tightly against the wall, she heard
his steps approaching, all at once he pulled the covers from
off the archduchess, and she saw a machine gun pointed at
her. In her shock she forgot everything that had gone before,
even the name of the German staff doctor, and in the seventeen
years since, she has wracked her brain for his name in vain,
unable to remember it again. She got up from the bed and
followed the Russian, the whole time under threat of the machine gun. Now I have only two choices, she thought to herself,
to die or to give in. Suddenly in the long corridor the roll
call started. Fighting was still going on: the Russian left her
standing there and ran to his unit. Russians could plunder

and take women, but when the roll call was read, they had to obey instantly or be shot. So she was saved; a miracle, said the father, a true miracle.

She stayed a while longer at the castle; Archduchess Stephanie's condition went rapidly downhill. The priest bought a horse for Sonia, and she rode for four days to Budapest. During those four days the value of the horse increased tenfold. She sold it immediately on arriving, and here she was lucky, for two hours later she would not have been able to sell it. From this windfall her two sisters lived for six months. That was what I heard of her story. Much more would have followed, but it had gotten so late I had to stop, and she had to go to bed. I have told only the most important parts, and in abbreviated form, and the story has lost all its color. When I visit her in Paris, I hope to hear more.

Interpreting a statement's meaning — all that remains of the tradition of consulting oracles. But since this takes place outside the scope of fear, not even that is left.

One book! Three-fourths of your life is there — your hope, your pleasure, your melancholy, your sorrow and your doubt. All of that you have now lost. Where are you? What is left of you? The crater your book left.

Yesterday this story of a young German woman's search for her father's remains. Her mother, brother, boyfriend and she drive from northern Germany to Collioure in Roussillon, on the Spanish border, where her father, who had been called up toward the end of the war into the field corps, was captured and died. He was taken to a prison camp in February 1945 and died at the end of the year. He did not know what had happened to his family, and vice versa. Late in 1946 they received a card saying, "Décédé." Four years later, from Paris, someone sent them his briefcase with scraps of paper on which he had occasionally written notes. On his daughter's birthday he had embossed her name on a piece of metal; she was nine then. The four traveled to Collioure in 1957 and looked up one of his prison guards. North of Perpignan they also found the cemetery where more than five hundred German prisoners of war were buried. There was his grave and his name. He had never previously traveled farther than Bavaria, where he had hiked on the Zugspitze with his wife. His imprisonment was his only foreign southern vacation.

The young woman now has an eleven-month-old child, and she keeps the scrap of metal that her father embossed with her name hidden in her home. She hardly dares to look at it and has hidden it so well that all of a sudden she will forget where she put it and will live in mortal fear that it is lost. At which point she conducts a complete search of her entire, very large apartment; on finding it, she immediately hides it again.

With friends we should keep an old-fashioned kind of distance, as if the telephone did not exist.

The people we don't miss we have seen too much of; there's nothing more to be done about it.

He sank three times, but to no avail—no one saw him. The fourth time he stayed up and no one saw him then either.

My friends showed me everything, their entire history, from the cloister at the university in Bangor, where they met, to the little registry office in Bala, where they got married, to the village houses where Eirwen lived during the war, waiting for her husband's leave, to the country road where one late night, extremely pregnant, she got caught in a thunderstorm.

The ancient farm of their friends who spoke English only with effort. The clock inside always an hour ahead. The eighty-year-old farmer, hands spotted with paint, coming home after nine from a sheepshearing at a neighboring farm. He had worked all day; they had shorn a thousand sheep.

Earlier, at supper, his son-in-law tells stories, with the emphasis of a Japanese actor; he has a face like a fox, but his eyes are piercing and kindly like those of a saint.

His exceedingly fat wife runs out of the kitchen, in rapid succession tosses various dishes onto the table, and before the guest has quite finished what was on his plate, hops up, insisting clumsily in her high-pitched voice that he help himself right away, eat, eat.

Afterwards she hauls out of the top drawer photographs that show the family members in all combinations. We are expected to become friends with each picture.

Her husband, who is missing both his thumbs, puts on his cap and disappears to fetch the old man, who is still at work. After a while he brings him in, a sturdy man with a mustache: he makes me think of pictures of old Georgian men; will he get to be 120 as well? He deserves to.

The couple's young son, his grandson William, slender and dark, comes into the house, so now we have a short visit with the whole family. Even the boy speaks broken English, or does it just sound that way?

The whole family walks with us across a few fields, asking us quite formally to come again, even me, the foreigner, and everyone waves a long time.

Don't say it's too late: how can you know you don't still have thirty years to begin a new life? Don't say it's too early: how can you know that you won't be dead in a month and that other people won't fashion lives for themselves out of the ruins of yours?

A man whom I had been avoiding used to go about on three words. The fourth was gone, but he enjoyed limping. He got around better than if he were whole. Sometimes he would sit at the roadside fixing and cleaning things. If one of his words gave him trouble, he put it in his mouth. Once a dog bit him in his best word, but its rabies did no harm; the other two words were afraid, though. This is the state I found him in. I heard a word foaming at the mouth and stopped in my tracks, and soon this wreck was at my side. The owner politely asked me for help. I took it on my shoulder and couldn't get rid of it again. Now I am carrying the three words that carry him—I hear them whining for alms.

He had a lover whom he visited only after funerals. She liked him then. "You are so different after funerals," she would say to him, "you love me more passionately. I don't like you any other way." She would read the obituaries for him and notify him by phone when she thought he should go. Right off, she would say, "Do you know who died?" Sometimes he wouldn't have heard from her for three or four weeks. "Who?" "N.N. You knew him. You'd better go." "What time?" "Monday at three in the crematorium. I'll expect you then." She would immediately feel better when she had found a funeral for him and would get everything ready for his visit. He went, saw and heard for himself, and he actually liked going, because he knew what was coming next. But he was not a cynic, or else the funerals would not have upset him. He thought about the deceased, he pictured him or her to himself, carried on old conversations with the person. The dead got to him so much that without cheering up he could scarcely have gone on living. Bent and aged, he would start off for her house. She would be standing behind the curtain and would see him on the street. Throwing the door open, she would say, "Welcome!" She would always wear something that reminded him of the special occasion, something small and quite discreet, but he always noticed it gratefully.

"Come," she would say, "you are exhausted. It's really taken a lot out of you." He would nod, come in and sit down, a bit timidly, in the best chair. She would sit near him but maintain a certain distance. "Tell me! Was it very bad? Maybe you'd rather not talk about it." "Not for a while," he would say—it seemed better that way. After all, he was no monster, he had feelings, he had to take a little breather before admitting to himself that life would go on. "Don't take it to heart so," she would say, with tears in her eyes: she was suffering with him. He was grateful for every move that demonstrated her understanding and concern. "Did it take a long time?" she would ask then. "Not especially. Luckily it was short. I don't like ceremony. It's such a terribly difficult thing in any case. You think you'll break down if it doesn't stop soon." "How was the minister?" "Not bad. Quite short and sweet. Afterwards he stood by the door and shook everyone's hand. I always wonder whether to give him something." "But you can't do that." "He has this way of holding out his hand. I think he could hide it well enough that nobody would notice." "Were there a lot of flowers?" "Mountains, but not as many as last time." "Must be beautiful, all those flowers." "Sometimes there are none, by request." "Yes, I remember. Time before last when you were here there were no flowers." "You have a good memory." "I only live for you. I share all your troubles with you." "That's true. I just don't know how I could go to funerals without you." "I hope you never do." "How could I deceive you?" "Sometimes I think you were someplace without telling me." "But you read all the notices. You don't miss a single one." "I'm not infallible. If I don't see you for six weeks, I think I must have missed something." "Hopefully you read more than one paper." "Sure, of course, but there are people who don't put a notice in the paper." "Then I wouldn't know about it either." "Do you get any private notices at home?" "I throw out anything with a black border. I leave everything up to you. Without you I'd be lost." After this little jealous scene, which he is used to and which only follows funerals, he puts out his right hand and clasps her knee.

To be more precise about the nature of *invention*: I think it always depends on your *starting point*. There do exist such things as the "germs" of invention; I know them and know they are irresistible. But I am not sure whether they differ from person to person or whether there is some kind of general supply of these "germs" that move all people everywhere to tell stories.

It is important to find belief, but in order to find belief, we must ourselves believe what we have invented. We can know very well that we are making something up and yet believe it all the same. The sensation of expansion that we

feel must be true, like another way of breathing, if we are to
believe what we bring forth.

To be believable, the story must first of all arouse our astonishment: only the astounding will be believed. Anything
obvious or everyday cannot be a story; since it doesn't arouse
our astonishment, it is not believed.

Invention is one of my most natural states of being, so it is
time I tried to define precisely what is involved in it.

Nothing is more crippling for the inventive person than the
presence of someone who is always asking; "And is it true?"
The question arises out of the listener's closed world, which his
fearfulness keeps him from leaving; he sticks to his own gut.

More than anything else, an inventor cannot abide people
who are unable to forget their own guts. He avoids them like
the plague.

The real creator gets bolder with age. He has more invention
germs within him; in the course of his life they have
multiplied. Of course, the danger for him is that he will be
embarrassed to astonish or will be ashamed of showing his
embarrassment. He is expected to know everything; nothing
should be new for him or the general opinion of idiots will
be that he hasn't experienced enough.

But the truth is that the more one has experienced, the
more there is to be astonished by. Our capacity for wonder
grows with experience, becomes more urgent.

— *translated from the German*
by John Hargraves

Two Poems by Marilyn Hacker

Broceliande

for Marie-Geneviève Havel

Yes, there is a vault in the ruined castle.
Yes, there is a woman waking beside the
gleaming sword she drew from the stone of childhood:
hers, if she bore it.

She has found her way through the singing forest.
She has gotten lost in the maze of cobbled
streets in ancient towns, where no lovely stranger
echoed her language.

Sometimes she inhabits the spiring cities
architects project out of science-fiction
dreams, but she illuminates them with different
voyages, visions:

with tomato plants, with the cat who answers
when he's called, with music-hall lyrics, work-scarred
hands on a steering wheel, the jeweled secret
name of a lover.

Here, the water plunges below the cliff-face.
Here, the locomotive purrs in the station.
Here, beneath viridian skies, a window
glistens at midnight.

Invocation

This is for Elsa, also known as Liz,
an ample-bosomed gospel singer: five
discrete malignancies in one full breast.
This is for auburn Jacqueline, who is
celebrating fifty years alive,
one since she finished chemotherapy
with fireworks on the fifteenth of July.
This is for June, whose words are lean and mean
as she is, elucidating our protest.
This is for Lucille, who shines a wide
beam for us with her dark cadences.
This is for long-limbed Maxine, astride
a horse like conscience. This is for Aline
who taught her lover to caress the scar.
This is for Eve, who thought of AZT
while hopeful poisons pumped into a vein.
This is for Nanette in the Midwest.
This is for Alicia, shaking back dark hair,
dancing one-breasted with the Sabbath bride.
This is for Judy on a mountainside,
plunging her gloved hand in a glistening hive.
Hilda, Patricia, Gaylord, Emilienne,
Tania, Eunice: this is for everyone
who marks the distance on a calendar
from what's each year less likely to "recur."
Our saved-for-now lives are life sentences
—which we prefer to the alternative.

Three Poems by Sidney Wade

Drinking Wine on a Hill Above the Confluence of the Bosphorus and the Golden Horn

High above the congregation of the laminated waters,
muscular and clear, that deeply and to great

effect reverse themselves in diurnal, layered turnings,
that lap between the Marmara, a heaving marble sea,

and the glassy Euxine, twice a day, at least,
the "cow ford," Io's refuge from the torment of the fly,

the Bosphorus, the blue veneer that "with one key"
says Gyllius, "opens and closes two worlds, two seas,"

and the black and stinking Golden Horn, where sludge
flourishes in sun, where black enamels all the piers

and boats and anchor ropes, where potent Ottoman fleets
once harbored, *Chrysokeras* (O gilded name), where
    subterfuge

bubbled up in darkness more than once to author
the splendid fall of fabled empire—up here, at night,

one scans the expanse of civil lights to try to see
what lies beneath the sheets, the film, the fine

and stratified detritus of significant events
to refine the figures, exfoliate the press of things,

to clarify the confluence of vessel and vexation
as the ferries skim the surfaces, as drops slip down the glass.

Bronze Dogs

Off Istiklal and up a winding street,
a dealer in antiques displays a pair
of dogs—enormous, placid, seated, bronze.
They frame the door which opens on a store
of artifice, of calm device to cheat
the past, which never dies. An étagère
reveals a wheel from Egypt, also bronze,
which purifies the soul, and a golden score
of vessels for the dying generations.
The dogs are blind and beautiful. A violet
moment hovers overhead, the evening
shadows fill with figured intimations.
O talismans, allusive amulets,
protect us from the dreadful closing in.

Dolphins in the Snow

Lines and sheets of white are blown, light conjugations,
in layered, flustered carousels and large

and hissing plates that skim and feint and charge
the pewter, mildly rolling scintillation

of the surface. Dolphins punctuate
the veneer, their dorsal fins appearing slow

and smooth, in cursive, off the starboard bow.
The light is thin and perishing and late.

These "incomparable wandering voices," these gray
and graceful constructs of another language

correspond in gloss, and passengers surround
the rails to scan the ample waterway

for signs, for the filaments of lineage
to something resonant, fluent and profound.

Carol Vanderveer Hamilton

Narcolepsy

> *Look, there is the sky, and here is the grass.*
> —Herman Melville

I

The sky flashes past us while we sleep,
deep in our beds, drowning,

cello-shaped in our linen sheets,
hands like petals on the pillows.

This morning we were ablaze,
breathing the foul light that streamed

through skyscrapers and subways,
rattling the coins in our pockets.

Someday I'd like to wake up forever from

the dreams I abjure,
toss on my railroad trestle, fall

past all recovery
into millions of loose stars, like dimes

freed from profit and exchange.

II

He was perplexed by all financial transactions,
could not recall his ATM number,

and arrived at the airport without his luggage
but left anyway — and never returned.

We remember him on Fridays, at the corner,
watching the kids play ball and whistling

Alle Menschen werden Brüder.

"You're all expendable," our boss tells us
when he catches us staring out the window

at the Goodyear blimp, or tracing
the Cape of Good Hope with a dazed finger.

And we are. I have been dead
since I first sat down in my cubicle, staring

at this screen in which I could not
see my face.

III

I could have lived in the suburbs

and read best-sellers, but instead
I play fugues on the glass harmonica in the subway

while accountants and receptionists
rush past me, their ticket stubs

tucked behind their ears.

The dead hold out their hands, imploring,
but impatient we brush past them.

We have nothing more to say to them,
except in our sleep; they are

tourists waiting at a bus stop
when the drivers are on strike.

I know where I am.
I feel like flotsam on a beach, detritus.

Then those postcards arrive
from born-again boroughs, threatening
that the world will end any minute.

If only it would.

Clayton Eshleman

Giverny

Nasturtium surplus.
     Water curls and lilies,
lily water. Vermilion and orange
flower flow, nearly stemming
     Monet's path,
the great division between
painting things and painting sensation.
If Yeats awakes one day
this will all be virtual. Tender
     green salad of the earth.
  Water curls and willows,
     a maggot belches

below the tourists' feet

No noun used to be safe here

A few roses trellis overhead.

Mucilaginous quince.

Karl Kirchwey

Syracuse

If you're thinking of going to Syracuse,
   be modest and do not expect
the bronze warriors of Reggio
   to blink at the prospect
with their limestone eyes,
or to whistle high-low
   through their silver teeth.
   There will be no one to go with,
because you decided suddenly
   on this trip. Friends won't change their plans.
Are you sure you won't be lonely?
   It often happens.

If you are still determined,
   remember that the Pensione Edelweiss
in Taormina won't give you a room
   for one night, even if there's space.
They will be insistent and bland
and sympathetic. You will hate them,
   as you climb back into your small
   underpowered vehicle.
Others will crowd, flash and swerve,
   pass you with a curse and a gesture
on a hill, in a tunnel, on a curve
   of a highway which is there and not there.

When you get to Catania,
   lava-cobbled and lava-corniced,
it will feel like a city in Hell.
   You will water the stones with your sweat
on a day of thick haze and humidity,

and Etna permanently invisible.
   Birds in cages and an idiot child singing
   will keep you awake all night long,
and though this is only a place
   on the way to your true destination,
you may feel, red-eyed and morose,
   discommoded and tense, that it is an omen.

At last you will arrive
   in the fabled city and find it dying,
sister, in its day, to Athens,
   swans and fish sluggish among
papyrus where Arethusa the nymph
once fled Alpheus; and the idea that the fountain's
   waters and the ocean's never mix
   is a fabulation of ancient hydraulics,
you will conclude, as you sit
   before a *granita di limone* in the square
when the waiter has fiercely knit
   his brows at your accent and your order.

And the disillusionment won't stop there.
   You won't get in to see *The Burial of Saint Lucy*—
in fact, no one will even tell you where she is.
   You will shuttle about looking ludicrously
for that throat, hacked as if by a serial killer,
then toned down. Truth will rise to the surface
   in your mind like a pentimento
   in the late work of Caravaggio.
Two brutes with their gleaming shovels
   in a slurry of shit-colored light
are digging a grave for your travels.
   Of course you won't like it.

In this place that knows no day without sun,
   you may begin to feel quite dark.
You may feel you are being laughed at
   by the little contorted terra cotta

temple antefix of a gorgon
face which you recently bought;
   and as for beauty, the citrus
   orchards, green in limestone quarries,
don't remember the bones of the army
   which perished there of exposure
because of hubris and treachery,
   so this shouldn't trouble you, either.

You may feel that life is all irony,
   Plato sold in the market for a slave
by a tyrant, the elder Dionysius;
   but really he ought not to have
come to Syracuse, so convinced was he
of the superiority of ideas to practice.
   But you don't have that problem—
   or at least you won't by the time
you depart, if, after all,
   you do. You won't be wrong to go
to Syracuse, that city of fable.
   Remember you were warned, though.

Three Poems by Timothy Liu

Action Painting

A canvas we cannot stretch across the frame
nor staple down to fact: a ladder leaning

against an awning, workers pitching tar
on the roof of a church packed each week

with swine — a chain of pearls dangling
off the limbs of an artificial tree

where boy scouts gather in a tool shack,
jacking off to the sounds of Perry Como

on a karaoke machine — a televised priest
gesticulating wildly at the pulpit again.

Against Nature

Those bottled fruit flies in Bethesda
(darlings of genetic research
    for nearly a century) waste no time
        in getting down to business —
    laboratory love now gone awry
(Ward Odenwald and Shang-Ding Zhang
    bewildered at the males in circles
        who start to link up end-to-end
    with a frenzy once reserved for females —
winged conga lines parading
    inside those gallon-size culture jars,

the buzz of homo love songs
filling the air)—a single gene spliced
into this scene responsible
for findings later published—a stretch
of DNA on human X
chromosomes said to affect our sexual
orientation according to
the NIH whose flies may offer clues
to the biochemical roots
of lust—the Rev. Louis P. Sheldon,
president of the Traditional
Values Coalition, already crying out
for "reparative therapy"
to correct those defects nature has left
undone (the amino acid
tryptophan wreaking havoc on the lives
of flies), serotonin levels
in the blood of Gorski's rats leading
to a study on human brains—
diomorphic nuclei left in the hands
of Simon LeVay, the calculus
for the survival of our species
yet to be solved for straights or gays
while furor in the media erupts
into churches across the country—
genetic tests to abort "abnormal"
fetuses the stuff of science
fiction (for now) while flies and rats
continue to get it on and on—

His Anus as Ventriloquist

"Your glance disrupts my ease, faces
painted onto asymmetric Asmat shields
   imported from Irian Jaya—
      relics to avenge those refugees
   hunted down by Klansmen just off
the coast of Galveston—razor burns
   round nipples nicked by double blades
      that attempt to resettle the body's
   wilderness. Another rice queen
nursing at my breast—that conquistador
   whose milk-toast smile noses into
      my ass meat's sweet abyss as natives beat
   their drums, navigating canoes
downriver in search of sago palm and game,
   the harpoon's arc zeroing in
      on some object of desire kneeling
   beside an ivory bowl—memory
now baiting us all with water-logged pages
   from a book fished out of the sea."

The Great Flood

Jane Avrich

The waters swept the East Coast from Maine to Florida.
Hourly broadcasts informed us that land was breaking off at
an alarming rate. In some places the coastline had regressed
to the Appalachians, sinking into the sea in chocolate-red
chunks. Heads of families invested in nautical compasses, diving gear and water wings in assorted sizes and colors. I took
to wearing my bathing cap at all times; other women chopped
off their hair entirely, fearful of strangulation. No one was
safe. Even the pool players who, days ago, had barely deigned
to glance at us in our wet suits, now flung their cue balls and
eight balls up in the air in a great black and white geyser and
fled in terror from the rushing spume. The few who thought
to clamber up the skyscrapers were found huddling in satellite
dishes, shivering in their jackets of soggy green felt. "Did you
think love would be easy?" I asked Hector who stood behind
me, his chin resting on my shoulder. Chess pieces lay strewn
around us, covered with algae and sea acorns. "I was naive,"
he murmured and nibbled my ear.

Since Saturday, Hector and I had been working for the
Flotsam and Jetsam Relief Unit, and if we outstripped all other

damage-control organizations it was because our methods bordered on militancy. We were neat and efficient, were well-oiled as seals; we could click our heels and pivot at a moment's notice. But our task was no easy one. Conditions in the city had gone from primitive to feral. There were no blankets to be had; waffle irons were a thing of the past. Looters and pillagers swarmed the city in droves. In the jewelry district, they grabbed tiaras by the handful and placed them rapturously on the heads of collies. Black pearls were dropped, fizzing, into glasses of anisette; toasts were made. With diamonds as big as herne's eggs, they scratched their names, tags, tic-tac-toe and hopscotch grids on a variety of surfaces — glass, pewter, chrome, steel and its various alloys. Walls, windows, escalators were shattered, the moving steps thundering down in blocks. In the garment district they made off with bonnets and tallises; in the plant district, ferns. Perhaps hardest hit was the poultry district. Youths were stuffing chickens, geese, loons under their greatcoats and running amok. Rumors, circulated by reliable sources, told of drumsticks and ostriches, of unsuspecting pigeons who were snatched from their statues and made into ladies' hats. "The time is now," I nodded to Corporal Spigot and leapt into the Hudson. I emerged with twins, one in each hand, and proceeded in the prescribed manner to shake them vigorously by the heels of their Oxfords, already puckering from the wet, and empty them of all they had swallowed. Beer cans, sea glass, variegated handkerchiefs, car parts, funnels and baby peas spilled out pell-mell, forming a pile so large that our packet boat sunk under the weight and we were forced to swim to shore. All around us the purple-veined blood coral grew in spreading stalks. I splashed like an otter, draped kelp on my breasts. I was a girl, an eel, a slippery nymphet. I waved to the dolphins that danced above and below me. And the more I dared to desire, the more I desired to dare.

Hector glided toward me, a sea anemone between his teeth, ready to tango. "My love is a rebel bird," he crooned. "She is eyes without a face, she is a limpid pool, she is a newspaper boat, she is baba au rhum."

"And mine is a fig leaf, a spool of spun flax."

"A trundle, a bundle, a categorical imperative."

"A crash of cymbals on a starry night."

"The sun never sets on my lady's buttocks." He was up close now, forehead pressed to mine.

"Nor rises in the shadows of my lord's downcast eyes."

There were different explanations for the flood. Meteorologists, millenarians, psychics and epistemologists all had their theories and were invited to colleges and talk shows where they were plied with rarebit and wine. Carpetbaggers and sponge-throwers conferred in back alleys; charcoal-browed beauticians stopped tending their tea roses to give out free samples and advice. Shampoo coursed in the gutters in still white peaks until it was sucked gurgling into the sewer. People thought it was a sign. But it is you who know the truth, know it as well as I do, you who hold my beating wrists as the tide crashes and spanks the shore. It is you whose eyes, concerned and dark, follow my spreading fingers and spreading hair. It is you whose words are always polite, always inflected, and even as the highways tumble like ribbons and the cars slide like beads into the sea, it is your tender fingertips that touch away my tears. I turned to Corporal Spigot. "What do you recommend?" I shouted, for the air was slipping into a vortex in the sky and the clouds had turned soupy gray; and while I am no meterologist, I know a tornado when I see one. It had been brewing for months, caused by inclement westerly winds, car exhaust and the wavy, ambivalent motions the go-go dancers had been making with their hands.

"The situation is tenuous," Corporal Spigot barked back. "The roots will not hold. Neglect and ridicule have weakened the foundation of critical land masses, namely North and South America. Already the Florida Keys have broken away and are drifting toward Portugal. They will arrive one at a time."

Armed with crates, barrels and pepper mills, we scoured the city. I was a woman with a mission. I knew I could take nothing for granted — not liberty, erotica, cheese, grouts, specialty shops or Naugahyde. Evacuation was the word of the day.

It was the word on people's lips as they bit into persimmons. It was the word whose syllables, vowels and flayed, spangled consonants were carried by the wind, the rain, by the hopeful blasts of aerosol sprays that pumped pine and potpourri into our bland gray air. And the more I dared to desire, the more I desired to dare. By the busload and without discrimination, we collected cardiologists, housewives and shoe-shine boys and sent them to where the earth was solid — New Zealand, Cape Hatteras, Tierra del Fuego. "In regions such as these, the sediment, rich with ore and fossils, is lodged firm," explained Professor A____, a small potato-bellied woman with shiny cheeks and flippers who, for reasons I can neither disclose nor comprehend, was known to us as Alma the Aquatic Animal. "These are the sites of mastodon burial grounds, oily with molasses and musk. These are places that will not crumble nor fritter away, places for our tired and our poor, our aged and our young, our lapdogs and pack animals, to dwell in safety."

On the Avenue of the Americas I found Hector filling his pockets with small luxury items wrapped in foil. "Look at the snug snug corners and the shiny, dapper sides!" he sang, turning one in the sunlight so as to lose himself in an ecstasy of metallic flashing. I had seen this before. "Hush, gypsy boy," I hissed and laid my finger on his lips; Hector had the tastes of a crow. In times of leisure, he used to stud my dresses with pocket mirrors and twirl me about like a disco ball. But that was then and now was now. Bailey and his diving corps had sent us long, sifting ticker tape reports to the effect that the sea had become uneven. There were advantages and disadvantages to this. On one hand, it was almost impossible to find smelts. On the other, new tide pools were there for the wading. Crampp found the wreck of a Spanish Man of War, complete with streaming-haired skulls, amethyst brooches, gold pieces strewn casually on the ocean floor, a mermaid whose flowing hair and painted wooden eyeballs recalled to me your maiden aunt and a Grand Inquisitor who, with a sweeping bow and flourish of his pearl-encrusted saber, introduced himself as Don Pedro del Gato y Cigarillo y Paella. I did not have time to answer his questions about metallurgy — the newfangled methods were far too numerous, too brittle — but I listened for a while to his discourse on torture, the rat, the hangnail and the oatmeal methods being, in his opinion, the most persuasive. In my opinion, he was merely flirting. He curled his mustachios, the two big and the two small and finally all four at once, producing a strumming sound not unlike a zither's. "Life is a lackluster cesspool," he declared. "Only zeal can keep us pure."

"And turpentine?"

"Turpentine," he murmured, caressing the heads of his rosary beads pensively and one by one, "has its charm, I concede you, my fierce and lovely cross-examiner, my minx, my sphinx, my pet. But like the Lutherans, it is shallow. You can stir it, but ultimately, it does not stipple."

I could take nothing for granted, I reminded myself. Rivulets of glacial runoff were trickling through the chinks between the skyscrapers. A unicycle boy — a rare sight these days, cowlicks and short pants having gone out of fashion — slapped a newspaper at my feet; City Hall was eroding, one wet brick at a time. In the Museum of Natural History the stuffed stags and bison had expanded on account of the moisture, they said, drastically, they said, until they burst without warning from their glass cases, terrorizing the chestnut vendors. The situation was critical. I brushed and flossed, changed channels and selected alternative routes for reduction, baking and paraphernalia. Crampp came with blueprints and flowcharts. After I had a chance to peruse them, licking my index finger as I turned the pages, he disclosed a plan which started with a rash assortment of soap flakes and ended with saffron and chintz. Before I could comment, the unicycle boy alerted me to an assortment of smoke signals shaped like a funnel, a rabbit and a copy of *Das Kapital*. There was plenty to do: there were life rafts, parasols and farfel for the counting; there were chicken bones and boluses, freshly disgorged. But even these lose their allure when I see you, my love, my buttonhole, my dream of green. It is you who find music, halvah and telephones, not just one but an entire assortment, and you bring them in boxes wrapped up in string. It is you with your horned-rimmed glasses forgotten for days on your forehead, it is your papers I long to smooth and your hair and the lines in your face. I struck Hector with a spatula. "Give up the goat," I whispered, chewing the starch in his cuffs. "We are meant for each other, you and I."

"Drainage is all," he replied. "Then we can clean house and gather pigeons, dice and spittle to our hearts' content."

"And marsh gas, too?"

"And marsh gas, too."

I climbed on his shoulders so I could kiss him on the forehead, leaving a star-shaped mark as only I knew how, but he had already released his parachute and was coursing away, hair, legs and arms streaming in the wind. I sprinkled confetti, Q-tips, crushed ice. I remember snatches of song from my days as a Catholic schoolgirl, as a cocktail waitress, as a mistress of ceremonies at a county fair. But that was then and now was now; the time had come to act. I knew it, the battalions knew it, the conquistadors knew it, even you, I maintain, you with your quips and glances, you with your games of jacks — you knew it too. I began to unwind the makeshift dam the concierges built out of safety pins, liver-colored bandages, chicken wire, nuts, bolts, hot crossed buns, funicular spinach truffles, Ajax bottles, pomade, locust jelly and playing cards that were red, ocher yellow, yellow with white spots, white with blue spots, plastic-coated, beveled or simply plaid. And the more I dared to desire, the more I desired to dare.

Wavelets scampered, grew, turned rabbit-like and fierce. They burst through the streets where bankers and barristers had strolled only a day before. They plunged down Nassau Street and Maiden Lane. They tore away stoplights, trash-can lids, candy-striped awnings with and without fringes. "Is this the end?" I asked Hector. "Have I caught you at last, like a kite?"

With a roar, the island city, its roots withered to a few mere threads, broke free. The El train halted, phone lines split; even the diehard members of the Thirteenth Rescue Unit grabbed their Stetsons and fled.

As we reached the shore in the final moments of the day, the last people were boarding the Intrepid and sailing off for Tanzania with bananas as their ancestors did so many years before them. I turned to my man Hector, for the wind had picked up, and with it, new decisions. "Here," I said; "here and now," he agreed, for this was our city, our island, our eyesore, and here we would stay, even if we were the last ones in the Western world. On the boat, the full-skirted women were crying and waving good-bye with their polka-dotted handkerchiefs; we waved back with our loofahs. I tore off my bathing cap and waved that, too, my hair streaming out like seaweed all around us.

"At last," breathed Alma the Aquatic Animal, her eyes growing moist as the boat finally vanished. "A meeting of two worlds, and no less."

Hector nudged me and pointed; dawn was breaking. We could just make out Cape Cod as it drifted out toward Greenland, a half-moon on the horizon.

NOTES ON CONTRIBUTORS

FICTION

Jane Avrich teaches English at Saint Ann's School in Brooklyn. Her fiction is forthcoming in *Harper's* and *Story*. This is her first published story.

Peter Matthiessen's new novel, *Lost Man's River*, is the second volume, after *Killing Mr. Watson*, of a planned trilogy about the life of E. J. Watson. He won the National Book Award in 1978 for *The Snow Leopard*. He is a founding editor of *The Paris Review*.

Rick Moody is the author of three novels: *Garden State, The Ice Storm* (a film version of which was released this fall) and *Purple America*. He received the 1994 Aga Khan Prize for Fiction from *The Paris Review* for the title novella in his collection *The Ring of Brightest Angels Around Heaven*.

Kate Walbert's first book, the short-story collection *Where She Went*, will be published in August 1998. She lives in New York and Connecticut, where she teaches creative writing at Yale.

David Foster Wallace is the author, most recently, of the novel *Infinite Jest* and a collection of essays, *A Supposedly Fun Thing I'll Never Do Again*.

FEATURES

Aldo Buzzi is the author of *Journey to the Land of the Flies*. Now eighty-three, he lives in Italy. **Ann Goldstein**'s translations include *Journey to the Land of the Flies* and Pier Pasolini's *Petrolio*.

Elias Canetti's (1905–1994) *Notes from Hampstead: The Writer's Notes 1954–1971* will be published by Farrar, Straus & Giroux next year. His translator, **John Hargraves**, is an assistant professor of German at Connecticut College.

POETRY

Michael Blumenthal's first novel, *Weinstock Among the Dying*, received the 1994 Harold U. Ribelow Fiction Prize from *Hadassah* magazine. He is also the author of five collections of poetry, most recently *The Wages of Goodness*.

Anne Babson Carter received the 1996 Intro Series in Poetry Award from Four Way Books, which will publish her first collection of poems, *Strike Root*.

Brad Davis received his MFA from Vermont College in 1995. He lives in Connecticut, where he is the chaplain and creative-writing teacher at Pomfret School.

Ben Downing interviewed Robert Pinsky for this issue.

Clayton Eshleman is the author, most recently, of *Nora's Roar* and the forthcoming *Scratch*. He teaches at Eastern Michigan University, where he edits *Sulfur*.

Marilyn Hacker is the author of eight books, including *Winter Numbers*, which in 1995 received a Lambda Literary Award and the Academy of American Poets/*The Nation* Lenore Marshall Prize. A collection of her translations of the French poet Claire Malroux was recently published.

Carol Vanderveer Hamilton's book on anarchism and modernism, *Dynamite: Anarchy and Modernist Aesthetics* is forthcoming. She teaches cultural studies and creative writing at Carnegie Mellon University.

Richard Kenney is the author of three books of poetry, most recently *The Invention of the Zero*. He lives in Seattle.

Karl Kirchwey's third book of poems, *The Engrafted Word*, will be published next year. He directs the Unterberg Poetry Center of the 92nd Street YMHA in New York City.

Kenneth Koch's most recent books of poetry are *On the Great Atlantic Rainway: Selected Poems 1950–1988* and *One Train*, for which he received the Bollingen Prize for Poetry in 1995 and the Bobbitt National Poetry Prize in 1996. The poem in this issue is from his new book, *Straits*, which will be published early next year.

Yusef Komunyakaa won the Pulitzer Prize for poetry in 1994 for *Neon Vernacular: New and Selected Poems*. His new collection, *Thieves of Paradise*, will be published next year. He teaches at Princeton University.

Timothy Liu's books of poems are *Vox Angelica, Burnt Offerings* and the forthcoming *Say Goodnight*. He lives in Iowa.

Joanie Mackowski is a poet and juggler living in Seattle.

Corey Marks's poems appear in such magazines as *The Antioch Review*, *New England Review* and *Raritan*. He lives in Houston.

Deborah Pease has published three volumes of poetry and four chapbooks. Her poems have appeared in such magazines as *The Gettysburg Review*, *Agni* and *Chelsea*. A poem is forthcoming in *The New Yorker*. From 1982–1992 she was publisher of *The Paris Review*.

Maura Stanton's fourth book of poems, *Life Among the Trolls*, will be published next year. She teaches at Indiana University in Bloomington.

Terese Svoboda is the author of *Mere Mortals* and *Cannibal* and the recipient of the Holmes Bobst Emerging Writers Award. She lives in New York City.

Wisława Szymborska received the Nobel Prize for literature in 1997. Her translator, **Joanna Trzeciak**, is a doctoral student in Russian literature at the University of Chicago and is at work on a collection of her translations of Szymborska's poetry.

John Updike's most recent novel is *Toward the End of Time*.

Sidney Wade is the author of *Empty Sleeves*. She lives in Gainesville, Florida, where she teaches at the University of Florida.

David Yezzi's poems and reviews are forthcoming from *Parnassus, Verse, Boston Review* and other magazines. He is the associate editor of *The New Criterion*.

INTERVIEWS

Henri Cole (Seamus Heaney interview) is the author of three collections of poetry, most recently *The Look of Things*. He is Briggs-Copeland Lecturer in Poetry at Harvard.

Ben Downing (Robert Pinsky interview) is the managing editor of *Parnassus*.

Daniel Kunitz (Pinsky interview) is the managing editor of *The Paris Review*.

ART

Pierre Constanca is represented by the Holly Solomon Gallery in New York City.

Betsy Rosenwald lives in New York City.

Frank Yamrus's work appears courtesy of Sarah Morthland Gallery in New York City.

The Paris Review
Put-on

Only $15

THE PARIS REVIEW♦45-39 171 PLACE♦FLUSHING, NY 11358
White with black. Quantity: _____
small ❑ medium ❑ large ❑ extra large ❑
NAME...
ADDRESS..
CITY..
STATE...ZIP.....................................
MASTERCARD/VISA #_____EXP._____
PAYMENT MUST ACCOMPANY ORDER
(New York State residents please add tax.)

STATEMENT required by the act of August 24, 1912 as amended by the acts of March 3, 1933, and July 2, 1946. (Title 39, United States Code, Section 233) showing the ownership, management, and circulation of *THE PARIS REVIEW* published quarterly at Flushing, New York, 11358.

1. *Editor:* George Plimpton, *Managing Editor:* Daniel Kunitz, 541 East 72 Street, New York, N.Y. *Business Manager:* Lillian Von Nickern, 45-39 171st Place, Flushing, N.Y.

2. The owners are: George Plimpton, Harold H. Humes, Peter Matthiessen, Thomas H. Guinzburg. All c/o Plimpton, 541 E. 72 Street, NY, NY 10021.

3. The known bondholders, mortgages, and other security holders owning or holding 1 percent or more of total amounts of bonds, mortgages, or other securities are: None.

4. Paragraphs 2 and 3 include, in cases where the stock holder or security holder appears upon the books of the company as trustee or in any other fiduciary relation, the name of the person or corporation for whom such trustee is acting; also the statements in the two paragraphs show the affiant's full knowledge and belief as to the circumstances and conditions under which the stock holders and security holders who do not appear upon the books of the company as trustees, hold stocks and securities in a capacity other than that of a bona fide owner.

5. Extent and nature of circulation: Average number of copies each issue during preceding 12 months (actual number of copies of single issue published nearest to filing date):

Total/number copies (Average): 10,452 (11,295 ¼) Paid and/or requested circulation (Sales through dealers and carriers, street vendors and counter sales): 6,065 (6,008 ¼) Mail Subscription: 2,871 (2,801) Free distribution by mail, carrier, or other means, samples, complimentary, and other free copies: 446 (484 ½). Total Distribution: 9,382 (9,293 ¾). Copies not distributed (office use, left over, unaccounted, spoiled after printing): 1,010 (1,259 ¾). Copies not distributed (return from news agents): 60 (741 ¾). Total: 10,452 (11,295 ¾).

Marjorie Kalman, Notary Public, State of New York
No. 4955336
Qualified in New York County
Commission Expires August 28, 1997

—Daniel Kunitz
Managing Editor

The Paris Review
Booksellers Advisory Board

Available now from the Flushing office
BACK ISSUES OF THE PARIS REVIEW

No.		
18	Ernest Hemingway Interview; Giacometti Portfolio; Philip Roth Fiction.	$25.00
25	Robert Lowell Interview; Hughes Rudd, X. J. Kennedy.	10.00
30	S. J. Perelman and Evelyn Waugh Interviews; Niccolo Tucci, 22 poets.	10.00
35	William Burroughs Interview; Irvin Faust, Leonard Gardner, Ron Padgett.	10.00
37	Allen Ginsberg and Cendrars Interviews; Charles Olson, Gary Snyder.	10.00
44	Creeley and I. B. Singer Interviews; James Salter, Diane di Prima.	15.00
45	Updike Interview; Hoagland Journal; Veitch, Brautigan, Padgett, O'Hara.	10.00
46	John Dos Passos Interview; Thomas M. Disch, Ted Berrigan, Kenneth Koch.	10.00
47	Robert Graves Interview; Ed Sanders, Robert Creeley, Tom Clark.	10.00
62	James Wright Interview; Joe Brainard, Christo Portfolio.	10.00
63	J. P. Donleavy and Steinbeck Interviews; Louis Simpson, Robert Bly.	10.00
64	Kingsley Amis and P. G. Wodehouse Interviews; Diane Vreuls, Thomas M. Disch.	10.00
66	Stanley Elkin Interview; Richard Stern, W. S. Merwin.	10.00
67	Cheever and Wheelock Interviews; Maxine Kumin, Aram Saroyan.	10.00
68	William Goyen Interview; John Updike, William Stafford.	10.00
69	Kurt Vonnegut Interview; William Burroughs, Ed Sanders, John Logan.	10.00
70	William Gass Interview; Peter Handke, William S. Wilson, Galway Kinnell.	10.00
72	Richard Wilbur Interview; Joy Williams, Norman Dubie.	10.00
73	James M. Cain and Anthony Powell Interviews; Dallas Wiebe, Bart Midwood.	10.00
74	Didion, Drabble and Oates Interviews; Vincente Aleixandre Portfolio; Max Apple.	10.00
75	Gardner, Shaw Interviews; Handke Journal; Dubus, Salter, Gunn, Heaney.	10.00
76	Ignatow, Levi, Rhys Interviews; Jean Rhys Memoir Louis Simpson.	10.00
77	Stephen Spender Interview; Mark Strand, Joseph Brodsky, Philip Levine.	10.00
78	Andrei Voznesensky Interview; Voznesensky/Ginsberg Conversation; Edie Sedgwick Memoir; T. Coraghessan Boyle, Tom Disch, Odysseus Elytis.	15.00
79	25th ANNIVERSARY: R. West Interview; Paris Review Sketchbook; Hemingway, Faulkner, Southern, Gass, Carver, Dickey, Schuyler, Gellhorn/Spender/Jackson Letters.	15.00
80	Barthelme, Bishop Interviews; Reinaldo Arenas, J. D. Salinger Feature.	10.00
81	T. Williams, P. Bowles Interviews; Wiebe, Atwood, Federman Fiction; Montale Poetry.	20.00
83	J. Brodsky, S. Kunitz Interviews; Gerald Stern/B. F. Conners Prize Poetry.	15.00
84	P. Larkin, J. Merrill Interviews; T. C. Boyle, Edmund White Fiction.	15.00
85	M. Cowley, W. Maxwell Interviews; H. Brodkey, Bill Knott Poetry.	15.00
87	H. Boll, Infante Interviews; Milosz, C. K. Williams Poetry.	10.00
88	Gordimer, Carver Interviews; Hill, Nemerov Poetry; McCourt, Davis Fiction.	10.00
89	James Laughlin, May Sarton Interviews; F. Bidart Poetry, Zelda Fitzgerald Feature.	10.00
90	John Ashbery, James Laughlin Interviews; C. Wright Poetry; E. Garber Fiction.	10.00
91	J. Baldwin, E. Wiesel Interviews; Morand, R. Wilson Fiction; Clampitt Poetry.	10.00
92	M. Kundera, E. O'Brien, A. Koestler Interviews; E. L. Doctorow Fiction.	10.00
93	30th ANNIV: Roth, Ionesco, Cortazar Interviews; Rush, Boyle Fiction; Brodsky, Carver Poetry.	15.00
97	Hollander, McGuane Interviews; Dickey, Kosinski Features; Dixon Fiction, Wright Poetry.	15.00
98	L. Edel, R. Stone Interviews; R. Stone Fiction; L. Edel Feature.	10.00
99	A. Robbe-Grillet, K. Shapiro Interviews; E. Tallent Fiction, D. Hall Poetry.	10.00
100	DOUBLE 100th: Hersey, Irving Interviews; Gordimer, Munro Fiction; Merrill, Milosz Poetry.	15.00
105	Calisher, Gaddis Interviews; B. Okri Fiction; A. Zagajewski Poetry.	15.00
106	35th ANNIV: Lessing, Yourcenar Interviews; C. Smith Fiction; Logue Poetry; Styron Feature.	15.00
108	A. Hecht, E. White Interviews; C. Baxter, J. Kauffman Fiction; S. Olds Poetry.	10.00
109	Mortimer, Stoppard Interviews; Burroughs, Minot Fiction; Mathews, Simic Poetry.	10.00
111	Fowles, Fugard, Spencer Interviews; Tucci, Gurganus Fiction; Proust, Rilke Translations.	10.00
112	Kennedy, Skvorecky Interviews; Malamud, Maspéro Fiction; Perec, Pinsky Poetry.	10.00
114	Sarraute, Settle Interviews; Matthiessen, P. West Fiction; F. Wright Poetry.	10.00
115	Murdoch, Stegner Interviews; Bass Fiction; Laughlin Poetry; Merwin Feature.	10.00
116	Angelou, Vargas Llosa Interviews; Perec Fiction; Ashbery Poetry; Stein Feature.	10.00
117	Atwood, Pritchett Interviews; R. Price, Stern Fiction; Kizer, Logue Poetry.	10.00
118	Bloom, Wolfe Interviews; Tolstaya Fiction; Ashbery Poetry; Carver, Burgess Features.	10.00
119	Grass, Paz Interviews; M. McCarthy Feature; DeMarinis Fiction; Bonnefoy, Hacker Poetry.	10.00
120	Hall, Morris Interviews; Milosz Feature; Brodkey, Mailer Fiction; Corn, Lasdun Poetry.	10.00
121	Brodkey, Price Interviews; D. Hall Feature; Minot, West Fiction; Z. Herbert Poetry.	10.00
122	Amichai, Simon Interviews; J. Merrill Feature; Konrád, Fiction; Montale, Zarin Poetry.	10.00
123	Mahfouz Interview; J. Scott Fiction; Ashbery, Sarton Poetry; Schwartz-Laughlin Letters.	10.00
124	Calvino, Paley Interviews; Grass, Johnson, Moore Fiction; Clampitt, Herbert Poetry.	10.00
125	Guare, Simon Interviews; Bass, Lopez Fiction; Hollander, Mazur Poetry.	10.00
126	Clampitt, Helprin Interviews; J. Williams, Eco Fiction; Goldbarth, Zarin Poetry.	10.00
127	Logue, Salter Interviews; Carroll, Shepard Fiction; Ammons, Swenson Poetry.	10.00
128	40th ANNIV: DeLillo, Morrison Interviews; Canin, García Márquez Fiction; Graham, Merwin Poetry; Cheever, Hemingway, Pound Documents.	15.00
129	Stafford Interview; J. Scott Fiction; Yenser Poetry; Salter, Trilling Features	10.00
130	Kesey, Snodgrass Interviews; Braverman, Power Fiction, Paz Poetry	10.00
131	Bonnefoy, Munro Interviews; Moody, Pritchard Fiction; Hacker, Merrill Poetry; Bishop-Swenson Letters.	10.00
132	Auchincloss, Gottlieb Interviews; Gass, Thon, West Fiction; Kinnell, Tomlinson Poetry; Kazin Feature.	10.00
133	Achebe, Milosz Interviews; Byatt, D'Ambrosio Fiction; Hirsch, Wagoner Poetry.	10.00
134	Hughes, Levi Interviews; Fischer, Schulman Fiction; Ammons, Kizer Poetry; Welty Feature.	10.00
135	Gunn, P.D. James, O'Brian Interviews; DeMarinis, Mayo, Prose Fiction; Rich, Wright Poetry	10.00
136	Humor: Allen, Keillor, Trillin Interviews; Barth, Boyle Fiction; Clifton, Updike Poetry; Bloom Feature.	30.00
137	Sontag, Steiner Interviews; Bass Fiction; Seshadri Poem; Russian Feature.	10.00
138	Screenwriting: Dunne, Price, Wilder Interviews; Díaz Fiction; Hecht Poetry; Southern Feature.	10.00
139	Ammons, Buckley, Cela Interviews; Davenport, Franzen Fiction; Kizer Poetry.	10.00
140	Ford, Oz Interviews; Butler, Eakins Fiction; Bidart, Olds Poetry; Cooper Feature.	10.00
141	Snyder, Vendler Interviews; New Fiction; New Poetry; Marquez Feature.	10.00
142	Theater: Mamet, Shepard, Wasserstein Interviews; McDonagh Play.	10.00
143	Le Carré, Morris Interviews; Oates, Powell, Smith Fiction; Merwin Poetry; Salter Feature.	10.00

Please add $3.00 for postage and handling for up to 2 issues; $4.75 for 3 to 5. Payment should accompany order. For orders outside the U.S. please double the shipping costs. Payments must be in U.S. currency. Prices and availability subject to change. **Address orders to: 45-39 171 Place, Flushing, N.Y. 11358**

MASTERCARD/VISA # _____ EXP. DATE _____

THE MOST HONORED LITERARY SERIES IN AMERICA
BEGINS ITS THIRD DECADE WITH ONE OF THE LARGEST SELECTIONS IN ITS HISTORY

THE 1997
PUSHCART
PRIZE BEST
OF THE
XXI SMALL
PRESSES

Edited by Bill Henderson
with the Pushcart Prize editors

*THE PUSHCART PRIZE XXI continues
as a testament to the flourishing
of American literature in our
small presses. Edited with the
assistance of over 200 distinguished contributing editors,
this volume is among the largest
in the history of the series
(69 selections from 44 presses).*

625 PAGES $29.50
HARDBOUND
JUST PUBLISHED

PUSHCART PRESS
P.O. Box 380
Wainscott, N.Y. 11975

"... a truly remarkable collection
of the finest small press poems,
essays, and short fiction."
BOOKLIST

"A surprising, vital collection that
should hearten all serious readers."
KIRKUS REVIEWS

"A fascinating peek at the vast
and largely hidden world of non-
commercial publishing."
TIME

"There is nothing else quite like
this labor of love... long may it
appear."
CHOICE

"Indispensable... Get it, read it,
lug it around with you; as always
this book is essential."
LIBRARY JOURNAL

"An exceptionally strong sampling
of contemporary writers."
NEW REPUBLIC

"Of all the anthologies that come
out each year, the one from the
Pushcart Press is perhaps the
single best measure of the state of
affairs in American literature today."
THE NEW YORK TIMES BOOK REVIEW

"There may be no better combina-
tion of overview, entertainment,
invention and play each year than
the Pushcart collections."
WORLD LITERATURE TODAY

"Of all the anthologies, Pushcart's
is the most rewarding."
CHICAGO TRIBUNE

You've heard about
SHENANDOAH
for years.
Why not subscribe today
and really get to know us?

(We'll send you a free 5" x 7" broadside featuring a complete poem
by a *Shenandoah* contributor to sweeten the deal!)

Betty Adcock, Neal Bowers, Fred Chappell, Philip Dacey, Brendan Galvin, Seamus Heaney, William ___, Andrew Hudgins, William Matthews, Jeanne Murray Wal___ ___rigley, Carolyn Kizer, Larry Rivers, Reynolds Price, John ___ ___icholas Delbanco, Kent Nelson, Margaret Gibson, A. Man___ ___ Rodney Jones, Charles Wright, Molly Best Ti___ ___orah Pope, David Borofka, Ruth Padel, W. S. Merw___ ___ Albert Goldb___ ___arry Humes, Colette Inex, William___ ___ne Boruch, Rachel Hadas, Rebecca ___ ___laser, Mary Oliver, Katherine Soni___ ___Katherine Stripling Byer, Hayden ___ ___ichael Longley, Scott Russell Sander___ ___ly, Robert Hill

Shenandoah seems about the best bargain in literature that one
could possibly find these days. It is just as sleek and thick as
journals twice its price, and has more beauty and life between its
covers than anything I have read in a long time.

-- *Literary Magazine Review*

SHENANDOAH
Washington and Lee University / Troubadour Theater, 2nd Floor
Box EX-A(B) / Lexington, Virginia 24450-0303

Name_____

PR

Address_____

City, State, Zip _____

Single issue: $5.00   Subscription: $28 / 2 years
                                            $15 / 1 year